Christmas at Maplemont Manor

A Novel

Julie Manthey

*Ceri & Rob!
Happy Christmas!*

Also by Julie Manthey

The Magic of Cape Disappointment

To Beth and Judi, superstars.

Contents

Title Page	1
Also by Julie Manthey	3
Dedication	5
Copyright	10
Noelle, Noelle	12
One Lord a-Leaping	20
Frost Impressions	27
Elvesdropping	41
No Time Like the Present	47
Decking the Halls	61
Oh Christmas Tree	68
Ye Merry Gentlemen	76
Plaid Tidings	87
An Eggnogural Tour	101
Gingerbread Elves	114
No Partridge in the Pear Tagine	125

Hark! The Mother in Maldives	134
Silver Lanes Aglow	139
Miracles and Mistletoe	144
On Comet and Cupid!	159
Tinsel in a Tangle	165
O Little Town of Matchmakers	172
Oh Ho the Mistletoe	180
Claus for Concern	189
Making Spirits Bright	196
A Cup of Cheer	206
Rockin' Around the Skating Rink	218
Christmas Dream	232
Reindeer Games	237
A Thrill of Hope	242
Did You Hear What I Heard?	249
Ho-ho-home Again	254
As It Snow Happens	262
Jingle Bales	270
Hearsleigh	277
The Fire is So Delightful	282
Everwreathing is Merry and Bright	287
Two Calling Birds	292
Dashing Through the Snow	297
A Rudolph Awakening	301

The Naughty List	305
Blue Christmas Eve	311
Then Arose Such a Clatter	316
Don We Now Our Gala Apparel	323
Season of Giving	327
Where the Love-Light Gleams	331
Elfterward	333
Book Club Guide	338
About the Author	340

Copyright

This book is a work of fiction. Names, characters, places, and incidents either are products of the author's imagination or are used fictitiously.

References to real events, establishments, organizations, or locales are intended only to provide a sense of authenticity and are used fictitiously.

Copyright © 2019 Julie Manthey

All rights reserved.

ISBN 978-1-08-101267-0 (pbk.)
ISBN 978-1-39-331691-6 (ebk)

Independently Published

Cover design by Julie Manthey
Author photo @Heather Crowder

"I should be playin' in the winter snow, but I'ma be under the mistletoe."
– JUSTIN BIEBER, NASRI ATWEH, & ADAM MESSINGER

Noelle, Noelle

The town's Christmas tree stood watch while Noelle flipped the bakery's door sign to 'closed.' She stopped for a second to smile at a photo of her sister, the original founder of the bakery, whose image had pride of place by the entrance where she could still welcome every guest. The aroma of maple fudge sweetened the air as Noelle tested out a new recipe that she hoped would be a contender for the gold medal of the prestigious Northeast Maple Tree awards.

    The Sugarhouse Bakery glowed in white twinkly lights after a busy day. A fixture at the far end of Main Street, the building started in 1853 as a maple syrup processing house, or sugarhouse. Snow piled up outside in big clumps, as the small town of Maplemont, New York glittered in lights. Maplemont had two claims to fame. The first that it was only three hours' drive from New York City and also to Montreal, Canada and the second, and by no means least, that it had the best maple fudge in the region at the Sugarhouse Bakery.

Noelle danced toward the kitchen, humming along to holiday music while totally engrossed in tasting fudge from a pan. With her long auburn hair pulled back neatly in a braid and long bangs framing her high cheek bones and hazel eyes, she could easily have been mistaken for a chic French woman. Chic, that is, until one noticed that her apron hid an ugly Christmas sweater from the bakery's contest earlier in the afternoon. The sweater's red sequins reflected the light as she moved.

Frowning after noticing another piece of fudge had been nabbed from the pan, Noelle looked up to find her employee, Skye, smiling in triumph.

"Is this for the contest?" Skye's hair was twisted into two side braids that made her look younger than she was, complemented by a polka-dotted green and white sweater of a cat wearing a Santa hat. Her signature scent of patchouli and violet scented the air around her. Usually the smell of cookies and maple fudge overtook the air in the bakery, but this close to Skye, the patchouli was unmistakable.

"I thought maybe, but it's still not right. I wish Carol was here, she'd know what was missing. I don't know. I should probably stick with Carol's recipe again this year."

"Tastes good to me," Skye said. "You

worry too much."

Noelle shook her head and thought that Skye didn't worry enough. "Maybe I won't submit my own recipe this year. The fudge has to be perfect, like all the best flavors of an upstate Christmas in maple fudge that is so good that Sugarhouse will win the gold medal again. This is only 'OK' maple fudge. It's still missing... something."

She sighed, afraid that she had run out of ideas. More importantly, she wanted to win the gold medal to know that Carol had made the right decision about giving her the bakery. Losing the first year she submitted her own recipe would make her feel like she was letting her sister down.

"You'll win, don't worry. You're the best chef I know." Skye mindlessly grabbed another piece of fudge, having gained ten pounds since she started working at the bakery but it only made her jollier. She frequently joked that being skinny was overrated.

"I'm the *only* chef you know." Noelle laughed.

"Like I said, you're the *best* chef I know. You'll win the gold medal and I'll meet my dream guy."

"Just like that, huh?" Noelle looked unconvinced.

Skye leaned on the counter and imagined her dream guy was walking in the door. "Someday he'll walk into the bakery and our eyes will meet." She sighed wistfully. "And next thing you know, we'll be off to dinner and the opera. You know, I read a book that said it's important to visualize for a dream to come true." Her gaze concentrated on the door, willing it to be opened by a handsome and cultured dream date. "Well, maybe tomorrow." Skye's optimism didn't end with thinking that her dreamboat would stumble into the bakery.

Noelle and Skye had met on a hiking trip in Spain, bonding on the trip as the only two women under fifty in the group. Skye, a free spirit who was always up for an adventure, worked on a fishing boat in Alaska, then at an art gallery in New Mexico, only to move to New York City where she became a taxi driver. She loved meeting interesting people. Noelle knew that she was trustworthy and a hard worker in whatever she put her mind to, so after her last employee quit and moved to San Diego, she asked if Skye might be up for a small-town adventure in upstate New York. Noelle wasn't sure how long Skye would stay, but so far she was grateful that she'd stuck around for the last year.

Noelle laughed. "Yes, maybe your dream guy will appear and it will be love at first sight."

Skye followed Noelle into the kitchen. Although they shared a sense of adventure, Noelle was far more grounded and realistic than Skye. She knew from experience that life didn't care what one's dreams were. When Noelle stopped to think about it, she couldn't remember the last time that she took a risk on a new adventure. Even now, she was terrified to submit her own recipe into the regional maple fudge competition. Noelle figured that she was simply getting older and becoming more responsible, although she felt like a coward.

Skye's glance was drawn to the many framed photographs on the wall at the far end of the kitchen. Castles, camels, and mountain glaciers covered the walls in a mix of scenes. "I love these photos. Where was this one taken again?" She pointed to a picture of a cobblestone street teaming with small cafes.

Noelle stopped briefly, smiled, and walked over to the wall. "That one is the view from Notre Dame in Paris and the street where I spent a year at the macaron shop." Having spent over a decade working around the world in different restaurants and bakeries, the pictures reminded her of life before Carol's accident when she was free to roam.

"You make the best macarons! And the camels?" Skye asked, pointing to an image with camels crossing radiant golden desert sands that almost looked orange.

"That was taken on a trek in Morocco. I was working in a restaurant in Fez and spent a week crossing the Sahara on an old salt caravan route." Noelle smiled at the memory which felt like it had happened a hundred years ago in a different life.

"Don't you miss traveling? Not knowing what's around the corner or who you'll meet and having to ask for directions sounds so romantic. Maybe I should move to Paris. I've never spent much time at all in Europe." Skye sighed. "I should learn French."

Looking thoughtful, Noelle waited a beat before replying. "Are you getting restless?" Noelle could completely relate to Skye. After almost four years in Maplemont herself, she missed the pull of the open road and the international airport, although her family kept her anchored to Maplemont's Main Street. She had a home now that she left for vacations, instead of her previous life where she was a traveler, slowing moving from one side of the earth to the other and 'home' was wherever she had unpacked her suitcase.

Skye stood tall and looked thoughtful. "I suppose I am feeling restless. Maybe I should take that trip to Cambodia with you next year."

"Yes, you should. That's exactly what I've been telling you." Noelle looked at her watch in alarm, clearly having lost track of time. "Oh no, I'm late! Can you close tonight, Skye? I'm catering a dinner tonight at Maplemont Manor and I can't be late. I hear that the new owner is a real bore; you know someone who is always working and thinks the rest of the world should wait on him hand and foot. But it gives me a chance to finally check out that kitchen and I can save the money from catering for the Cambodia trip," she said quickly.

"No problem," Skye said. "You know, I've heard he's handsome, single, a millionaire, and that he's moved back to Maplemont Manor to finally settle down. You'll get to meet the most eligible bachelor upstate. I'm so jealous! I bet he loves opera and Paris in the spring." Skye put one hand over her heart and the other over her forehead as if she would swoon.

Noelle shook her head. "I'm sure he's a spoiled, entitled jerk and I'll probably not meet him because he'll have 'staff' to deal with the help."

"Or he'll be a smoldering Darcy to your feisty Elizabeth," Skye said and they shared a laugh. "I've been re-reading the classics and I'm simply falling for the romance of them."

Glancing at her watch nervously, Noelle worried about being late. "Oh, I've got to run. See you tomorrow! Take that fudge home with you, please. I don't want it sitting there in the morning, reminding me how mediocre it is." Before leaving, she grabbed the plastic containers holding the dough for the dinner rolls that she'd prepared earlier.

Skye grinned, happy that the bakery kept her so well stocked up on treats that quickly made her the most popular member of her book club. "Wait, Noelle!" Skye yelled out, as Noelle was putting on her down parka and hat. "Your ugly sweater! You can't wear that to Maplemont Manor."

Laughing, Noelle looked down at her garish sweater of a reindeer's face with a sparkling red nose that shimmered in sequins. "I don't have time to change. It's no big deal; I'll be in the kitchen the whole time with an apron. Besides, the 'lord of the manor' hired a server." Wrapping a scarf around her neck, she waved quickly and flew out the door in a rush.

One Lord a-Leaping

At the local Moonlight Theater, Grant Fitzgerald tried not to doze off in the plush red velvet seat, listening to a classical music quartet that included two violins, a viola, and a cello. The charity concert supported the restoration of the local museum after the roof caved in last year when historic snows blanketed the region. He looked comfortable, albeit bored, in his full tuxedo that he wore as a uniform to the many charity events on his social calendar. His thick, wavy hair seemed purposefully disheveled, as if he had just left the beach, in contrast to his strong jawline that made him look serious.

Checking his watch, he wondered whether his mother would notice if he slipped out to leave early. Glancing over to her, she glared back as if reading his thoughts. He returned his gaze to the quartet, wondering how many hours of his life he'd spent at events like these. While being the 'lord of the manor' in Maplemont had its privileges, Grant often found his new life here to be very dull and isolating.

At the end of the concert, he stood up quickly while a young woman rushed up to him gushing about the music and the benefit for the museum. Word had quickly spread that Grant was the most eligible bachelor in the area, having recently moved into the enormous and historic Maplemont Manor that he inherited from his grandfather. The gossip mill's description that he was also tall, dark, and handsome added to the frenzy. Having already amassed a fortune, he allegedly planned to settle down at Maplemont where the only thing he lacked was a wife.

His mother smiled, while a flock of potential partners encircled her son in varying colors of silk and velvet, vying to gain his attention. She and his stepfather, William Smythe, lived nearby in another grand historic mansion, Highgate House, in neighboring Mount Briar. Although having remarried decades ago, she decided to keep the Fitzgerald last name, hyphenating it to 'Fitzgerald-Smythe,' since she then benefitted from the double prestige of both well-known and wealthy names.

Grant's mother strolled over, arm-in-arm,

with the beautiful and very blonde, Imogen Prescott. Imogen, heiress to the estate of the Mount Briar Prescotts, had never worked a day in her life, attended only the best private schools, and made all the charitable events she attended fashionable.

Mrs. Fitzgerald-Smythe had already judged Imogen to be the perfect match for her son. "Look who I found," she announced. "Imogen has agreed to join us for dinner. Isn't that lovely, Grant? You two have so much in common."

Imogen smiled and grabbed Grant's hand, as the tide of ladies receded in her wake. "You simply must join us this summer, Grant. We're taking the yacht to the vineyard for the summer and staying at the house there for three weeks. It will be gorgeous. You're coming!"

Grant's face maintained cool composure while he thought of an excuse. "I'm planning a trek across the Atlas Mountains in Morocco this summer. I'm sure that you'll have a great time though," he said knowing that someone like Imogen would never agree to any trip that included the slightest lapse of luxury.

"Morocco?" Imogen made a face. "Oh, you can't be serious! You're teasing me!" Imogen proclaimed it to be the truth, and to her, it was. She had a habit of adjusting reality to the way she believed things should be. Between her wealth and her beauty, she usually got her way anyway.

"You'll love the vineyard and the beaches. We Prescotts go every year."

"Sounds wonderful, doesn't it, Grant?" Mrs. Fitzgerald-Smythe chimed in. She'd wanted nothing more than to see her son settle down with an appropriate wife from the right family who would provide structure and a social path for Grant to follow. She regretted that her son didn't understand the privilege that she'd sacrificed so much for, to give him access to all the right people for him to thrive. Routinely, she congratulated herself as the primary driver of his success. Had she not remarried to an even wealthier and more prestigious man than Grant's father, their position in society would be very different. Instead, he had been provided all of the best connections and the world was his to conquer.

Conveniently, she forgot that his grandfather's money paid for everything although she never saw a penny of it for herself and wasn't allowed to live in the manor. Grant's grandfather made it very clear when his son died, that the 'money grabbing' wife he left behind would never see a penny. He ensured Grant received the inheritance that his father should have had. She knew though that all the social opportunities that she married into did not come without a cost, mostly resonating as a cool rift between them since his father died. The more she tried to be a part of his life these days, the more distance he managed to put between them. By choosing the right wife for him who would be her ally, she'd seal her position in Grant's life.

"If you'll excuse me," Grant said, walking toward the bathroom. He looked over his shoulder to find his mother and Imogen laughing over some comment and then darted for the door like a thief. He slipped out where his driver waited as if driving a getaway car.

"Will Mrs. Fitzgerald-Smythe be joining us, sir?" the driver, a young burly man of maybe thirty years old asked about Grant's mother. He used 'sir' out of habit from his military days.

"No, Dean, her driver is waiting. They'll meet us at the manor," Grant said stiffly.

"Roger that, sir." Having worked for Grant for several years, Dean knew that he typically didn't appreciate long conversations. While some interpreted that as rude, most quickly learned that Grant was always very busy and surrounded by work so he appreciated his quiet time. Once Dean understood that, the quiet time they spent in the car became a comfortable silence.

Grant had taken a chance on hiring Dean, given his post-traumatic stress disorder, most commonly referred to as PTSD after his time in the service, when it was difficult for him to hold an office job. Dean performed terribly as an administrative assistant but, instead of firing him, Grant took time to find another job that would be more suitable for him. Dean knew from experience that level of effort and care was rare, making him very loyal to Grant.

"Have you ever been to Nantucket, Dean?"

"No sir, that's not really my thing," Dean said.

"Me neither," Grant replied, still working out the scene with Imogen in his mind. "Oh, please stop at the kitchen entrance of the house. I need to tell the chef that there will be one more for dinner."

"Of course, sir." Grant felt annoyed that his mother had invited Imogen to dinner. It was bad enough that she had invited several members of the museum board, but continuing to give Imogen hope that she'd someday be the lady of Maplemont Manor made him irritable. All he wanted was a quiet night at his new home and time to think. His opened his phone to catch up on business, mostly the final negotiations of the sale of his multi-million-dollar business.

It was important to him that his staff were taken care of after the transaction and he replied with another strongly worded email that, yes, he was serious about the new company providing one week of paid holiday leave for all of his employees this year. He used the phrase 'non-negotiable,' hoping to drive the point home. He knew that several companies were interested in the app his company developed and that his terms for the sale were very reasonable. Once he decided on a path, Grant rarely veered from it.

    As the car left the parking lot, Grant's laser focus on his phone and business meant that he missed the holiday lights and the town Christmas tree. After the car stopped in the driveway, it took Grant almost a minute to realize that they had reached the manor. Dean forced a cough to alert him to their arrival. As requested, instead of the usual front entrance stop, Grant entered the house via the kitchen back door.

Frost Impressions

Noelle gazed in wonder, driving down the tree-lined lane toward Maplemont Manor, a ten-bedroom Tudor style brick mansion sitting majestically on twenty park-like acres. With the wide courtyard and limestone accents around the doors and edges, Noelle thought that the manor looked more like a fancy university complex than a home. Although the manor's property shared a fence with the Maplemont River Farm where Noelle lived, she'd only been inside the manor once or twice in her life when she was a little girl.

Each tree along the drive was lit up with white lights and every window of the house held a candle lantern, flickering with light that made each room look as if it glowed. Even the service entrance door at the back of the property had a massive evergreen wreath and large red bow, that smelled of pine as she approached the door. The snow looked as if it had been directed to only fall outside of the walkways.

Following the directions from the house manager, Noelle quickly took stock of the kitchen, finding all of the ingredients already in the refrigerator as previously arranged. She squealed with delight in the kitchen, touching the wide stone hearth that met the ceiling's wood beams. Despite the enormous footprint of the kitchen, it felt cozy with the custom maple cabinets, large marble island, and original wood stove in the corner that stood proudly in front of a river stone feature wall. Noelle could not have imagined a more perfect kitchen, although she did find it strange that the interior of the house did not appear to include the slightest decoration for Christmas.

The exterior holiday decorations hid the fact that inside, the house was beautiful, but felt more like a cold museum. Before anything else, Noelle found some wood to start a fire in the old wood stove and then she set to work by preparing the beef tenderloin with a rich cognac butter sauce. After the sauce was ready and the tenderloin in one of the double ovens, she then started prepping a spicy Moroccan-style harissa glaze for the sliced carrots. Opening the other oven, she added the cardamom roll dough that she brought from the bakery and set the timer for fifteen minutes.

For the appetizer, she quickly threw together a spinach, feta, and grape salad drizzled with a maple-soy vinaigrette. A few minutes later, a man entered the kitchen from the service door, dressed in a full tuxedo. Noelle assumed that he was the waiter that the house manager had hired. She couldn't help but notice how handsome he was and hoped he wouldn't ruin things by pulling out his phone to play a game.

The kitchen smelled like cardamom, cognac, and butter while the fire flickered in the wood stove, warming the room. Grant felt as if he'd finally arrived home after a long journey on the moon.

"Great, you're here! I was starting to think that I'd have to serve the dinner myself," Noelle said glancing at her watch. Grant stood in the kitchen with a bemused look on his face. "Well, come on, don't just stand there. Grab an apron and pull the rolls out of the oven, then I'll need some help with slicing the tenderloin and plating the salad." He didn't move, unsure of what to do. "Come on!" Noelle urged impatiently and it was clear from her slightly disheveled braid, flour-streaked apron, and dishes overwhelming the sink that she needed help.

Grant put on an apron and stepped into the kitchen. He opened the oven and stopped for a moment to take in the heavenly smell of the freshly baked cardamom rolls. Noelle soon pushed him aside with a sigh, efficiently pulling the rolls out with one hand and replacing them with a pan in the other. For dessert she planned to serve maple gingerbread mousse and black cherry clafouti. She rolled her eyes.

"Sorry, they smelled incredible," he said, speaking for the first time. "What's in the cake pan?"

"It's black cherry clafouti."

"I'm going to need more nouns." Grant's eyes twinkled with an intrigued look.

"A clafouti is a baked French dessert. Usually with fruit covered with a thick flan-like batter. Black cherries are the most traditional."

"So, it's a cake then."

Noelle bristled. "No, it's a *clafouti*. Maybe you could help with the mousse instead. Pour the cream mix in that bowl into the processor and run it. Can you handle that?" The tone of her voice indicated that she was clearly annoyed and stressed.

Grant looked unsure and she walked with him over to the island and explained how to dump the creamy mixture for the maple gingerbread mousse into the processor. Grant put the top cover back on the food processor.

"Don't forget to—" Noelle started before Grant hit the button on the food processor and the top flew off and cream and maple syrup mixture rained over them. Clumps of the mousse mixture dripped all over their hair, faces, and aprons. Wiping the mix off from her eyes, Noelle finished her sentence, "—lock the top."

"Well, it's certainly mixed." They both started laughing almost completely in sync with each other. Noelle couldn't breathe, she was laughing so hard. Grant reached over to scoop some of the mix off of her face and they stopped laughing as they shared a quiet moment, standing close. Noelle's heart beat faster and Grant seemed unable to move, before Noelle came to her senses and got back to dealing with the mess. She wondered for a second why he stepped away and then realized that she was the one who had moved back first. Still, it wasn't like her to kiss men she didn't know, even charming and handsome ones. For about a second though, she almost made an exception.

Snapping back to reality, she was sure that she was fantasizing and that he hadn't wanted to kiss her since they didn't know anything about each other. Noelle used her apron to start cleaning up the floor. "Don't worry about it. I'll get this cleaned up." She tried to think about anything but the potential kiss, which only made her wonder more. Noelle couldn't help but wonder if he had been leaning in or if she imagined it.

Shaking her head, she chalked it up to a side effect of all the romantic Christmas movies that she'd been watching and that it was nothing. The last thing she needed right now in her life was a relationship, regardless of what her sister thought. Further, she knew nothing about this waiter other than his blue eyes reminded her of the ocean and he looked handsome in a tuxedo. He probably was serially unemployed and still 'finding himself,' having only been hired because he looked good in a tux.

Grant wondered if he had chickened out of something or if he had really been leaning in. Mostly he wanted to know why she pulled back first. For months now he'd had beautiful women thrown into his path, yet there was never a spark like that moment which left him wanting to stop time. Still, he realized that kissing the kitchen help wasn't ever going to be appropriate for someone in his position of society. While it wasn't the 1800s, there were still expectations, especially from his mother. He figured that he had only imagined that there was a moment, given that so many women have been vying for his attention recently. This woman didn't seem to be that impressed, although he still thought there was a moment. Grant tried to scoop away some of the mousse mix that had covered his hair, unsuccessfully. "Let me help you clean this up," he said.

Nodding in agreement, Noelle pointed toward the extra dish towels by the sink and Grant stepped toward the sink but slipped on some cream. He fell onto the floor. Noelle covered her mouth in shock, trying desperately not to laugh. "Are you OK?" she asked, helping him to stand.

"I'm fine. I think my pride took the brunt of it." He touched his head gently. "Am I hallucinating or is your sweater glowing? No offense but that is, very possibly, the ugliest sweater I have ever seen."

Noelle looked down at her holiday sweater, now revealed because she had used her apron to clean the floor and they both got the giggles. "I'll let you know that this is an award-winning ugly sweater, thank you very much." She sat up straight to model it proudly, stretching her arms out widely so the sequins could catch the light. Looking unconvinced, Grant asked what award it had won. "Most sequins! Oh wait, take off that jacket. I have another sweater here for my brother-in-law, but he had to work late. You can wear this tonight instead. It's not as professional as your penguin suit, but it's clean and...festive."

Before Grant knew it, he was wearing a dark green sweater that featured a Christmas tree. Noelle clicked a hidden button on the cuff and small lights on the tree started to blink. "And this one would have won the 'most lights' award, I think." She giggled and noticed how strange it was that he looked more uncomfortable in a sweater than he did in a tuxedo.

"Sorry, about this mess. I don't really cook much." He sat down on the floor to help clean up the spill and was soon joined by Noelle.

"Don't worry, neither does the family who

own this house. The wealthy inherit houses with amazing kitchens like this and then, of course, have no idea how to cook in one. It's all for show. Then people like you and me get stuck with making it all work so they can have fancy dinners in houses they only stay in once a year."

Grant kept wiping up the floor, trying not to react. He couldn't help but want to defend himself. "Maybe the owners don't have time for cooking because they have busy jobs that help pay for others like you, and uh me, to have these jobs. I mean, I'm sure they are really good people, if you got to know them."

Noelle scoffed. "Like I want to meet the most eligible bachelor of Maplemont," she said sarcastically. "I'm sure he's a spoiled, boring suit who spends all of his time reading emails and ordering other people around. I mean the owner of this house and his family actually spent tonight at an expensive museum fundraiser concert, only because their family is in every exhibit. Meanwhile the hospital's roof leaks so badly that they've closed the cancer clinic and patients have to drive all the way over to Ridgewater for their treatments. No, it doesn't make any sense. People like the Fitzgeralds don't actually *care* about the community. They simply *decorate* it."

Grant was shocked. No woman had ever spoken to him like that in his life. "The Fitzgeralds contribute a lot of money to this community. I suppose that's hard to understand for someone who's spent their whole life in this postage stamp town with their glory days behind them and thinks that an ugly sweater contest is a cultural event." His anger surprised both of them and silence fell across the kitchen that previously rang with their laughter.

Noelle looked stung by his words. Grant regretted them almost the moment they were deployed, knowing that Noelle hadn't known who her words were hurting. At that moment Grant's mother stormed into the kitchen.

"Grant Barclay Fitzgerald! What are you doing cleaning and what on earth happened to you? That sweater is hideous. Go change this instant into something respectable. Imogen is waiting and you can't possibly present yourself like this." Her focus then zoomed to Noelle. "We'll have nine tonight, not eight. You can begin serving as soon as my son joins us at the table, as the server we had hired couldn't make it tonight." She spun out of the room with a bustle of silk fabric the only sound.

"You're Grant Fitzgerald," Noelle said slowly, closing her eyes as if by doing so he could no longer see her.

"Yes."

"But…you…why didn't?" Noelle stumbled awkwardly.

"I think we've both said enough for this evening. Miss? I'm sorry, I didn't get your name."

"Krin—"

Grant left the room before she could finish. Noelle sighed, covered her mouth with her hands and leaned against the countertop as another blob of maple gingerbread mousse mix fell onto the floor.

Noelle straightened up her braid in the reflection of the oven door, splashed some water on her face, and cleaned her sequined sweater as best she could before going into the dining room to serve the meal. She picked up the plates from the island and set them onto a rolling serving cart, taking a deep breath before leaving the kitchen. When she arrived in the dining room, the Fitzgeralds and six other guests were seated at a long, mahogany dining room table that stood on a beautiful red and mustard wool kilim rug, reminding Noelle of the grand rugs she had seen when living in Morocco. She thought it was the best part of the room.

A young woman who looked like a movie star sat next to Grant. Noelle recognized her immediately as Imogen Prescott, someone she'd

Christmas at Maplemont Manor

rather avoid. Seeing them together, Noelle thought that they looked like a pharmaceutical commercial of a happy scene subtitled with a list of terrible side effects.

As she set each plate down in front of the diners while avoiding eye contact with anyone else, Noelle was painfully aware of how shabby she looked in comparison to the diners in evening gowns and tuxedos. She wished that she knew how to get the perfect 'smoky eye' look that Imogen had mastered, before realizing that she couldn't remember the last time she bought or used mascara.

Noelle overheard Grant tell his mother that he planned to match the donations for the museum and send the same amount over to the hospital. "The funds should help the hospital reopen the cancer clinic," Grant said.

Looking up for the first time since entering the room, Noelle was shocked to find his eyes on her. She remembered the contempt in his voice essentially calling her a 'townie' and refused to acknowledge him.

Imogen called attention to her ugly sweater. "Well, that is certainly a festive sweater, isn't it, Grant? It literally lights up the room with those sequins. What's that on the right sleeve?" She effortlessly lobbed an attack on Noelle after having noticed how Grant's attention shifted the second that Noelle entered the room. Sensing enough interest to be jealous,

Imogen was obviously trying to inspire Grant to dislike Noelle. Noelle was surprised that she had even bothered to try at all and she checked the sleeve in a glance.

Imogen sat at the table daintily pulling pieces off of a cardamom bun that she piled elsewhere on the plate, pretending that she ever ate carbohydrates. The entire table now stared at Noelle's sweater with the large reindeer face with a sparkling red nose that shimmered in sequins. Standing up straight she addressed them with confidence and mettle.

"It's only a little preview of the mousse for dessert. The blender got away from me earlier, but no worries, everything will still be perfection." Noelle feigned a smile along with the confidence. She wasn't going to give Imogen the satisfaction of seeing how her words had injured her. Noelle's courage always rose at moments like that.

"Wait, aren't you Libby Kringle's daughter?" Imogen asked, already knowing the answer. "I believe Libby worked at my father's house as a maid for some time." She knew very well that Noelle's mother worked for her family for twenty years. Imogen had even played with Noelle and her sisters when they were all children. Of course, she only wanted to point out to Grant that not only was Noelle part of *his* staff, but her mother had worked for Imogen's family for a long time as well. She painted a thick line between upstairs and downstairs.

"Yes, Imogen, that's true. How kind of you to remember her," Noelle replied before returning to the kitchen. She waited in the kitchen for what seemed like an eternity, until they finished the dinner. She then returned to the dining room with the cart to clear the dinner dishes and serve dessert. Usually she would have done so via multiple trips, but she did everything at once to spend the least amount of time in the dining room. As Noelle explained the dessert options, she congratulated herself for managing to avoid Grant's gaze and any additional grilling from Imogen.

Her sister, Holly, soon arrived at the back door to find Noelle at the sink washing dishes and pans that couldn't go into the dishwasher. Noelle greeted Holly with a hug. The two resembled each other closely and they could never deny that they were sisters, although Holly was always the most reliable and responsible of the two. She ran the Maplemont River syrup farm on six hundred acres at the edge of town that made the best maple syrup in the county.

"I'm sorry that it took me so long to get over here. Ava insisted on 'one more story' and then another after that. Todd got home late also," Holly explained.

"Thanks for coming, I owe you one. Everything's mostly done, all you need to do is finish these dishes, clear the dessert course in about a half hour, once they leave the dining room and run the dishwasher."

Elvesdropping

After the dessert was delivered, Grant had gone up to his room to get the holiday sweater and return it. He stopped at the kitchen door out of sight, after hearing the sisters talking. While Grant knew that he should have gone in or made himself known, he had a suspicion that they were talking about him and he wanted to hear if Noelle mentioned anything about the kiss that almost happened. He justified his eavesdropping with wanting to see if she felt the same spark, which for him felt more like lightning.

"I can't believe that you said, what you said...that you said." Holly smirked. "And to Grant Fitzgerald, of all people! Only *you* would mistake him for a waiter." Shaking her head, she put on some gloves to help with the dishes.

Noelle sighed. "Me? What about *him*? He had no right in talking to me like that! Postage stamp town...glory days...and then lie about who he was! Even if he was the last man in the world, you couldn't convince me to go out with him. Besides, it looks like he's dating some perfect society drone who is meaner than a junkyard dog, so exactly his type I'm sure. Rich snobs like him only date other wealthy jerks."

Noelle didn't bother mentioning that it was Imogen Prescott, because that would only make Holly upset and she probably wouldn't see her tonight anyway. Silently, Grant set the sweater down on a nearby table, having overheard enough and returned to the dining room.

Holly pulled some hardened cream cheese from her sister's hair that she had missed earlier and tried not to laugh. "Come on, you know that you don't mean that. He probably feels terrible for what he said and I'm sure he didn't mean it. I doubt anyone has ever spoken to him like you did in his life and he simply reacted." While she had heard about his privileged upbringing, Holly remembered how well her parents spoke of his late father and grandfather, saying that they were very kind-hearted men. She also knew that Noelle's past experience with a wealthy ex-boyfriend had more to do with her opinion about Grant than anything else.

"How can you take his side?" Noelle was annoyed that her sister always saw the best in everyone, a trait which they didn't share.

"I'm always on your side and you know that. But you know very well that you can often judge others a little too harshly, especially

Christmas at Maplemont Manor

if they injure your pride. Remember when that customer called your macarons 'quaint cookies' and you kicked her out of the bakery? Sometimes you overreact. And you can't be sure that this isn't about Ewan."

"You weren't there, Holly. I was a saint compared to Grant. I can't believe you'd bring up Ewan." Ewan was Noelle's long-term boyfriend of almost two years when she lived in Scotland and Noelle assumed that they were going to be married until it was made painfully obvious to her that wasn't going to happen.

"I'm sure you were a saint, but this house and the whole 'laird of the manor thing' had to have thrown you. Now why don't you go home, take a nice bath, and try to forget about tonight. I'll close out everything here and tomorrow morning we're decorating at the hospital. We'll have cocoa and decorate the trees..." Holly knew that Noelle loved to decorate at Christmas, so the thought of their annual tradition would cheer her up.

Her sister started to calm down and nodded. "This entire evening has been a dumpster fire. Thank you for doing this." She put her jacket on and pulled the car keys from her purse. "I would have called Skye but tonight is her book club. I can't stay here. I've had enough humiliation for one evening."

Holly nodded supportively as she watched Noelle walk out the door, yelling behind her, "Don't forget, you owe me fudge for Ava's school on Friday!" Noelle waved with the back of her hand as she walked out into the snowy night. She agreed to fill in for Holly at Ava's community history day to talk about the history of the Maplemont River syrup farm.

Noelle rushed home to the neighboring farm where she and Holly lived. The post and beam farmhouse built in 1791, where Holly and her family lived, had been updated a few times over the years yet it still retained character with the deep red, traditional farmhouse color and navy-blue shutters.

The farm included the farmhouse, a sugarhouse, and a large garage with an apartment above it where Noelle lived. Collapsing onto the sofa, Noelle sighed loudly and turned on the television to watch an old movie and try to forget about Maplemont Manor.

∞∞∞

Holly loaded the dishwasher when Grant walked into the kitchen after the rest of the party had adjourned into the living room. "Miss Kringle?"

Holly stood up and turned to face him. She couldn't help but notice that the town gossips had not underrated how handsome Grant looked. "Noelle left. I'm Holly, her sister...I know, the names, right? Noelle, Holly, and Carol—our parents really loved Christmas and I suppose with the last name of Kringle, they couldn't help themselves. Poor Uncle Chris got the worst of it. Although I'm Holly Mitchell now so I'm married, but Noelle is...still single. She works at the Sugarhouse Bakery. They have the best maple fudge in the world. We're neighbors actually. I run Maplemont River Farm down the road. Sorry, I talk when I'm nervous," she said.

Grant nodded, trying to hide any emotion. "Here's the payment for tonight. Please let Miss Kringle know that we won't require her services again." In his experience, it was best to keep things short.

Holly took the envelope and shook his hand with a smile. "I'm not trying to excuse my sister, but you should know that it had nothing to do with you. Her heart was broken by this rich guy. He basically grew up in a castle and she thought they were really serious, but his family never approved of 'the American.'" Holly mimed air quotes with her hands. "My sister really is a good person."

Grant continued to look unmoved and then he turned around and left the kitchen. Holly watched him leave and shook her head. Her gut instinct told her that he played things way too cool which meant that he must be interested in Noelle. Turning over the envelope in her hands, she noticed it had a stamp in the corner

45

and was likely supposed to be mailed the next day by his staff. Holly knew that he delivered it in person on purpose. She smiled, remembering how his face fell perceptively when he realized that Holly wasn't who he expected to see. She loved knowing a secret, especially when the other people involved had no idea what it was...yet.

No Time Like the Present

In the morning, Grant woke up early and completed his usual morning routine of running on the treadmill and then cleaning up for day. Without thinking about it, he got dressed in a charcoal gray Italian wool suit. Looking out the window of his bedroom he saw the snow pile up and made a mental note that he should go into the city today to get the rest of his clothes. With only suits and two tuxes at the manor, he hardly had any appropriate winter wear and he wanted to go skiing.

He had been excited about the prospect of going into the city that day because he was already bored in Maplemont. With the sale of his business, all he had was some minimal contract negotiations to complete since his partner Porter was taking care of everything else. The manor felt cold and empty. Grant didn't sleep well the night before and he felt tired. Something in Noelle's words had rung true to him—he wasn't a part of the community.

He didn't really belong in Maplemont; so much as he occupied it. As he stood in the grand hallway with a view of the main living room, he knew that he had everything that most people would imagine wanting. He lived in a mansion, had millions in the bank, beautiful women flocked to him, and he had the freedom to do whatever he wanted. Yet he found himself feeling depressed; a lonely man disconnected from the world.

He wondered how having spent only a few minutes with Noelle, that she was able to shine a light into his life that made him reevaluate everything. He wanted to be a better man. After dedicating his life to being busy with work and school, he now wanted to dig in to Maplemont and grow roots. He would start by not going to the city that day.

Making his way to the manor's kitchen, he found the green holiday sweater that Noelle had given him on the table and he sighed. Grant decided to make toast and coffee, surprising the usual house chef, Fiona Edwards, when she opened the door to find him already eating toast at the kitchen island. Fiona was in her late sixties and had worked for Grant's grandfather most of her life.

Originally from England, Fiona visited the Finger Lakes in New York with her family on vacation in her twenties and fell in love with an American lumberjack. They eventually settled in Maplemont and she got the job at the manor since it was especially stylish to have staff from 'the continent' at the time. The Fitzgerald family and, by extension their staff including Fiona, previously spent every Christmas at Maplemont until Grant's father died over twenty years ago and then the house stood quiet at the holidays when the family typically travelled anywhere else instead. Grant was sent to boarding school and his mother eventually re-married a man who never had much interest in her son. Eventually he started spending Christmas at school.

"Oh, good morning, Mr. Fitzgerald." Fiona looked surprised to see him in the kitchen this early, since usually she had to track him down in the office or somewhere in the manor with his laptop. "Would you like me to make you something else for breakfast this morning? Perhaps some eggs benedict or beans on toast?" Her British accent remained strong and crisp, as did her breakfast options that always included beans on toast which was a childhood favorite of Grant's that always reminded him of Maplemont. She hurriedly put on an apron then quickly went to pour more coffee to warm up Grant's cup.

"Thank you, Fiona, please call me Grant. And please sit down. Have some coffee."

Fiona eyed Grant suspiciously. "Is something wrong, sir?"

"Grant," he reminded her.

"Mr. Fitzgerald, I'm sorry but I'm an old

bird and I can't possibly call you anything else despite these modern times. When you were four and got a marble stuck in your nose, I still called you, 'Mr. Fitzgerald.' Please don't expect me to change." Fiona shrugged and Grant sighed as a dramatic sign of capitulation. "Now, tell me what's wrong."

"Nothing is wrong. I simply realized this morning that I never cook when I'm here. I figured that I'd make some toast and coffee this morning only to prove that I could." He looked down at a piece of charred toast that he was determined to eat anyway. Fiona smiled and then helped herself to a cup of coffee. "Do you think I'm a snob, Fiona?"

Sitting across from him, Fiona looked concerned. "Certainly not, sir! Why would you ask such a thing?"

He picked at his toast and wished there were leftover cardamom buns from the night before. If only Imogen hadn't dissected two without eating them, there would be leftovers. He remembered how the kitchen seemed like a mirage of his dream of what a home could be the night before, only to find it a cold and lonely place first thing that morning when he struggled to get the coffee maker to work and burned his toast. Mostly, he tried not to think about Noelle and the tone of her voice when she said that she wouldn't date Grant even if he was the last man on earth. His mind swam around that phrase all night.

"I don't know. I guess being in Maplemont is not as easy a transition as I thought it might be. To me this is home, but no one here knows me."

"I know you, sir, and you are anything but a snob. You remind me so much of your dear father and grandfather! They were the best of men, I dare say, the best! I think your grandfather thought he had been Santa Claus in a past life. It was his favorite time of year. He'd be right proud that you moved here permanently."

Grant remembered the Maplemont Manor Christmas parties that were his favorite childhood memories. The entire town seemed to cram into the manor and his grandfather would appear in a Santa suit and dance around with his wife, always dressed as Mrs. Claus. "Those Christmases here are some of my best memories."

"Your grandfather loved this town and this house. I suppose he wanted to pass that along to you. Oh! The school called yesterday. They asked if you would speak at a community history day for the first graders this year. It's this Friday. I can let them know that you are busy." Fiona knew that the school called annually as a courtesy, but Grant never agreed to attend. The Fitzgeralds were always invited to everything, if only ceremonially. No one ever expected to be taken up on the offer, at least not since Grant's grandfather had passed away.

"They must have someone else going also?" He instinctively planned to say no, as usual, but he wanted to make sure that someone else had already agreed.

"Yes, Noelle Kringle from the Sugarhouse Bakery has agreed to be there to talk about the history of Maplemont River Farm and maple syrup production in the region. She's bringing maple fudge and will explain to the students how many local sugarhouses, including Maplemont River, were built by abolitionists. Many people don't know that part of history anymore. Anyway, I believe that you met her last night. Isn't she lovely?" Fiona had already heard about the two of them laughing in the kitchen from Dean.

"Indeed." He didn't want Fiona to pick up on anything else and he hoped a short response would help to camouflage the fact that all Grant could think about since last night was Noelle.

"We were lucky to get her for the dinner last night. I know that she's usually so busy during the holidays. I sometimes think that she stays so busy on purpose, but I shouldn't gossip," Fiona said. Mrs. Fitzgerald-Smythe had already called Fiona earlier that morning and given her an earful about Noelle serving them in an ugly sweater, but Fiona didn't care. She knew Noelle was an outstanding chef and they had often exchanged recipes.

"What do you mean?" Grant was intrigued.

Fiona figured that everyone else in town knew anyway, so it wouldn't hurt to bring Grant into the loop. She reasoned that it wasn't gossip if it was relaying the facts. "You two have something very unique in common. Her father also passed away over the holidays when she was a teenager and then her mother shortly after. Her oldest sister didn't go to college, so they could stay together in Maplemont. She raised Noelle during a very difficult time."

Grant's eyes softened, as the pang of his father's death when he was young never seemed to leave him. He still had his mother, although without the smoothest sailing, but he didn't lose both parents like Noelle. His grandfather was also always there for him. To have been parented by her sister as a teenager while also dealing with such grief must have been incredibly difficult for her. "I'm sorry to hear that we have that in common."

"I think Christmas can be a difficult time for them with all the memories, but those girls really pull together. There is not one holiday event in town that you won't find both of them working in the background somewhere. Noelle once told me that the best way she could think of honoring their parents was to share the joy of a season that they loved so much."

"Last night she mentioned that her mother worked at the Prescott's in Mount Briar."

Grant remembered Imogen's remarks.

"I almost forgot about that, but yes, I remember now. Libby Kringle was in my book club." Fiona knew there was some sort of attachment between Grant and Imogen, so she treaded carefully, minimizing the information. "It was terrible, poor Libby. She had been fired under suspicion of theft, but later they found the item. She refused to return to that house again though, after having her integrity questioned by people she'd spent decades working for." Fiona neglected to include that everyone suspected a lie from Imogen sparked the drama. "Such a nice family, the Kringles."

Grant finished his coffee and put the cup in the dishwasher. He stopped for a second to think. He told himself that today was a new day and the first of his new life here in Maplemont. "Tell the school that I'll be happy to attend on Friday. I'd like to get a big tree for the living room this year—maybe even have a holiday party like grandfather had. I think I'll go out today for that after I stop at the hospital. Could you ask Dean to bring down the decorations?" It bothered him that Noelle thought he didn't care about the community, mostly because she said out loud what probably many others thought.

"Yes, of course. I'll call the decorator to return for a tree."

"Don't call that decorator—she has mother's style of everything over the top with gold ribbons. I want to decorate the tree and the manor myself. And take the day off, I can manage on my own. I'm sure you must have some holiday things to catch up on. I'll be staying in town today." He liked New York, but the city's constant beat made it hard for him to think. Maplemont Manor was the closest thing that he had to real home and he wanted to think that the community thought the same.

He had been under the mistaken impression that all he had to do was show in Maplemont and be a Fitzgerald and the town would embrace him, only to realize that was an unreasonable expectation. A part of him also wanted to prove Noelle wrong, to show her that he was more than his family name and bank account. Her criticism still echoed and he couldn't get her out of his mind.

Fiona was shocked to hear that from Grant, yet she managed to agree and grin while he walked out to the car. Dean soon appeared in the kitchen. "Aren't you driving him today?" Fiona asked.

"He gave me the day off," Dean said, clearly shocked. "I was supposed to drive him into the city today. I thought he wanted to be there to sign the papers."

"This morning he made his own breakfast, burned the toast, and then put the dishes in the dishwasher. He's going to buy a tree today and then is going to decorate it...himself."

Dean poured himself a cup of coffee and sat down across from Fiona. "I think it has something to do with that lady chef from last night," he said. "I told you that I heard them laughing up a storm in the kitchen as I walked past. I've worked for him six years now and yesterday was the first time I've ever heard him laugh like that." Dean and Fiona exchanged a knowing glance.

"Well, Christmas is a time of miracles," Fiona said conspiratorially.

∞∞∞

Before leaving the house, Grant spent time in his office reviewing the latest counter-offer from the bidding company. He called his partner and best friend, Porter, to discuss the changes.

"Hey Porter, I told you that they'd comply with the condition to keep all our current staff and give them a week off over Christmas!" Grant congratulated himself with his victory.

"I thought you were pushing the line with that, to be honest. I guess they were infected by the holiday spirit. Once we sign on the dotted line, the little company we started from our dorm room to make it easier to order pizza is theirs and we walk away with five million dollars each! Man, am I grateful that I took a chance on the roommate lottery and ended up with this quiet geek from upstate New York," Porter said.

Grant laughed and likewise couldn't believe their good fortune. Porter was the closest thing he ever had to a brother and after years of working eighty-hour weeks, they could now both retire in the prime of their lives. "I'm signing it now and it'll be in your email in two seconds. Done!" Grant loved technology.

"Got it. All right, adding my signature and sending it over to the lawyers. See you at lunch today at the usual place to celebrate?"

"No, I'm staying up here today. I'm going to get a Christmas tree and maybe a dog."

"Hmmm...OK. I say we celebrate by flying out to Saint Moritz for our annual ski trip, or do you prefer Chamonix?"

"About that, I was thinking that instead you could come up to Maplemont and we could ski up here. There's a ski hill twenty minutes away and I think you'll agree that this is the place to start our next business."

Porter scoffed. "The ink isn't even dry on the sale of the company and you're already thinking about our next business? Are you really serious about moving to Maplemont? I thought you were kidding. I'm still thinking about moving to Los Angeles."

"I hear that the skiing is terrible in LA," Grant joked. He knew why Porter wanted to go there, but had hoped he'd come to Maplemont instead.

"Very funny. Wait, what's her name?" Porter asked.

"Who?"

"The mystery woman you must have met to make you think that Christmas in Maplemont is better than Christmas in Saint Moritz." Porter knew that Grant never turned down a ski vacation to Switzerland.

"Whatever. Maplemont is growing on me. Why don't you get out of the city and get some fresh air? You're going to like it up here. Besides, I could use your help on a project that I'm planning." Grant purposefully kept the true purpose vague and mysterious because he knew Porter loved surprises.

"A mystery woman and a mystery project? I'm intrigued and you know I can't pass that up." Although Porter's family lived in Massachusetts, he preferred to spend the holidays with Grant than any of his actual family. Grant and Porter were their own tribe and as close as brothers, having spent most of their lives in boarding school then college, and bonding together as boys left alone on an island. "Wait, we won't have to deal with the dragon lady, will we?" Porter asked, referring to Grant's mother.

The last thing he wanted to deal with over the holidays was parents of any kind. Christmas was never a 'family' holiday for him or Grant, outside of the Christmases Grant spent at Maplemont before his father died and before being sent away to boarding school.

"Nah, you know my mother prefers to spend her holidays at that resort in the Maldives. She and William left today and they won't be back until the end of January. Of course she couldn't leave without setting me up with that pretentious society drone," Grant complained.

Porter laughed. "She's still throwing Imogen Prescott in your path, then hoping against hope? You would think when our parents sent us away to boarding school and basically ignored us for a decade that meant they shouldn't be congratulating themselves for our success and trying to arrange marriages." Porter's parents had likewise been trying to set him up with another 'suitable' match, as they called her. He couldn't imagine being tied down to anyone that his parents chose.

"Your dad still bragging that the app was his idea?"

"You know it. OK, of course I'll get upstate. You're the only sane person in my life and if you need my help, then I'm there, brother. I'll take the train up soon," Porter agreed. If Grant thought that Maplemont was a good town, then it probably was. He'd pack two big suitcases that would be unwieldy on the train, but the convenience of having everything there would be worth it. One thing that Porter could count on after all of these years was that Grant never steered him wrong.

"Cool, see you later. And Porter—thanks." Hanging up the phone, Grant was pleased that Porter would be coming up. He couldn't imagine setting down roots in Maplemont if his best friend wasn't there also.

Decking the Halls

Noelle woke up after a restless night. She felt tired after not having slept much. The exchange with Grant still bothered her. In the last four years she hadn't created one new recipe, sticking to the standards. While she had added some new things to the bakery's menu, like rye bread and currant scones, they were well-honed recipes from her travels abroad. Otherwise, she managed Sugarhouse as a memorial to her sister Carol and as each year passed, she became more and more reluctant to change anything.

As mad as she was when Grant implied that her glory days were behind her, her heart knew a pang of truth. She used to be audacious and fearless, moving to a new country with only a backpack and an inspiration, but now she was afraid to try a new recipe. Looking in the mirror as she brushed her teeth, she wondered what happened to that brave girl. The thought of submitting a new maple fudge recipe to the annual competition seemed crazy.

Every year for the last four years she'd start a recipe and then chicken out to end up submitting Carol's award-winning 'Christmas Carol' maple fudge. She canceled more vacations than she actually took and the last time she left Maplemont was for a New England cruise with a well-scripted itinerary. She used to take chances. Now she found excuses not to. The old Noelle would have kissed the waiter when they shared that moment in the kitchen. The old Noelle would have taken a chance.

∞∞∞

Noelle and Holly met at the Maplemont General Hospital later that day, decorating the waiting rooms and nurses' stations. A small army of volunteers, all wearing Santa hats, helped them as Noelle and Holly coordinated everything and everyone. Noelle giggled with a nurse as she held up a picture of Santa while Noelle secured it to the wall with tape.

"Is it straight?" the nurse asked.

"Hold on, let me step back a bit to check." Noelle stepped backwards slowly down the hallway. She bumped into someone and she quickly stopped and apologized. "Oh! I'm so sorry," she said before looking up. "We were—"

Seeing Grant in a fitted dark suit and crisp

Christmas at Maplemont Manor

white oxford shirt, she couldn't help but gape. He was more handsome than she remembered, but she reminded herself that he was a complete jerk.

"Grant. What are you doing here?" Noelle then addressed the hospital administrator, Stan, who stood nearby. "Hey Stan, Merry Christmas."

"Nice hat." Grant pointed to the Santa hat on her head. "You really do love Christmas. I was here about some business." He noticed how her hazel eyes reminded him of magical dark forest with their deep moss green mixed with a dark brown like tree bark that included flecks of golden amber like sunlight. He wanted to get lost in that forest.

Noelle cringed, feeling self-conscious about once again resembling a Christmas ornament instead of a chic and confident woman. She mostly wished that she didn't care what Grant though about her, but she knew that she secretly did.

"My mom always used to say that if Kringles can't go overboard at Christmas, then who can?" She wanted to play her wardrobe choices off as something endearing and not embarrassing. Another volunteer asked about where to get some more garland for the hallway and Noelle said that she had more in the truck. She was grateful for an excuse to leave Grant because he made her nervous. "I have to..."

"Sure." He watched her walk away with a

focused attention that didn't go unnoticed by Stan. Grant didn't expect to run into Noelle again so quickly or in a scene with so much frenetic activity. He cringed, thinking about how she basically ran away after noticing he how he got lost in her eyes. He wished that he had Porter's charm to smooth things over.

"I didn't realize that you knew Noelle," Stan said. "She and Holly really make this place special around the holidays."

"We met the other day." Grant pretended that his interest was casual.

"They volunteer every year in honor of their father. He spent a lot of time here toward the end and they spent Christmas here that year. They came back the next year and it became a tradition for the community. Good people, the Kringles."

Grant noticed that Noelle had returned down the hallway with her arms draped in garland that she was untangling along with help of another volunteer. "Yes," he said, thinking about how his only annual holiday tradition was skiing in the most expensive and exclusive Swiss resort he could find. He felt as if he'd spent too much time building his company and not enough time building a life in a community. Having spent most of his life standing outside of a group and looking in, he wanted to belong somewhere...he wanted to belong in Maplemont.

Christmas at Maplemont Manor

"It's this type of community that your donation supports. Thanks again, Mr. Fitzgerald. That money is urgently needed and we'll put it to the best use."

"I know that you will." Grant nodded, returning his attention to Stan and finding that he had to put effort into not looking for Noelle. "Will it be enough to re-open the cancer clinic?"

Stan shook his head. "I'm afraid not. The roof leak damaged all of the equipment and replacing everything will require close to twenty million dollars. Our patients will have to commute over to Ridgewater for several years until we can even get the funding together, not counting the time to rebuild. I've applied for grants, so hopefully something will come through."

Grant looked frustrated, having wanted to be able to wave a magic checkbook and solve the problem for the town; however, even he didn't have the funds available to cover that amount. Not one to give up easily, he had an idea—he knew a lot of people, especially people with money.

"I'd like to host a charitable gala at the manor to help raise more funds. My grandfather used to have a holiday gala at the manor every year and I'll bring back that tradition, only using it to help raise money for the hospital. With the right guest list, support from the community, and an internet campaign I think we might be able to cover the difference." Grant's eyes lit up at the challenge and he realized that being able to find funding for a startup wasn't any different from raising it for charity.

Stan looked surprised at the offer. While it wasn't unusual for a Fitzgerald to write a check to the hospital, it was very unusual for them to volunteer to do anything else. Noelle and Holly had started caroling down the hallway, leading a jolly group of volunteers between rooms and singing joyfully, although off-tune, as they added small wreaths to the doors. Grant's attention wandered toward their voices and he smiled. Stan followed his gaze and became more suspicious that Grant's sudden interest in the hospital and community had more to do with one very specific person as opposed to general philanthropy.

"I'm sure Noelle would be happy to help you with the holiday gala at the manor," Stan suggested.

Grant seemed startled at the mention of her name and looked thoughtful without responding. "I'll be in touch with your staff about the details. I'll schedule it for Christmas Eve, like the ones grandfather always hosted."

Stan's eyes widened. "Christmas Eve? But that's barely two weeks away!"

"Don't worry, I have a great team," Grant said confidently, mostly referring to Porter who was a genius when he focused his attention on a goal. "You'll have a state-of-the art cancer center before you know it."

Oh Christmas Tree

At the Christmas tree lot, Grant toured the trees and sought out the biggest one he could find to be the centerpiece for the manor's decorations. He always hired a decorator every year for the exterior, but he left the interior of the manor untouched since usually he didn't get up to Maplemont to celebrate anyway. He and Porter typically spent the holiday skiing min Europe.

He realized that he hadn't checked his phone all day, which was unheard of in his busy, work-filled life and then he was even more surprised to discover that his pocket was empty and that he must have left his phone back at the manor. Grant picked the biggest tree that they had and requested it be delivered later that day. Unfortunately, he learned that they didn't deliver.

"I'm afraid that this isn't New York City, Mr. Fitzgerald. You buy it and then you haul it. We'll help you load it onto your car though," the tree lot manager said. After some careful maneuvering, they had managed to get the tree onto Grant's sports car which looked comical considering that the tree completely overwhelmed the car it covered since it was almost twice as long as the car.

"Drive slowly now," the teenage boy from the lot cautioned. "This tree is about as stable as we can make it, but it could still slip off if you take a corner too quickly or something."

Crawling through town in the Christmas sports car, Grant couldn't believe what he was doing. He felt like he was driving inside a Christmas cartoon. He could barely see the road over the tree boughs.

Despite his careful speed, when the road curved tightly a wind gust pushed the tree in exactly the right way that it fell off the top of the car and he was still a mile or two from the manor on the quiet road through the maple syrup farm acreage.

Getting out of the car, he stood by investigating the options and realized that he could take the car *or* the tree to the manor, but not both at the same time. Without his phone, he also couldn't call for help. A vintage red truck soon pulled up behind him on the side of the road and Noelle got out.

She thought about driving past him, but knew that she'd been raised better than that. "Looks like the tree won." She wondered why

Grant had bothered to get a tree by himself, and then cheered herself with the idea that his staff had probably mutinied and deserted him. He wore a full suit which seemed out of place for someone who had planned to pick up a tree, but then again, this was Grant Fitzgerald. She figured that he probably wore a suit to the gym.

Grant laughed. "Yes, you could say that. I didn't realize that they don't deliver and, of course, I bought the biggest tree they had." He was freezing and realized that he didn't plan very well.

"And the smallest sports car." Noelle didn't put any effort into not being judgmental.

"Only the best," Grant said. They shared an awkward silence, both waiting for the other to bring up the other night or to apologize, but neither was willing to budge. The longer the silence, the more entrenched in their positions they became. It soon became clear that they would not be talking about the other night.

"Well, good thing I have the truck. Here, help me put the tree in the back and I'll meet you at the manor." The two struggled a bit to get the unwieldly, twelve feet tall tree into the back of the truck, where almost four feet still hung off the edge so they tied a little red garland trail on the tree's stump for safety.

Christmas at Maplemont Manor

∞∞∞

At the manor, Noelle wordlessly helped Grant get the tree from the truck and propped it next to the kitchen door. "Don't you have staff to do this for you? I mean, you wouldn't want to get sap on your expensive Italian suit."

Grant thought it strange that she referred to his suit at all. "I gave everyone the day off. It's the holidays." What had been a spontaneous and nice gesture now sounded like something he had been forced to do by some sort of manor house workers union. Grant had never been good about taking credit for his ideas, and he usually let Porter take the credit, because he preferred to be outside of the limelight.

Noelle crossed her arms, clearly having an internal debate with herself about whether or not to help him setup the tree inside. She bargained with herself that by helping him with the tree then she didn't need to apologize because that good deed would cancel any other obligation. Besides, she reasoned, if anyone needed to apologize it was Grant, because she had only spoken the truth, albeit rather harshly.

"I'll help you set it up inside," she said. "It would be a shame for a majestic tree like this to die in the driveway because its owner didn't plan ahead."

Grant looked surprised at the offer. He was also too proud to apologize and wondered what exactly he would need to apologize for in the first place. All he did was tell the truth as he saw it, although he knew that he didn't package the message very well. Porter was always the smooth talker who could clean up any situation. In contrast, Grant was the straight talking 'muscle' who spoke truth to power. Grant was always the one to fire employees if they weren't working out, while Porter hid in his office to avoid the confrontation.

Still, Maplemont was a small town the size of a postage stamp and Noelle had been wearing a ridiculous sweater and crowing about the award that it had garnered her. She had also lectured him when she didn't even know him. He looked at the tree, which was almost twice as tall as he was, and silently wished that he could manage getting it into the tree stand inside by himself. He chastised himself for having to buy the biggest tree on the lot, because he wouldn't need her help if he got a regular tree.

"Thanks. There's no way I could get that tree inside by myself." He realized that turning down the offer of help would only add fuel to the fire and that he couldn't otherwise get the tree inside by himself.

They struggled to bring the tree into the main living room and set it up in the stand that Dean had brought down earlier that morning.

Once inside, Grant took off his suit jacket to reveal a perfectly pressed white oxford shirt. He carelessly rolled the sleeves up at the elbows. A trail of dense, spiky tree needles traced their path and they almost broke a table lamp trying to get the tree into the stand. Grant lay on the ground like a soldier elbowing through a muddy field as he tightened the stand braces, while Noelle held the tree up straight.

"Leave it to me to pick the biggest Christmas tree in the world," Grant grumbled and then spit out one of the tree's needles that had fallen into his mouth. He coughed. "I'm pretty sure that I swallowed a pine needle."

"Actually, it was a spruce needle. This is a Norway Spruce, not a Scotch pine, city slicker."

Grant's exasperated sigh could probably have been heard in Norway. "How does it look now? I tweaked it tighter on the left."

"It's leaning *left* now." Last time he asked, she told him that it was leaning right.

"It can't be!" Grant scooted out from under the tree to look at it himself. Noelle took a deep breath after they stood back to appreciate the result of the hard work.

"See? It's still leaning." Feeling exhausted and dispirited after almost a half hour of struggling with the evergreen beast, neither of them really cared anymore. "I feel like the tree is toying with us now."

Grant stepped back a few more steps to

check and he laughed. "I think it might be easier to rebuild the room at an angle around it, so that the tree looks straight in comparison." Noelle couldn't help but smile at his remark. "No one else will notice once it's decorated, right?" They both agreed that no one else would notice that the tree leaned a little left of center. "If Pisa can have a leaning tower, then I can have a leaning Christmas tree."

"Well, I've got to get back to the bakery and you've got a tree to decorate." Noelle started for the door. She planned to spend the evening at the bakery testing out a new fudge recipe. She'd been thinking about maple eggnog fudge, maybe with pecans or walnuts, with a little bit of nutmeg. Unfortunately, so far all of her tests ended up with a sort of blah-tasting maple fudge or something that tasted like maple-flavored nutmeg.

She felt like she had a winning idea, but no clue on how to actually make it work. She needed time in the kitchen to experiment. When she walked out to the truck, she was surprised to find that Grant had followed her.

"Thanks, again. I probably would still be stuck on the side of the road if you hadn't stopped."

"Probably, not many people use this back road. You should be more careful. This isn't the big city." Noelle started up the truck and the engine roared to life. "Bye, Mr. Fitzgerald." Putting the truck into gear, she pulled out of the driveway.

Grant watched the truck until it was out of view. As he turned back inside, he walked quickly annoyed at being called a city slicker twice in one hour. Slipping on a patch of ice, he fell flat on his back and groaned.

"What am I doing here?" he asked himself out loud.

Ye Merry Gentlemen

Porter arrived later that evening to find Grant surrounded by boxes in the living room while white twinkly lights lit up the tree. "Did you do this yourself? Don't you have staff for this?" Porter asked, setting his suitcases in the corner. He'd been to the manor on several occasions in the years since Grant had inherited it.

"I gave them the day off." Grant moved a box from the sofa, while having to shimmy between others to get back to the tree. The two stumbled over a couple of boxes and grabbed each other in a hardy embrace. Grant slapped Porter on the back. "Thanks for coming. Can you help me find the star? I think it's in one of these boxes." He motioned toward two boxes by the coffee table.

"It looks like the North Pole exploded in here." Porter laughed, surveying the mess of boxes, garland, and holiday decorations strewn all over the place. "What exactly is happening with all of…this? I find you not only living in Christmas village here in Maplemont but also decorating your own tree and hosting a holiday gala? Who are you and what have you done with my best friend? We were supposed to be skiing tomorrow and now you want me to help you raise twenty million dollars for the hospital in a town that we don't live in?"

"When's the last time you decorated a tree, Porter?"

"I'm guessing it was the same time you did. That first Christmas in boarding school, when you got the lucky opportunity of being my roommate and we decided to decorate a tree in the common room."

Grant continued searching through a box to find the tree topper. "Found it!" He raised his arm with the star high above his head. Porter looked on, clearly amused. "Pull that ladder over. My dad loved this star. He said that it's been in our family for over two hundred years." Grant turned the star over in his hands to inspect it more closely. Looking at his friend suspiciously, Porter moved the ladder and watched Grant climb to top the tree with the star.

"Uh huh," he said knowingly, "What is the name of the girl whom you're trying to impress by decorating your house into Santa's living room?"

"Noelle," Grant said quickly without thinking and then tried to double back. "No, I mean, she only helped me put the tree up. It fell off my car. She was driving by and—"

Porter smiled. "Sure, so this...Noelle is involved in the gala?"

Grant picked up an angel ornament and carefully found a spot for it on the tree. "Well no, I haven't asked her yet." Grant sighed. "She's not like anyone I've ever met. She's beautiful and... frustratingly impossible. I can't stop thinking about her. It doesn't make any sense."

He felt irritated and unable to control the situation. He wished that he had Porter's natural charm so he could have already been able to ask her out and at least find out if he really liked her. Mostly he wanted to go back to that moment in the kitchen when they stood so close and leaned over, pulling her into his arms without a second thought. He sighed again.

Porter laughed and nodded his head at his best friend's predicament. "You always go after the impossible ones."

The doorbell rang and Grant rushed over to the door, thinking that maybe Noelle had decided to check in on him and the tree. Imogen stood in the doorway.

"I thought I would drop in and say hello."

Grant opened the door and she barged into the living room to find Porter adding an ornament to the tree. He turned around and walked over, assuming she was Noelle.

"So, you must be the woman that Grant

Christmas at Maplemont Manor

can't stop talking about." Porter charmed with a smile as Grant's eyes opened wide in panic behind Imogen's back. While Porter had heard his complaints about Imogen, he hadn't actually ever met her or even seen a photo.

"Oh Grant! You've been talking about me, huh?" she teased, clearly pleased to hear that. "Well, I knew there was a connection between us. I'm Imogen and you are?"

Porter realized that he had made a mistake, having caught Grant's eye. "Porter, I'm Porter Cage—Grant's business partner and former best friend." He joked, realizing his mistake. Grant nodded, clearly wishing that he had a time machine.

"Oh, Porter! I can't believe that we haven't met until now. Grant has spoken of you so often that I feel like we are old friends." Imogen gushed, happy to finally be meeting Grant's best friend.

"Likewise. I have no doubt that Grant is rather deeply regretting having not introduced us sooner so that I would be able to recognize you." Porter shared an understanding look with Grant.

"Are you decorating the tree yourselves? Grant why haven't you gotten a decorator to manage that?" Imogen asked. "It looks a bit... rustic."

Stepping into the fray and completely in front of Imogen in order to help take the heat off of his friend, Porter responded. "That was my idea, actually. I told Grant that I wanted to decorate a tree this year because we haven't done it since boarding school. Of course, I should have realized that he'd buy the biggest one on the lot and that it would take hours, maybe even days, but that's part of the fun."

Imogen smirked, disapprovingly, stepping around Porter. "Well, boys will be boys, I suppose. Actually, I came by because Daddy said that he heard you were planning a gala on Christmas Eve?"

"News travels fast." Grant couldn't believe that the speed of gossip in Maplemont appeared to be faster than a bullet of light.

"Well, you simply must let me help. I know how to make any event fashionable. After all, I'm basically a professional influencer. We'll need a theme. I was thinking either 'Winter Wonderland' or 'Hearts of Christmas,' but a benefit really should reflect the colors of the season. I dislike all the cold whites and blues this time of year. People think it's elegant, but it's so last year." Imogen was now pretty much only talking to herself at this point. "Yes, 'Hearts of Christmas' with red and green tartan and cream candles. Oh, can't you see it? We'll have to get a decorator in to re-do the tree of course, but you won't mind."

"Actually, I would mind, Imogen. We're decorating this tree ourselves," Grant said.

"And it's...charming, but for a gala? No, it

won't work. Oh, we could get little hearts instead of candy cane stripes on the napkins. Of course for the music you must hire that classical quartet from the museum event the other night. They are probably booked, but a call from me and I'm sure that they'll change their plans."

Imogen knew that all Grant needed was for her to step in, especially since everyone had expected for years that she'd be the lady of Maplemont Manor. She merely played her part in a role that had been earmarked for her since birth. Although she didn't exactly receive much encouragement from Grant, he was known to be reserved and serious.

"Those are all really terrific ideas." Porter interrupted and stepped in front of her again. "We will absolutely bring those up to the event manager that Grant hired. I'm sure they have everything under control. All you need to do is to decide what gorgeous dress to wear and how much to donate to the hospital!" Porter took Imogen's hand in his and smiled his trademark dazzle that never ceased to charm, along with his well-chosen words.

Grant saw the opening and took it. "Exactly, everything is already planned so it's too late for changes, especially with such little time left."

Imogen took her hand from Porter. "But who is managing the gala? I don't know of any local event planners who could possibly manage such—" In a way, she found it charming that Grant didn't want her to lift a finger, already playing his role as the doting spouse, however it did vex her that she couldn't be more involved. Events like these would typically be managed by the lady of the manor, a role for which she was certain had already been granted to her.

"I hired Noelle Kringle from the Sugarhouse Bakery. We've already signed the contract." Grant surprised himself with this assertion as if saying Noelle's name to Imogen had cracked a window open into his genuine intentions. Ironically, the only woman in the world who didn't want the title of lady of the manor was Noelle; yet she was also in Grant's eyes, the only woman whom he was beginning to believe that it should be bestowed upon. He thought about how pretty her hair looked pulled back into a haphazard braid and how her hazel eyes sparkled when she laughed.

"Didn't she cater your event last night? I thought the tenderloin was overdone and the clafouti left a lot to be desired. And that ugly sweater! Please tell me that there will be a dress code."

Imogen made no effort to display her horror at Grant's lack of understanding for how important the details at these society events were. She realized that perhaps she had allowed Grant to remain a bachelor for too long and that she should devise the situation to rectify that. She also remembered feeling a stab of jealousy when she saw how Grant looked at Noelle.

Porter was on his phone, pretending to be talking to someone important, and soon waved over at Grant. "Of course, ma'am, hold on I have Grant right here. I'm sorry, Imogen, but I need to steal Grant. We have hours of work to go over tonight and an important conference call. Please be a doll and excuse us this evening," he said while reaching out for her hand again.

Imogen didn't stand a chance at not being charmed by Porter or doing exactly what he asked her; no woman did, outside of Porter's sisters and mother. His charm was absolute. Imogen thought it a pity that Grant was so taciturn compared to Porter. She'd have to change him to be more outgoing once they were married. Imogen said that she understood and didn't want to interrupt their important work.

She kissed Grant on the cheek quickly and walked out to her car, already with a foolproof plan that would resolve everything. She turned to take another look at the manor and her future home, thinking how she knew they would spend all their time in Manhattan instead.

Grant shut the door behind her and shook his head. Porter dropped his phone on the sofa. "Sorry, how was I supposed to know? In all these years of hearing you talk about her, I can't believe that I've never seen a photo or met her. Of course the dragon lady approves of her; Imogen is basically your mother."

"There's no way Noelle will agree to be the event manager for this. She hates me." Grant fell onto the sofa and lightly punched Porter on the shoulder.

In Grant's mind, he was again standing at the kitchen door hearing Noelle say that he was the last man in the world she could be prevailed upon to date. He wondered if it was only the challenge that had inspired him, but then remembered the almost kiss between them and palpable connection that had probably registered on a Richter scale somewhere.

Mostly he remembered what it felt like walking into that kitchen, where the smell of cardamom and warmth of Noelle's smile welcomed him home. That moment felt as if he had the opportunity to be taken by a ghost of Christmas Future where he was rewarded for making all the right choices.

"Well, we will have to find a way to convince her, won't we? Seems to me that Imogen is clever enough to determine pretty quickly if we have actually hired Noelle or not, so we will have to meet up with Noelle first thing tomorrow to close that deal. Otherwise, you're stuck with Imogen." Porter threw his hands up in the air dramatically.

"You did this, Porter, and I need you to undo it." He slapped his lifelong friend on the knee and stood up. "Deploy that Porter charm on Noelle tomorrow and get her to agree to help."

Porter laughed. "You make it sound like my charm is the equivalent of a nuclear option."

"That's because it usually is."

"OK, but you know the rules. I can't fix anything until I know exactly what happened. So give me all the details, everything."

Grant walked into the library and Porter quickly followed. Pouring two glasses of scotch neat, Grant started to bring Porter up-to-speed. As Grant fully expected, Porter soon devised a plan.

"Well, it is obvious isn't it?"

"What is?" If Grant thought the solution was obvious then he wouldn't have called Porter in for help.

"We need to show her the real you; make her realize how wrong she is. You're not a spoiled suit who spends all of his time reading emails and ordering other people around."

"Don't forget boring." Grant rounded out the description that he'd already memorized.

"You're not a boring suit, Grant—you never were. All we have to do is create the conditions for her to see that and also make sure you don't wear another actual suit for a while. Do we need to go shopping?" Porter asked.

"Uh, well, yeah. I only brought my suits and a few tuxes for social events. Oh man, I even wore this suit to pick up the Christmas tree."

Grant smacked himself on the head. He realized how much Noelle's perception of him was based on reality.

Porter narrowed his eyes, indicating that obviously didn't help Grant's case. Standing up, he patted his friend on the back. "Don't worry about it, you can recover from this. You are Grant Fitzgerald, the lord of the manor and catch of the county. Tomorrow we go shopping and then to the bakery. I guarantee that by lunch time she'll be falling for your charms."

Plaid Tidings

The next morning at the bakery, Skye and Noelle enjoyed a coffee during a well-deserved break after the morning rush. Noelle was talking about the gingerbread house competition when the bells on the door's wreath jingled to announce Porter and Grant had arrived. Porter looked well-dressed in a finely tailored suit, while Grant wore dark jeans and a fitted plaid shirt that still had creases on it from being folded in the store. They had purposely coordinated the contrast, to make Grant look relaxed in comparison.

Upon seeing Grant, Noelle looked over at Skye with a knowing glance only Skye's eyes were locked elsewhere, on Porter who likewise seemed transfixed on her. Noelle could smell trouble over the wafting scent of gingerbread.

"Good morning, very beautiful ladies," Porter announced, his voice smoother than the caramel. "Grant, you didn't tell me that Maplemont was home to such goddesses, no doubt to keep that secret all to yourself." Porter winked at Skye and she blushed. "While Grant has already had the honor of meeting at least one of you, I haven't yet had the pleasure. Please forgive our barging in today; I'd like to introduce myself. I'm Porter Cage and this is Grant Fitzgerald."

Skye reached out her hand, which Porter gently leaned over to kiss. "I'm Skye and this is Noelle."

"Absolutely charmed," Porter said, still holding Skye's hand. "So, Skye, what do you recommend that we buy this morning? I have no doubt that you will know exactly what it is that I most desire."

Noelle watched as Skye fell for Porter's words, hook, line, and sink...her. She knew that Skye would no doubt attribute the appearance of this snake charmer to her recent reading about how visualizing what one wants results in all one's dreams coming true. Arching her eyebrows in curiosity, Noelle wondered how someone as serious and generally unpleasant as Grant could have such a smooth-talking friend. Mostly she wondered why they were at the bakery at all.

Noelle decided that whatever it was they wanted that she wouldn't be a part of it. Skye recommended a hand-picked selection of macarons with two pieces of award-winning maple fudge to go along with it.

∞∞∞

The two men sat at a table by the window and Noelle retreated to the kitchen as if it were a protective bunker from the outside world. Skye tended to a group of older ladies who had dropped in for their usual coffee and cookie morning meetup, while their voices filled the room over the holiday music.

"I didn't think that there was a woman alive who was immune to the Porter charm," Grant said quietly across the table to Porter. Although surprised that Noelle didn't find Porter charming, he was also pleased.

"I'm as shocked as you are. Noelle appears to be immune not only to my legendary charm, but also to yours. Here you are, the most eligible bachelor in all of New York, *literally* the handsome millionaire next door and—"

"She couldn't care less." Grant finished his sentence and waved a hand.

"We have our work cut out for us."

Grant stared out the window and thought of Noelle's eyes, his gaze giving himself away. "Most women only like me for my bank account or for my family's name. If they disagree with me when they don't know who I am, then they quickly change their minds once they do. Noelle's not like that. She's a...unicorn. I can't get her out of my head." He didn't want to fall for Noelle, but he couldn't seem to help himself.

Porter smiled and nodded in agreement. "Well, let's go and talk to your unicorn."

∞∞∞

In the kitchen, Noelle focused on adding an eggnog cream instead of regular cream and then she finally started feeling good about the recipe. Her latest idea was for golden maple fudge that was smooth but not sweet, with maple syrup, an eggnog cream, dark chocolate, vanilla, cinnamon, and a salted caramel glaze.

While Carol's go-to maple pecan fudge was always a hit, this new version elevated the treat with a unique twist. The biggest challenge was balancing out the flavors and she worried that the salted caramel would be too overpowering. Noelle poured the mixture on a baking sheet and was deep in the thought, evening out the fudge in the pan as the men appeared in the doorway.

"Noelle?" A man's voice asked tentatively. Noelle looked up, surprised to see Porter and Grant standing inside the kitchen door; the relative quiet safety of her bunker, breached.

"Is there a problem with your order?" She couldn't imagine what other reason would cause them to disturb her in the kitchen. She noticed Grant's gaze drawn to her travel photos on the wall and walked over to them to block his view. Since he assumed that she was a 'townie' who hadn't seen the world, then she didn't want to let him in any further. Men like Grant, or Ewan, saw the world the way that they wanted to and nothing could persuade them otherwise.

Porter continued. "We were hoping that you might be able to help us out of a tricky situation."

Noelle looked unconvinced. "Unless your 'tricky situation' involves cookies or maple fudge then I don't think that I can help you." She started to step away into the shop area.

"Wait, Noelle!" Grant reached out for her sleeve and she stopped. "It does, well sort of. We need your help to plan the Christmas Eve holiday gala at the manor. It's for the hospital and Stan said you might be willing to help."

Skye soon appeared around the corner, looking guilty, as if she had already aided and abetted the two men by letting them into the kitchen in the first place. Noelle considered the problem. Christmas Eve was around the corner and she could barely keep up with the Christmas orders she had already, not to mention working on the recipe for the fudge competition.

"I can donate some fudge, but that's about it. Probably throw in a few dozen macarons. You can have your staff pick them up on the twenty third." She crossed her arms as if that ended the conversation.

"They were hoping that you could help with the planning," Skye said.

Noelle narrowed her eyes in a glare. Skye's inability to see through Porter's charm as manipulation was now a major inconvenience to Noelle.

"Planning an entire gala in less than two weeks, while I'm also behind on holiday orders and the fudge competition? And the gingerbread house event is this week. It's impossible. I don't have time. I'm sorry." Noelle knew that although men like Porter and Grant probably were never turned down for anything, she had assumed that this second 'no' would stick. They were businessmen and they should at least understand and appreciate her situation from a business owner's point of view.

Grant leaned on the island and somehow managed to tip a small bowl of pretzels and cranberries that Noelle had set aside for a snack onto the cooling fudge. Noelle pushed him out of the way and then realized that there wasn't anything she could do. Half of the pan was salvageable which would be fine for testing the recipe, so it wasn't a complete disaster. Her eyes narrowed and looked at Grant who had since moved to the doorway.

"You really should have to get a permit to be in a kitchen."

"I'm sorry. I have no idea how that happened."

"We could help you at the bakery!" Porter volunteered. "We'll do whatever you need us to do, since you are so busy, wouldn't having two extra staff at your beck and call be invaluable? And we'll do all the work on the details of the gala. We only need your advice on local things like bands, theme, decorations, and stuff like that."

Noelle looked at Porter. It was clear that he was only going to annoy her until she agreed to help and she was too busy for that, so she weighed her options. She could use help with the gingerbread house event and it would be a kind of punishment to them for bugging her. They also seemed strangely desperate for her help and not asking much of her.

"You'd be willing to work the gingerbread house competition this week and help package the holiday orders?"

Both Grant and Porter nodded, not knowing what either task implied yet confident that it sounded easy enough. They would have agreed to build an extension on the bakery if she only asked. Skye smiled, knowing how much work the gingerbread competition was. Noelle shook her head. While she could use the extra help and it would be fun to watch them squirm during the gingerbread house event, she didn't want to spend any more time with Grant than necessary.

"No, I'm sorry, I can donate some fudge, but that's all. You will have to find someone else."

Skye looked almost more disappointed than Grant and Porter. The bakery door wreath's bells jingled as Imogen Prescott entered the bakery. Noelle turned to greet her, noticing that Imogen looked like a celebrity who had left a spa that had a hair salon and clothing boutique.

Her look was inexplicably perfect and Noelle was sure that Imogen's coat alone probably cost more than the espresso machine she wanted to use the competition money to buy. Imogen immediately zoomed over to Porter and Grant, giving Grant a once over that clearly indicated she found his plaid shirt wanting. She hugged Grant and pecked a kiss on his cheek, then did the same for Porter.

"Grant, Porter, darlings! I was hoping to see you here. What is this, Grant? Going off with the lumberjacks later?" She laughed at her own joke. "Oh good, Noelle is here also. It is lovely to see you. No holiday sweater today? I suppose it's only for special occasions." Noelle looked up at Imogen as she did with any rude customer or theatrical four-year-old, which was basically not a frown but not a smile either. "I pulled some strings and found an expert event planner who's agreed to take on the holiday gala at Grant's house, which I am certain is a relief to you, Noelle. I mean, not that your work isn't fine for a basic family dinner, but an event like this? We really must have the very best. I'm sure that you understand."

The men were both about to speak before Noelle responded.

"I appreciate your concern, Imogen, however, the contract has already been signed and I'm committed to the gala. I'm sure that you can understand the importance of a legally binding contract. If we didn't all meet our obligations, well, there would be chaos in the streets. How kind of you to try to help Grant though. I'm sure he's wondering what exactly he ever did to deserve having someone like you in his life. Did you want to purchase anything today? Perhaps some croissants or maybe a few pieces of maple fudge?"

Noelle finished, while both Porter and Grant stood silently, both completely shocked. Imogen smiled aggressively, her plans having been sunk so effortlessly by Noelle, while Grant stood by with a shrug, as if saying there was indeed nothing that could be done.

"No thank you, I find that most baked goods outside of the city aren't worth their trouble in calories. A woman must watch her figure, after all." Noelle answered that by grabbing a croissant and taking a bite. Imogen looked as if pistols had been drawn at high noon. "I must get off to my yoga class, Grant, be a dear and pick me up for lunch in an hour." She behaved as if their meeting later had been pre-arranged.

"But Grant, I thought we were going to go

over the music options. I mean there are still so many decisions to make, it will probably take most of the day," Noelle said.

Porter looked at Imogen as if he were watching a professional ping-pong match, between ninjas.

Grant nodded, still a bit dazed. "Yes, of course, forgive me Imogen but we'll have to meet up at another time. The gala must take priority. I'm sure you understand." Grant almost couldn't believe what had happened. Not only had Noelle agreed to work with him but she'd also basically told Imogen to go pound sand.

Straightening the collar on her very expensive jacket, Imogen continued smiling aggressively as if in a beauty pageant. "Of course—another time then, darling." She kissed him on the cheek and glided out the door.

Once her coat could no longer be seen from the bakery's large windows as she turned the corner, Porter gave Noelle a long and impressed look.

"I'll expect you both here at two o'clock sharp to set up for the gingerbread house competition the day after tomorrow," Noelle said simply. Skye grinned broadly, happy to know that she would be seeing Porter again.

Grant nodded. "We wouldn't miss it." In the last year of dealing with Imogen, he had never successfully routed her as Noelle did. Instead, the only trick that ever worked was simply disappearing, like he did at the concert earlier when he pretended to look for the restroom only to head to the car. His regard for Noelle only grew.

"Noelle, would you mind coming to manor tomorrow to help us generally figure out the floor plan and decorations? Very high-level input but we could use a feminine point of view. It would only be maybe thirty minutes of your time, say lunch tomorrow?" Porter felt impressed by how quickly he was able to set this up.

"Fine." With that single word, she then turned to leave for the kitchen.

∞∞∞

When they got inside the car, Porter started to laugh. "I think I'm in love!"

"With Noelle?" Grant looked shocked that his friend would even consider going after someone he'd already mentioned himself. They had an established rule about that.

"No, Skye, but yes, that Noelle of yours is truly gifted. The genius of her phrasing! *'I'm sure he's wondering what exactly he ever did to deserve having someone like you in his life.'* Noelle really is your unicorn. I think you were right that we should move here. I'd be willing to relocate only to see Skye again. I think it's love at first sight!"

Grant chuffed. "You always think that. Still, the only reason that Noelle agreed to help us was to spite Imogen, it had nothing to do with me. She didn't even notice that I wasn't wearing a suit." The more he thought about it, Grant realized that perhaps less progress was made than Porter thought.

"I have a feeling that very little escapes Noelle's attention. She noticed. I'm sure of it. Besides, you have another chance to wow her at this gingerbread thing. I mean, how hard can it be?"

Neither of them had any idea about what Noelle had in store for them.

∞∞∞

Back at the manor, Fiona chatted with Dean while he got ready to move the tree decoration boxes back into the attic and she dusted the living room. "Today, he left the house wearing a flannel shirt and jeans!" she said. "Can you believe it? A flannel shirt!" Fiona laughed.

"I haven't seen him wear anything but a suit or a tuxedo since I started working for him," Dean replied. "And today, out of the blue, he walks out in jeans!"

"Jeans!" Fiona repeated, as if he had instead worn an avant-garde outfit made of only toilet paper.

"Mrs. Fitzgerald-Smythe would never approve." Dean lifted up a box and got ready to take it upstairs.

"I saw Skye at yoga last night and she said that it was Noelle who helped him put up the Christmas tree. Evidently, she found him on the side the road and helped him not only get the tree to the manor, but also set it up."

Dean stopped to look at the tree before going up the stairs. "That explains why it's crooked—neither of them was paying close enough attention." He winked and Fiona giggled.

∞∞∞

Before closing the bakery for the night, Noelle tasted the fudge with the new recipe. After it had cooled for three hours, she added a salted caramel glaze on the half that didn't get hit by the pretzels and cranberries. It wasn't right. The caramel glaze overpowered everything and it was not possible to taste the eggnog cream.

To confirm her suspicions, she then tried a piece on the pretzel end to see if the eggnog came through. The salt from the pretzel and the sweetness from the cranberry worked in harmony with the eggnog and maple to create almost exactly the flavor she had been looking to create.

"Well I'll be! It's missing the smallest thing still like pecans, no…pistachios." Noelle laughed out loud, alone in the bakery and turned up the holiday music for a victory dance. She had figured out the recipe.

An Eggnogural Tour

Noelle arrived at the manor to discover Porter leaving at exactly the same time. He opened the door for her and Grant stood in the foyer.

"Aren't you staying?" she asked.

"I'm afraid that I can't. I've run out of shampoo and the closest salon that carries the brand is in Ridgewater. Grant can fill you in on our plans though. See you later!" With a quick wave, he popped into the back seat of the car that Dean magically pulled up in.

It didn't occur to her to suspect they had pre-coordinated the departure word by word. Of course someone like Porter would drive one hour to get his favorite shampoo dressed to the hilt in a suit, she thought. She waved and walked inside.

Grant wore a crisply ironed gingham shirt with dark jeans, perfectly fitted. Noelle couldn't help but notice that he also wore socks with a Santa on each foot for a little holiday 'pop' to his otherwise put together look. She found that surprising and endearing. In the car ride over, she had already promised herself that she wouldn't be intimidated by Grant or the fancy manor. She repeated a mantra in her head that it was nothing to stress about.

"Hey."

"Noelle, thanks for coming over here. I know that you are very busy." Grant closed the door behind her and Noelle took off her snowy boots in foyer. "Have you been to the manor before, outside of the other night I mean?"

Shaking her head, she replied. "I did come here a few times when I was a kid. Your grandfather used to host a big Fourth of July party with fireworks, but we weren't allowed inside the house. Otherwise I've only seen the kitchen and dining room, aside from struggling with the Christmas tree."

"Why don't I give you a tour? You'll be able to help us plan the gala better once you understand the layout better." Noelle agreed and Grant felt as if he'd acquired some of Porter's smooth-talking charm, however pre-planned. "This is the main living room. I don't spend much time here. Usually I'm in the TV room or the library."

Noelle raised an eyebrow at the mention of a library, while she thought about how her entire apartment would easily fit into the manor's foyer. Her eyes were drawn to four plush

Christmas at Maplemont Manor

red and white stockings that hung on the stone fireplace where only one Christmas card, a handmade card of red paper and a crayon drawing of a Christmas tree, stood on the mantle. She wondered why only one card was displayed and who the child involved was.

The tree lights flickered in front of the large window, where the slightly leaning spruce tree held center stage in the large room and scented the air with a fresh, earthy scent. The tree had unique ornaments dotted throughout with white lights and a charming popcorn garland. The star at the top looked like it had been handed down through the generations.

"Grant, the Christmas tree looks beautiful. I like that it looks understated and not like a decorator threw up on it. I love these antique ornaments."

He looked pleased. "Porter and I made the popcorn garland ourselves. It took us a *very* long time. We were just talking about it though and maybe we should get a decorator to redo it for the gala." Grant thought of Imogen's disdain for their handiwork.

"Don't you dare! It's perfect." She noticed how he seemed to relax a little.

"We thought that the band could go over there and then the dance floor right over there." He motioned to the large area on the side of the tree, currently filled with a variety of plush chairs and antique tables sitting on wool rugs near another fireplace that was big enough to house a sofa. The end effect made it look like a posh hotel lobby area with limestone walls and maple wood floors. "Do you think there's enough space?"

Noelle looked like it was a trick question. The room was so large that there was enough space to host a basketball game. "Probably."

"Obviously we'll move the furniture and roll up the rugs. We can store everything we don't need in the garage. I've also ordered some side chairs to line the walls."

"That sounds like a great plan. If you remove the dining table, then you'll have space for two long side tables for the food and it will be easier for traffic flow." Noelle found it difficult to imagine the size of the garage that could store all of that stuff, but if it was anything like the rest of the manor then it should be no problem.

"We hadn't thought of that, Noelle, but it makes sense to store the dining table as well. Good idea."

"How long have you owned it now, Grant? Ten years?" she asked, remembering that it had been about ten years since his grandfather passed away.

"Longer than that, grandfather gave it to me when I graduated from college. He didn't want to worry about estate planning or something about inheritance taxes."

"You got a mansion on twenty-acres for

a college graduation gift? Wow. I got a luggage set." Noelle found it difficult to relate to him, given their wildly different life experiences.

Grant suddenly realized a flaw in the plan of dazzling her with a tour of the manor. Noelle wasn't like the other women he had dated, who were impressed by his wealth. He was a little uncertain in this new territory and nervous about showing the rest of the house.

"The library is one of my favorite rooms." She followed him down a wide, formal hallway lined with oil paintings in gold frames that were probably all by famous painters. "I spend a lot of time here because it's my new office."

Noelle was impressed by the floor to ceiling wood built-in bookcases, large desk, and huge window with a view of the garden. A grand piano occupied a corner. She couldn't stop herself from running a hand along the hardcover antique books that decorated the room. "It's incredible."

Noticing the piano, she asked if he played although she knew the answer would be no. People like Grant only had concert pianos for decoration. He surprised her by nodding in confirmation that he did play and then sat down at the piano bench, tapping the bench for her to sit by him.

"Any requests?"

"Something festive."

Grant started playing a jolly holiday tune

that showcased his expertise on the piano and Noelle had to remind herself not to be impressed. After he finished, she clapped politely. He removed his hands from the piano and motioned for her to play something.

"Your turn, Noelle."

She shook her head. "I never learned."

He showed her a simple tune and she copied him, playing a repetitive beat. He added the melody and it sounded like an actual song, which made Noelle laugh as her face beamed with pride at the achievement.

"We make a good team," he said softly.

Noelle stopped playing the piano, feeling a little unnerved at how easy it was to spend time with him and she was not about to fall into that trap. She noticed a large oil painting of a man wearing a blue military jacket and black tricorn hat that somewhat resembled Grant across from them, mostly from the strong jaw.

"Who's that?"

"That is my five-times-great-grandfather, Henry Fitzgerald. He fought in the American Revolution."

Noelle stood up to inspect the painting and Grant followed her. "And who's in this one?" She pointed to a neighboring painting of a man also in a blue uniform but with a short blue cap.

"He's my three-times-great-grandfather, George, who fought in the Civil War. My grandfather liked to brag that in every American military conflict, one could always find a Fitzgerald. Grandfather was in the Army in World War II and his father, the first Grant Fitzgerald, served in World War I."

"Wow! That's kind of intense, actually."

Grant nodded in agreement. "Indeed. It's a lot to live up to."

She noticed that he seemed to almost retreat into himself, as if he didn't mean to say that out loud. They proceeded further down the hall to a massive room with windows on both sides and two large brown leather sofas.

"I mostly use this as a TV room, but I thought that maybe for the gala this could be where we serve drinks."

Noelle wanted to know more about how the Fitzgerald's ended up at Maplemont Manor. "How did your family end up founding Maplemont?"

Grant sat down on one of the leather sofas and she copied him, sitting across from him. "After the Revolutionary War, Henry bought a large tract of land here and started the maple syrup farm that your family manages now. He wanted a quiet life. His son worked on the Erie Canal and speculated on a risky steelmaking venture that ended up paying huge dividends. He's the one who founded Maplemont to bring in staff for the steel plant in 1825 and he also had the manor built after selling the plant at the height of the market in 1901 and then selling the maple syrup farm then also. Listen to me, I sound like a history book. What about your family? How did they end up running the farm?"

"My family didn't fight in the Revolutionary War; they came over from Ireland during the potato famine. Somehow they ended up in Maplemont, working at the farm until they eventually bought it. My grandfather used to joke that they jumped a train to get out of the New York slums and took it as far as they could. Evidently back then the train line ended in Maplemont."

"So, Kringle is...an Irish name?" Grant asked in disbelief, raising an eyebrow.

Noelle giggled. "No. We think it was due to poor penmanship. My family came from the Dingle peninsula in Ireland. Dad always thought that the real name was originally Kavanagh, but somehow when they immigrated it became Kringle. As far as I know we don't have any military heroes or anything." She thought about how even their family lineages were on completely opposite ends of the spectrum.

Standing up, Grant smiled and reached out hand to help her up. "I must apologize for not being a very good tour guide. I get distracted too easily."

Noelle noticed how when he winked at her, his eyes seemed to twinkle. Quickly, however, she dismissed it as unlikely. "I will take that into account on my internet review of the tour today, Mr. Fitzgerald," she teased.

They toured the billiard room that held two pool tables and three card tables, where the walls were painted a deep scarlet and crystal chandeliers created unique shadows on the ceiling. Upstairs they peeked into eight different guestrooms, one that had been converted into a gym.

He stopped in the hallway at a framed old photo of his father and grandfather in relaxed cashmere sweaters, while eleven-year-old Grant stood between them next to a Christmas tree. It was the last photo Grant had of him and his father, before his father died in a car accident.

"This is one of my favorite pictures. That's my dad and my grandfather." A part of him wanted to Noelle that it was the last photo of all of them together, but he wasn't ready to share that yet.

Inspecting the photo closely, Noelle observed, "It's the same star on top of the tree. You look so happy."

Grant smiled at the memory. "My dad was so much fun and my grandfather was always there for me. Did you ever meet him, my grandfather?" Since Noelle had grown up literally around the corner, he wondered if she had met his grandfather or gotten to know him in his later years.

"I didn't. I traveled a lot and wasn't around. My sister went to his funeral though."

Julie Manthey

"I wish I could have made it to the funeral." Grant's eyes narrowed, as if stung with regret. "I couldn't get away from work."

This news upset Noelle. She knew that his grandfather had given him so much, including the manor, and it made her a little angry to learn that Grant didn't make it to the funeral because he was busy with work. Although he was handsome and rich, she could never excuse something like that.

"What job was so important that you couldn't get away?" She couldn't help herself.

Grant looked surprised and offended by her question. She didn't know him or the situation and yet assumed the worst. He knew that she still saw him as a spoiled jerk, regardless of how many casual shirts he wore with jeans instead of suits.

"My grandfather would have understood," he said sharply and then continued down the hall, ending the conversation.

They returned to the main living room down the grand staircase quietly and found Fiona dusting in the living room. She had heard them talking and managed to find a way to get in the middle.

"Hello, Noelle! It is lovely to see you again. Has Grant taken you on a tour of the manor? What do you think?" Grant's eyes watched her response closely, although he pretended to not care about her response.

"It's very grand. How big is it?" The scale of the manor almost defied Noelle's definition of a home.

"The manor is twenty-one thousand square feet." Grant's words were crisp and staccato like throwing knives. Fiona looked at him in surprise at how harsh his response was.

"That's big…for a place to live. I mean, it's amazing and gorgeous. You must love it here." She tried to backpedal on her initial reaction to the manor's size. "I think you're right about the location for the band and moving the drinks to the TV room is a smart idea. That gives a lot of space for people to spread out and really talk."

She hoped he didn't take her comment too negatively and something in his manner had changed distinctly since looking at the photo upstairs. Noelle understood that they weren't simply different people; they were like different planets in their own universes. She had to remind herself that, especially whenever he smiled at her. She wouldn't need to worry about that for the moment, however, as he seemed to wish her to leave.

∞∞∞

Porter returned to the manor sometime later. He had spent the afternoon in Ridgewater, mostly to have lunch at a farm-to-table restaurant he read about and also to do some Christmas shopping. He bought Grant a very garish holiday sweater that featured gingerbread men running away from an outreached hand and a new hockey stick as well. He found Grant in the TV room, watching a hockey game and yelling at the TV, as if personally arguing with the referee.

"You know that they can't hear you." Porter shook his head and smirked at Grant.

"Well they should be able to! There is no way that was a penalty!"

"How did the tour go?"

"I don't think she was impressed. She seemed overwhelmed by the size of the place." Grant summarized his understanding of Noelle's point.

Porter looked concerned. "Do you think that's a good thing or a bad thing?"

Grant shrugged. "My grandfather always told me that I should marry a woman who loves me in spite of the manor and not because of it." In most of his dating experience so far, he'd only met the latter that is, until meeting Noelle. She seemed to bring out the worst in him and yet, she also challenged him more than anyone.

"So…it's a good thing that she was overwhelmed by the manor house? Is that what we're thinking?"

Grant yelled at the TV again, annoyed by another call that he thought should have been a penalty instead. He sighed. "I guess. I don't know.

When she doesn't think about it, we get along effortlessly and have fun. But then something will happen and she'll be simply impossible and judgmental. The craziest part is that I still want to be around her, all the time, even when she's being...insufferable."

"Sounds like you've met your match, Grant."

Gingerbread Elves

Noelle left Skye in charge of the bakery while she ran out to get some last-minute supplies for the gingerbread competition. Her mind turned over the meeting with Imogen and the deal she had struck with Grant and Porter. Imogen reminded her of Ewan's sister, and having had two years of learning the art of polite verbal dueling with the best, dealing with Imogen was a cake walk.

She wondered what Grant thought of her and then tried not to think about it. She figured that he probably thought of Imogen as the 'right' sort of woman that he should marry, and clearly Imogen had her sights on him as well. Of course his mother probably set the whole thing up when they were born, Noelle thought. Noelle knew that there wasn't anything between her and Grant and the only reason he asked her to help on the gala was most likely because of Stan at the hospital.

Stan probably assumed that it would

be good exposure for the bakery and Noelle reasoned that he meant well. She only agreed to annoy Imogen. That she also had the opportunity to mess with Grant and Porter at the gingerbread house event today was the cherry on top. As she walked to the boutique grocery store on Main Street, she was intercepted by Betty who was writing a new holiday message on the chalkboard sign in front of her clothing store. A large and bubbly woman in her sixties with a short, pixie haircut who always wore bright red lipstick, Betty always seemed to sparkle in Maplemont's limelight.

Betty's small store sold a combination of sweaters and flannel, mostly items geared for living in their cold climate. In the summer, she switched over to Maplemont T-shirts and postcards for the tourists. Everyone in town knew her and she knew everybody's business. The mayor was known to drop by to see 'Miss Betty,' as she was known in town, at least twice a week to keep his pulse on the goings on.

"Miss Noelle! You will simply not believe it. Come inside out of the cold." Betty pulled on her arm and Noelle giggled. Betty never called anyone by their first names directly, always adding a 'Miss' or 'Mr.' as a prefix and it would take her at least one year before she addressed someone by their first name. She called Noelle 'Miss Kringle' for almost two years before making the switch. Betty was the first of all the Main Street merchants to welcome Noelle to town after she arrived. She had arrived at the bakery with a basket of wool socks as a welcome gift. Noelle always enjoyed chatting with Miss Betty because it made her feel truly part of the community.

"Miss Betty! How are you?"

"I have the most exciting news!" Miss Betty clasped her hands together and jumped a little in excitement. "Mr. Fitzgerald is going to host a gala on Christmas Eve at Maplemont Manor, like the old days. A gala! Isn't that something? He came into the store the other day and almost bought me out of plaid and flannel shirts. And oh, if he isn't the most handsome man in the county then I don't know who is." She winked at Noelle. "He's also single."

"Actually, he asked me to help him with the gala." Noelle now understood where the plaid shirt had come from and why it had looked so new.

"He did *not!*" Betty clasped her hands on her face in excitement. "Well, yes, that makes sense. He's cozying up to the local merchants. First with me, of course, when he bought me out of flannel. He's a man who knows quality when he sees it, that much I know. Who could throw a gala in this town without also serving the award-winning maple fudge from Sugarhouse? Do you know what this means? Let me tell you, I am sure that he means to settle down in Maplemont. I heard from the mayor as much.

Did I tell you how handsome he was—like our very own movie star in Maplemont, that's what it is."

Noelle nodded in agreement, as that was typically the best response with Miss Betty where anything you said would be shared with the entire town later. The last thing in the world Noelle wanted was Miss Betty telling the whole town that she also found Grant to be very handsome, even if it was the truth.

"His friend is so charming. A Mr. Cage, I believe was his name, like a charming rogue from a novel. He was helping Mr. Fitzgerald soften his look and Mr. Cage implied it was to impress a local woman. Of course, I'm dying to know who she is. Imagine one of our own Maplemont residents becoming the lady of the manor!" Betty sighed, almost swooning at the romance of the idea.

Noelle thought that perhaps he was trying to impress *her*, but then quickly disregarded the idea because it was ridiculous. Besides, she knew that horrible Imogen Prescott was more his style. A bright green and red sweater caught her eye next to tartan pajamas. "Is that an elf sweater, Miss Betty?" She walked over closer to inspect it.

Betty giggled. "Aren't they precious? I tried to convince Mr. Fitzgerald and his friend to buy them, but they wanted to think about it."

Noelle grinned knowing that an elf costume was very possibly the last thing in the world that Grant Fitzgerald would ever wear. "They are indeed the most precious of sweaters."

"Look over here. I have matching elf ear hats that tie it all together." She tried on the little green hat that made it look like she had elf ears and Noelle laughed. "Mr. Fitzgerald said that he prefers to be called by his first name, but you know that's too informal for me. I suppose that I'm old fashioned. I had to remind him to call me 'Miss' Betty not once, but *twice*. I suppose they only had time to shop for shirts as they seemed to be in a bit of a rush…probably to see you!" Her eyes twinkled as she pieced together the chain of events.

A mischievous thought crossed Noelle's mind. "I'll take three of the sweaters, including the ears." If Grant's brand-new flannel shirt and jeans had been an attempt to show that he was like everyone else, she thought she'd see how far she could push the envelope.

∞∞∞

At the grocery store, Noelle found the additional decorative gingerbread supplies like licorice, sprinkles, and jelly beans. She also picked up two extra boxes of candy canes and more coffee for the bakery. Porter and Grant arrived at the bakery fifteen minutes earlier than

Christmas at Maplemont Manor

agreed, which surprised Noelle. She showed them where the extra tables and chairs were and where to set them up, resulting in four long rectangular tables being set up in the bakery while the other smaller tables were moved in the back room.

Porter spent time flirting shamelessly with Skye, eventually bringing up his opera ticket subscription which made Skye even more certain that they were meant to be. Grant tried not to notice and was always amazed at how easily Porter fell into relationships. Noelle soon appeared with the elf sweaters and hats.

"The tables look great, thanks. Here are your uniforms for the event, please put them on quickly because the kids should be arriving soon." Skye squealed with glee at how cute the elf uniforms were, while Grant stopped in his tracks.

"There are only *three* here, why aren't you wearing one of these...ensembles?" Grant remembered seeing them in Betty's store that morning and wondered when Noelle bought them.

"Because *I'm* the boss." Noelle's eyes sparkled. "Of course, if you don't want to wear the uniform, then I'm sure Imogen's event manager would be happy to take over. I am very busy, as you know."

Grant and Porter quickly pulled on the elf sweaters and put on the hats that made it look as if they had pointy elf ears. Noelle stifled a laugh, but her eyes showed her delight.

"What exactly do we need to do here?" Porter asked.

"Sugarhouse hosts the annual gingerbread competition every year. We're expecting about twenty kids to participate and you'll need to generally be on hand to help them with the house construction and make sure they have all the supplies that they need," Noelle explained.

Grant stood up confidently and pulled up his sleeves. "Sounds easy enough." He thought that Porter was right earlier when he asked how hard an event like this could really be.

Skye laughed. "I don't think you were listening closely to the numbers. Twenty children under the age of six and three adults while the kids eat sugary treats and argue about their design plans."

Porter gave Grant the 'thumbs up' and made a hand motion for him to smile. Both men realized that Noelle had set them up, evidently hoping they would give up.

"Dig deep," Porter whispered to Grant. "We got this."

The very loud and energetic children started to stream in the doors and Grant felt completely out of his comfort zone. He'd never babysat in his life, let alone built a gingerbread house.

Skye tapped Grant on the shoulder. "Smile

—they can smell fear." She winked. Once all the children had arrived, Noelle provided them with a quick overview on how to build their houses and the materials available to them. She then slipped back in the kitchen to perfect the fudge layers for her recipe. Grant and Porter exchanged worried glances, as if suddenly they were left in charge of a mental institution.

The kids ran around from table to table, 'borrowing' supplies from other groups and comparing design plans. Chaos ruled the day and when Grant checked his watch after what felt like two hours, he was horrified to discover that they had only been at it for about ten minutes. Every child seemed to need help with gluing together their house with frosting or trying to landscape the 'yard' with chocolate and jelly beans.

As more candy was consumed, the tempo of the room increased into a fever pitch until soon Noelle was called in to deal with a little girl who was in tears and completely inconsolable. Grant had been trying to help her with the roof of her house, but it was still crooked and then a little boy had eaten what was supposed to be the chimney piece.

Skye yelled for Noelle over the already noisy room. Noelle rushed in to find Ava in tears and Grant sitting next to her while their gingerbread house looked like it had been toppled by a tree.

"What happened?" She knelt down to Ava's eye level. Ava's eyes ushered forth big tears and she struggled to speak in between sobs, taking deep breaths.

"The roof is crooked and Tommy ate the chimney. He knew it was my chimney and he ate it anyway! And... this elf can't fix anything. He's not very good at building gingerbread houses." Ava listed out the many problems of her world while she continued to cry.

Noelle hugged her and wiped the tears from her eyes. "Ava, honey, take a breath. Now, let me look at that house. Oh, I see what happened." She took some chocolate and a couple of reindeer candies and placed them on the roof, along with a small licorice piece to serve as a new chimney. "Look, Ava, Santa's sleigh was so heavy with gifts that he dented the roof!"

Ava laughed and her eyes lit up with delight. "You fixed it, Auntie!" She hugged her tightly.

Noelle smiled. "OK, now I think we have an apology to make to this nice elf who was trying to help you, Ava." Grant shook his head, but Noelle insisted.

"I'm sorry, Mister Elf. It's not your fault that you don't know how to fix gingerbread houses," she said as a back-handed apology that made both Grant and Noelle laugh.

Noelle took out a piece of fudge from her apron and handed it to Ava. "Well, I'm not going

Christmas at Maplemont Manor

to let the perfect be the enemy of good, as your mom used to always say. Here, try this fudge and let me know what you think."

Ava grinned and ate the whole piece at once. She made a face. "Too sweet, Auntie. I don't like it." She then returned to her seat and started added gum drops around the door frame.

Noelle nodded and looked at Grant, "She's my best taste tester. Ava doesn't worry about sparing your feelings with food—she's like her mother that way."

Grant smiled. He looked a little sheepish, leaning over to talk quietly to Noelle. "Thanks for that save. I had no idea how to fix that and she wouldn't stop crying. Ava is Holly's daughter?"

Ava interrupted, happy to be the center of conversation. "No, my mommy is Carol and that's her picture by the door, but she died." Ava blew a kiss toward the picture. "Auntie Holly is my other mommy now, and sometimes Auntie Noelle. Mister Elf get me more chocolate chips! I need them for the roof."

Grant's eyes softened once he realized that Noelle and Holly had lost their sister. He mouthed a silent 'I'm sorry,' to Noelle and she nodded.

"Ava Caroline Mitchell that is *not* how we ask someone for help. Don't be bossy." Noelle waited.

Ava patted Grant's shirt and directed all of her attention at him. "Mister Elf. What is your name?" she asked sweetly.

"Grant."

"Elf Grant, pretty please could you get me some more chocolate chips? I'm sorry that I was so bossy."

He fell instantly for her charm. "That's OK, Ava. I'm bossy too sometimes." He winked at Noelle which took her off guard. "More chocolate chips coming up!" He stood up and hurried across the room to check out the other tables and their stockpiles.

Noelle's eyes couldn't help but follow him. Across the room, he and Porter shared a laugh and Noelle noticed a different side of Grant—a lighter and more casual version of him that reminded her of their kitchen mousse escapade. She wondered if maybe in the kitchen she had seen and known the real Grant and the boring suit was a separate persona that he maintained for others. Ava tugged at her sleeve and Noelle turned her attention back to the girl.

No Partridge in the Pear Tagine

Before leaving for the day, Fiona was tidying up in the kitchen when Grant appeared wearing the elf sweater and elf ears. Her eyes twinkled as she stifled a laugh. Noticing her response to him entering the room, Grant took the elf ears off and set them on the kitchen table.

"Oops! I forgot that I had these on," he said with a chuckle.

"Working on a special mission for Santa, sir?" Fiona asked.

"You could say that." Grant smiled broadly. "We helped Noelle with the gingerbread house competition. She'll be helping us with the Christmas Eve gala, so it was the least we could do."

Fiona nodded, wondering if Noelle knew that Grant was falling for her. She had noticed a change in him since he returned to Maplemont.

"I've set aside two dinner plates in the refrigerator."

"Thank you. You always take such good care of me and I really appreciate it. Without you, my diet would consist only of coffee and burnt toast." His appreciation was genuine.

"It's my pleasure."

"Did you know Noelle's sister, Carol?" Grant was curious to learn more about the family.

"Yes, everyone knew Carol. She was sweeter than fudge and far too young when she passed. Noelle and Holly dropped everything to be there for Ava and to keep the bakery and farm going. Those girls are so much like their dear mother Libby; they are always willing to help. I do worry that Noelle might be lonely in this small town, though."

The last comment intrigued Grant. "Really? Why?" The implication that Noelle was not dating anyone was not lost on him.

Fiona pretended as if she hadn't planned her words very carefully. "Oh, it's only my speculation. I shouldn't have said anything," she demurred, putting on her tweed jacket and wool scarf. "Have a good night, sir."

He started humming a Christmas carol and walked upstairs. Fiona watched him with a smile. She would delight in her report to Dean about the conversation later.

∞∞∞

That night, Noelle cooked dinner at Holly's house, which was their regular routine. Noelle lived across the driveway, in the separate apartment that their parents had built for their grandmother. Carol lived there when she cared for their mother and then she inherited the house. Holly moved in after Carol passed away and Noelle decided to live in the apartment so she could help Holly and Todd with Ava. Because Holly and Todd could find a way to burn water and the apartment kitchen was small, they usually had most meals together in the house with Noelle cooking and Holly doing the dishes.

They wanted Ava to grow up with family around her and hoped that would be enough for her to learn about her mother. The house smelled of cinnamon, honey, and saffron, as Noelle prepared couscous while a Moroccan tagine of lamb, pears, garlic, and onions steeped in the oven.

After setting the table, Holly returned to the kitchen. "We haven't had a tagine night in a while." Her tone seemed to be an accusation, mostly because they both knew that Noelle only cooked tagines when something was bothering her.

Noelle ignored the remark. As the only

person who didn't really cook in a family of chefs, Holly had learned early on to pay attention to the subtle cues each recipe represented.

"Why don't you call everyone to the table, dinner will be ready in about two minutes," Noelle said.

Holly looked frustrated, but not defeated. "Fine, then don't tell me." She wrangled her husband, Todd, from the office where he was researching last-minute Christmas gifts, but pretending that it was something for work at the hospital. She also yelled out for Ava whose footsteps could soon be heard on the stairs.

Noelle placed the tagine in the center of the table and lifted off the top dramatically. "Ta da!" Everyone at the table clapped before taking a deep breath to smell the sweet and spicy combination.

"Ooh!" Ava exclaimed, clearly impressed by the presentation. "What's in it?"

"It's lamb, onions, pears, and yummy spices," Noelle said.

"Do I like lamb?" Ava asked with curiosity.

"Yes! You love lamb, remember? It's caviar that you didn't like," Noelle said reassuringly, knowing that Ava hadn't ever tasted lamb or caviar. While it was dishonest, she had learned it was the easiest way to help Ava develop a more refined palette that included more than chicken strips and grilled cheese sandwiches. It also avoided any battles at the table.

"Yah! Lamb and pears in a...what's that thing called?"

"It's a tagine. That's the name for this type of pot that they use all the time in Morocco."

As they each filled their plates, Holly looked at Noelle and wondered what was bugging her. With both of her sisters and parents being chefs, she'd learned early on that they communicated more clearly through food instead of words. Holly knew that in Noelle's cooking language, a tagine meant comfort food to ease stress where macarons meant being in love. Vanilla cake would alarm Holly because it always meant sadness tinged with ennui; it meant that Noelle was moving away.

Some families talked about their feelings, others ignored them, but the Kringles turned them into food. Carol's maple fudge always meant love, which is probably why it won every award.

"Ava, honey, how did it go with building the gingerbread house today?" Holly asked.

"My house's roof was crooked and Tommy ate the chimney, but Auntie fixed it. She put Santa's sleigh on the roof so all the gifts make the roof crooked! I had an elf to help me and at first he wasn't very good, but then he was my favorite elf because he was so nice to me...even when I was bossy," her voice trailed at the end, saying the part about being bossy a little bit softer as if it wouldn't be picked up by Holly.

Julie Manthey

"There were elves helping out?" Holly pried, more surprised by that than by Ava being bossy.

"Yes, and they wore elf sweaters and hats with elf ears! Grant was my favorite."

Holly raised her eyebrows and looked at Noelle, noticing an almost imperceptible blush in her sister's cheeks. "Grant Fitzgerald was dressed in an elf costume at the bakery today?"

Todd perked up at the name. "Grant Fitzgerald? Really? Did you know that he donated over seven hundred thousand dollars to the hospital? Stan told me at work and swore me to secrecy, by the way, so you can't tell anyone. Evidently Grant doesn't want people to know the actual amount. Stan only told me about it because, well he was so surprised, and he needed my advice on the most critical equipment on the list for replacement at the cancer clinic."

Both Holly and Noelle looked surprised at the news. "Did you know about this?" Holly looked at Noelle.

"Grant said that he planned to donate to the hospital, but nothing about the amount." Noelle was surprised that Grant had donated so much money without almost a second thought after she mentioned the problem to him offhand in the kitchen the other night.

"Stan told me that not only did he donate that much, but Grant is also hosting a gala benefit for the hospital on Christmas Eve with the hope of being able to raise the twenty million dollars needed for the complete overhaul." Holly's eyes widened. "Imagine that, hon, someone hearing about the hospital needing twenty million dollars one day and then creating a plan to get that amount within two weeks! Stan said that most people in the community have no idea how much we owe to him because Grant doesn't want them to know. He prefers to keep his contributions anonymous. For example, did you know that last year Grant personally paid for the entire refurbishment of the gym at the school and the kitchen remodel at the community center a few years ago?"

Noelle looked like a piece of couscous could have knocked her off her seat. She had no idea that Grant had been contributing so much to the community over the last several years, or that he had been involved in any of those projects. The mayor and other community leaders had always only mentioned grants as the source of income for these projects, never a mention of Grant. Noelle also remembered what she had said to Grant that night in the kitchen, saying that the Fitzgeralds didn't actually care about the community but instead they simply decorated it. Her stomach turned.

"Sounds like Maplemont has a guardian angel," Holly said, her attention drawn to Noelle's reaction. "Maybe someone owes somebody an apology." Noelle glared.

Ava sighed. "But I already apologized for being bossy."

Holly smiled and said that was good of her to do. "How exactly did Grant end up helping out at the gingerbread house event?" Holly prodded, knowing that the tagine was certainly somehow related to Grant.

Noelle waved a hand. "He and his friend came to the bakery today asking my help for planning and catering a Christmas Eve gala at the manor, to help raise money for the clinic."

Holly looked confused. "But you are already overbooked with everything else—you can't possibly also manage a gala in two weeks." Holly wondered why he went to Noelle in the first place. That night at the manor, he had made it clear that he didn't plan on hiring her for anything else. Then she remembered that he did protest a little too much.

"I said as much and told them no. Then Imogen Prescott came in."

Holly rolled her eyes. "The ice princess of Mount Briar," she groaned. "I'll never forgive her for how she treated mom in that house." Holly remembered how decades before, Imogen had created a story about stolen jewelry that she herself had personally lost, which resulted in Libby being unceremoniously fired by the Prescotts.

Imogen was almost eighteen years old at the time and she thought she lost the necklace at a party, but couldn't admit that she'd been to a party so she manufactured a tale that blamed Libby Kringle for theft instead. Months later, the driver found the necklace in the back seat of the car and, although the Prescotts apologized profusely for the accusation, their mother refused to return to work there.

Noelle nodded in agreement. "Imogen made this big deal that Grant shouldn't hire me and that she had found some other event planner, implying the whole time that my work and food were subpar."

Holly shook her head. "And you couldn't let that stand, so you agreed to help them to spite Imogen." Holly didn't disapprove of the decision. She had started to think that Noelle had likewise protested too much about being paired up with Grant though.

"Yes, I agreed as long as they helped with the gingerbread house event. They were very persistent and promised that my role would be limited."

Holly understood what had inspired the tagine night now. Noelle had agreed to take on this big event and to work closely with Grant and his friend over the next two weeks. Holly also knew that Noelle couldn't back out of it now.

Hark! The Mother in Maldives

Grant received a late-night call from his mother, while he and Porter were working on the website for the gala. "Mother? Is something wrong?" Grant asked, since usually he never received a call from her once she was on vacation, with the exception of Christmas day.

Porter made a face. Grant put her on speaker phone so that Porter could hear the conversation, knowing that he would tell him everything later anyway so it was more efficient.

"Grant, dear, can't a mother call her son without there being something wrong?" She sat on the veranda of their luxury resort hotel, with a view of crystal blue water in the background. A broad brimmed hat shielded her from the sun as she finished her breakfast.

Sighing, Grant sat down on a nearby leather lounge chair. "Yes, of course, although you very rarely do."

"Well, now that I think about it, I did hear a disturbing bit of news from Imogen. She's very concerned that this gala you are planning for Christmas Eve will be...what did she say? Oh yes, more 'ugly sweater' than elegant cashmere." Rosalind laughed at the description. "That Imogen is such an eloquent writer."

Grant shook his head. "Mother, I have everything under control. It's a benefit for the hospital and a holiday party like the ones grandfather used to throw. There's no reason for you, or Imogen, to worry," Grant assured her. Since he moved to Maplemont, only striking distance from Mount Briar, his mother had taken a more passionate interest in his life than ever.

"But darling, we have a reputation to maintain and your actions reflect on the rest of the family, and of course, on Imogen." Porter made a face and Grant rolled his eyes. "As you very well know, it has always been the wish of her mother and me that you two marry. She's beautiful, accomplished, and exactly the type of woman that you should be with. I don't know why you—"

Interrupting her, Grant replied sternly, yet not without patience. "The gala will be a success, mother. You have nothing to worry about." Grant shook his head and Porter gave him a gesture of encouragement.

Rosalind sighed, exasperated. "Don't

think you can simply change the subject. Grant, you have responsibilities to your family and the Fitzgerald name. Imogen is exactly the right type of wife for you and she has been since you were born." She could not understand why her son dallied away his time as he did. He should have married Imogen four years ago and already been a father of at least two children. Her plan for him had been made clear and his deviation from it was incomprehensible to her.

Porter aped an understanding look with his friend, since his family had similar views and they would also not approve of his attentions toward Skye. "Your concern has been duly noted, mother. Enjoy the rest of your vacation." Grant hung up the phone. It quickly rang again and he ignored it.

Porter patted him on the back. "We knew it was only a matter of time for the dragon lady to strike back after that scene with Imogen."

Grant nodded. "Still, her point has been made. Even if Noelle does eventually fall for me, my mother will never accept her. If I married Noelle, she'd be in for a lifetime of passive aggression from my mother and any of her acquaintances."

"If you *married* her, huh?"

"It's a figure of speech." Grant waved a hand.

"I don't think so. '*Time is money*' or '*heart of stone*' are figures of speech. '*If I married her*' is an imagined condition, and in this example, first conditional where you believe that situation is quite likely."

"Sometimes I forget that you were an English major."

"Language is power, my friend! Already thinking about marrying Noelle means you are, at least subconsciously, more serious than I thought." Porter rubbed his hands together, pretending to look serious while stifling a laugh. He enjoyed putting Grant on the spot.

Grant sighed. "I don't care what your grammar thinks I'm subconsciously or consciously saying. I'm attracted to her and I like spending time with her. It makes sense to think about what direction that could go in the future, that's all. It's nothing more than that. Maybe I shouldn't pursue this if that would mean committing her to a lifetime of passive aggression from mother and her circle of society snobs."

"Remember how deftly Noelle handled Imogen? Don't underestimate her; your unicorn can hold her own. Besides, name one married person you know who has a perfect relationship with their in-laws." Porter waited.

Smiling in appreciation for Porter's support, the knowledge of his family's disapproval still weighed heavily on Grant's thoughts. "The night that I met Noelle, Holly tried to apologize on her behalf. She said that Noelle's heart had been broken by some rich guy whose family never approved of her. Maybe she isn't as resilient as we think." Grant worried that he had become too involved with the idea of Noelle in his life and that it had zero chance of working out.

"There's only one way to find out." Porter crossed his arms.

Silver Lanes Aglow

The next evening, Noelle walked to the local grocery store on Main Street to pick up some extra butter and a few other essentials before heading home. She loved how the town glittered when decorated for Christmas and preferred to walk, despite the cold weather. Upon leaving the grocery store, she bumped into Grant who had stepped out of the local realtor's office.

"Grant!"

"Noelle, this is a nice surprise. I met with Kevin about buying an office space here on Main Street. He said that the old shoe store building down the street might be a great option."

Noelle pointed to her small grocery bag. "I was picking up a few things before heading home. My car is at the bakery."

"I'll walk with you there. I wouldn't want you to get mugged."

Noelle laughed at the absurdity, given that they had never had one mugging incident in all of Maplemont's history. "That's really not necessary—"

"I insist."

"OK." Noelle agreed and they walked along a few steps in an awkward silence.

"I don't like the idea of opening an office in a former shoe store. I'm worried it will remind me too much of my ex-girlfriend who was obsessed with shoes."

"Well, I'm sure that you can renovate it so that it doesn't look like a shoe store."

"Yes, but everyone giving directions for years will still say 'the old shoe store.' But I do want to be on Main Street."

Noelle nodded in agreement. Maplemont didn't change much and there were still many people who referred to the bakery as the 'old sugarhouse' when it was a maple syrup processing facility in the late 1800s.

"She really must have left a scar."

"I thought it was love and she was more interested in my check book. When she found someone with deeper pockets, she broke it off without a second thought." Grant didn't bother making himself sound more pathetic by adding that had happened to him several times in the last decade. While he had come up with all of these 'dating tests' over the years, he still had a difficult time finding anyone who cared more about him than his spending power.

"I'm sorry. Ironically, my ex broke up with

me because I didn't care about his money. He grew up in a castle in Scotland. I thought we were really serious and I asked him to move to Maplemont when Carol…passed. He stayed in Scotland and now he's married to the heiress of another grand British estate. He wanted to secure his future and keep the castle which requires a lot of money. His solution to the problem was to marry someone as rich as he was."

"Sounds like he was only interested in her because of her money. He sounds like a jerk to me." Grant better understood the scar left behind from that breakup.

He knew that Noelle would need to overcome that before she would agree to date him. He also knew that there weren't enough plaid shirts in the world to make him seem like the 'guy next door' when he lived in the closest thing Maplemont had to a castle. Her prejudice against dating a wealthy man, combined with his concern of their long-term relationship prospects, nearly made any potential relationship between them seem doomed from the start. Yet, he was never someone who cared about the odds.

"Thanks, yeah I agree." Noelle stopped in front of an empty building that the town still had decorated with a Christmas wreath on the door and lights across the window. "This is the… potential real estate opportunity." She stopped herself from calling it the old shoe store.

Peering into the window, Grant tried to look past the empty wall stacks and window display area. He noticed maple hardwood floors and exposed brick walls. He tried to imagine areas for a few desks and a waiting area for visitors. "It looks like a great building and the location is exactly what I wanted. Perhaps it's time for me to move on and not allow myself to continue being haunted by a ghost of Christmas Past."

She understood his reference about the importance of moving on with life. Ewan marrying Lady Seraphina Breckenridge had made her think that any relationship with Grant would be destined to fail. She wondered if Holly was right and she had put too much trust in the past repeating itself. Noelle thought that perhaps it might be time to release the ghost of Christmas Past from determining how she lived in the present. "It is a great location."

Two young boys rushed past them, pulling a sled as they giggled and hurried toward the park to meet their friends. Miss Betty waved to them from across the street, greeting them with a 'Merry Christmas' as she pulled her sidewalk sign in for the night. They continued walking toward the bakery and Noelle asked him how he was finding life in Maplemont.

He commented about how he enjoyed the slower pace of life and how Maplemont was the only place he ever knew as 'home.' She could relate. Grant gestured at the holiday lights draped above them.

"I love Maplemont. I mean look at this street, all lit up for Christmas as the snow practically floats down. It's idyllic. In the city, there would be unending noise from traffic with honking cabbies and people pushing to get by on the sidewalk."

Arriving at the bakery, they stopped by Noelle's truck in the parking lot. "Thank you for seeing me safely here." Noelle grinned.

"My pleasure. There were a couple of dangerous thugs that I think we managed to avoid," he teased.

Noelle giggled. "Barely made it out with our lives. See you tomorrow."

He nodded and closed the truck door for her with a wave. After watching her truck disappear down the street, Grant spun around and started the walk back toward his car at the grocery store. He stopped for a few seconds at the park to watch a pack of rambunctious boys chase each other and then screech down a small hill with their sleds around the large town Christmas tree.

He decided to buy the shoe store. Although the manor was certainly big enough to house an office, he preferred to have a place for clients to visit that was completely separate from his house. He also liked the idea of being within easy walking distance of the bakery.

Miracles and Mistletoe

The next afternoon, Noelle closed the bakery early so she and Skye could attend the gingerbread house competition event judging. Grant and Porter had already helped that morning to deliver all the gingerbread houses to the community center where they would remain on display for a few days and then the children would take their creations home with them. The event started with the children singing a few Christmas carols for the crowd and it continued with the mayor making a short speech and explaining the rules of the competition.

"I personally want to thank everyone for coming today and especially to Sugarhouse Bakery for helping to make this event possible," the mayor said as the crowd clapped in appreciation. He was a tall, husky man who towered over the podium, dressed casually in jeans and a plaid shirt. "This event is a cornerstone of support to help keep this community center serving as the heart of our town. These children spend time here after school, we also serve lunch daily here for our senior citizens, and the center also supports several community classes from English as a second language to plumbing basics for those like me who need a little help on anything DIY."

The crowd laughed hard at this last remark, as the mayor's work on renovating his 1880s Victorian house on Maple Avenue was a constant source of stories from him, including his latest problems with replacing the lead pipes. "Basically, this center is our home for everyone and today's gingerbread competition not only recognizes the work of these children, but it also helps raise funds for the center. Remember, you can buy tickets to vote at the table over there."

Miss Betty and Jocelyn sat at the table and waved their hands. "You can vote as many times as you want. This is to raise funds, after all," Betty said.

The mayor smiled. "Voting is open until the Christmas Cookie Swap and the winner will be the house that receives the most votes. I highly encourage you all to 'vote early and often! Also please don't forget that we'll be meeting here later this week for the Cookie Swap and to wrap up toy donations for those in need."

Again the crowd clapped, dispersing to

buy tickets and vote with the ticket stubs in the small boxes in front of each gingerbread house. Grant and Porter soon caught up with Skye and Noelle, as they were putting tickets into one of the voting boxes in front of a gingerbread house scene. They all laughed at the house where the roof had caved in overnight and a clever parent saved the day by setting a plastic dinosaur toy next to the house. The dinosaur had a piece of gingerbread inside of its mouth, standing over the house nefariously.

The mayor came over to shake Grant's hand and Grant smiled and laughed. "Absolutely! You know that I wouldn't miss it for the world. Victor, I don't believe you've met Porter—this is my business partner, Porter Cage. Porter, this is Victor Rivera." Porter reached out to shake Victor's hand. "Of course, you already know Noelle and Skye."

"Yes, and ladies, thanks again for all your work to make this happen," Victor said. "This one," he pointed to the dinosaur house, "is my favorite!" Victor laughed heartily. "See you tomorrow, buddy." Victor stepped over to talk to a group of senior citizens.

Noelle gave Grant a curious look, wondering what the men were talking about and surprised that they were so chummy. She realized that it probably had something to do with all the donations Grant made over the years to the town, so naturally the mayor knew him, but their relationship was much more like friends than Noelle had expected. Grant noticed her interest.

"Impressed that I know the mayor?"

"Hardly - everyone knows Victor. I am a bit curious as to what you are helping him with tomorrow though," Noelle admitted.

"Why don't you come with us? I can tell you that it involves the best nachos in Maplemont." Standing so close, Grant couldn't help but notice that Noelle smelled like cinnamon and vanilla.

"You're helping the mayor with something at El Toro?" she asked, referring to the best Mexican restaurant in town. Grant winked.

"No, I said the *best* nachos in town. I can pick you up at seven o'clock tomorrow night?"

"OK, sure, but what exactly will we be doing?" Noelle's curiosity was getting the better of her.

Grant smiled. "It's a surprise."

Noelle wondered what she had agreed to, but then didn't worry about it because she assumed it was some sort of volunteer project with the mayor. Porter asked about band recommendations for the gala and Skye said that she knew of a great cover band that was playing at the Old Stein bar that night. She recommended that they all go out to listen to them and check it out as an option for the gala.

As soon as Skye mentioned the band type,

Noelle thought that Grant would instantly disapprove and probably instead recommend finding a classical quartet or something similar and higher brow for the gala. To her astonishment, Grant said that it was a great idea and that he wanted the gala to be fun and not a typical, stuffy charity event.

"At the end of the day, it's a big holiday party and people should have fun. I'd like to feature the winning gingerbread house in the decorations also, allowing people to continue to contribute money towards the community center. Boy, I sure hope this one wins." He pointed to the dinosaur house. "It's hilarious!"

They all agreed to meet later at the bar to see the band and then Porter and Skye slipped off on their own, looking at the gingerbread houses. Grant put all of his fifty tickets into the box at the dinosaur house and Noelle laughed.

"You surprise me," she said.

"In a good way, I hope."

Noelle smiled, "Yes, I suppose you're *not* a boring suit," she said as a way of an apology.

"And, based on your world traveling photos at the bakery, you aren't someone who has spent their whole life in this postage stamp town," he offered likewise in lieu of an apology. "Skye said that you took them all yourself. She told me about many of them when we were cleaning up after the event yesterday."

Noelle nodded. "Holly likes to say that I

took the long way around, but I moved back here after Carol passed away." Grant listened. "It was a plane crash. She and her husband went on a big trip for their wedding anniversary to Alaska. Holly came up from the city to babysit Ava. I was in Scotland and flew back the next day. I've been here ever since…almost four years ago."

"I'm so sorry, Noelle. I can only imagine how difficult that must have been for you."

"Thanks. We do OK here in Maplemont." She quickly changed the subject. "Do you really think a cover band is right for the gala?"

Grant stopped a second to think. "I suppose that it depends on the covers. I'd like to hear them first and see if they are good and what their range is. It's a holiday party, so we definitely want dancing and people to have fun. I'm keeping an open mind."

"For decorations, Suzanne at Downtown Flowers has always been great about helping out with the hospital decorations. I'm sure she'd be happy to help."

"I'll call her tomorrow then. So, we have flowers, a gingerbread house, a crooked Christmas tree, and possibly a cover band. All we'd really need are some other Christmas decorations, which we have at the manor already, and food. Perhaps you might know someone who could help?" Grant asked.

Noelle laughed and Grant smiled, happy to make her laugh. "You make it sound so easy.

Julie Manthey

We still need a theme, staff, and for sure we'll need a Santa Claus. Perhaps you might know someone who could play Santa? Didn't your grandfather always play that role at parties?"

"I'm sure Porter would make a great Santa." Grant ducked out on the implied invitation. "He's much better with people than I am."

"Don't sell yourself short. Ava said that you were her favorite out of all the elves, which is high praise."

Grant almost blushed. "Where is she? I expected that she'd be here with the other kids."

"They'll be here. They are running late. Todd, Holly's husband, had a work party that they went to first. What type of theme were you thinking about for the gala? Knowing that will help with the rest of the decisions we need to make about decorations, flowers, and the food."

"Oh, Porter has already come up with one. He's been telling everyone it's the 'Miracles and Mistletoe Gala.' We've already sold all three hundred tickets and our online campaign is also doing rather well—raised almost two million dollars," Grant said casually as if he had said ten dollars.

Grant had always bragged that Porter was the best 'money man' in the business world. They worked with a web designer on the page and sent it around to their friends and other influential acquaintances. Porter had even managed to get the hashtag of *'mistletoemiracles'* trending.

Noelle stopped short and suddenly felt the pressure of the event acutely. She knew that people spending a lot of money on tickets and donations wouldn't be impressed by a dinosaur gingerbread house and cover band. She worried that it would reflect badly upon Grant and she wondered if Imogen was right. Imogen would know how to throw a gala for that type of crowd and she would make sure it was elegant.

With her confidence diminishing, Noelle spotted Holly, Ava, and Todd entering the room. Ava ran up to Noelle and Grant and hugged them both. Todd and Holly soon caught up. "Grant, you've met Holly before and this is her husband, Todd," Noelle said, introducing them.

Grant said it was nice to see them both and they also laughed at the Jurassic house. As they chatted about the competition and walked between the different houses, Holly focused entirely on Grant, especially noticing how Grant looked at Noelle as if she was all he wanted for Christmas. Holly wasn't the only one to notice.

Betty walked up to the same gingerbread house that they were looking at and naturally joined the conversation. "Don't you love this event? It's so much fun to see everyone out to support the community center. My sources tell me, Mr. Fitzgerald, that you and Mr. Cage helped the children build these gingerbread houses."

Betty mostly wanted to check the accuracy of her information, but she was also fishing for the identity of the local woman that Grant had his eye on. She first suspected it was Zoe Davis, a nurse at the hospital who had been selected as Maple Syrup Queen three years running. Zoe was not only the town beauty but also recently single after breaking up with the art teacher at the high school last month. Betty presumed that the hospital connection for the gala resulted from Zoe's influence; however, the only women that anyone had seen Mr. Fitzgerald with were Imogen and Noelle.

Stepping back for space, since Betty stood a little *too* close to him, Grant confirmed her information. "Your sources are correct, Miss Betty. Porter and I helped the children build these houses, although the dinosaur wasn't our idea unfortunately."

Betty was pleased that he remembered to include the 'Miss' when he addressed her. "We are all very much looking forward to the gala, Mr. Fitzgerald. I must say that your grandfather would be proud to see you bring back the tradition. Who are you taking as your date?" Betty often found the best route to information was asking a direct question.

Grant's gaze drifted to Noelle who was listening to Porter brag about the gingerbread house that he played a key role in building. Noelle laughed as Porter pointed out how much frosting they used to get the graham cracker door to stick to the house. Grant smiled and looked back at Betty. "I've been too busy to figure that out yet, Miss Betty. Perhaps like my grandfather I'll decide to go as Santa Claus."

"Grant, are you planning to stay in Maplemont, or move back to the city? Forgive me for prying," Holly said. Betty also listened closely to his response.

He caught Noelle's eye before answering, catching her off guard. "Well, it's not prying if we are friends and I do hope that we are. I plan to stay here permanently. I've decided to buy the old shoe store for my new office space. Porter and I plan to start a new company." Grant hoped that he conveyed how very serious he was about staying in Maplemont and also being around Noelle.

Noelle needed to get some air. Between Miss Betty and Holly, she'd been on the receiving end of too many nuanced glances. "I have some work to do at the bakery," she lied, walking out toward where her coat hung near the door. Stepping away, Grant followed her while Todd and Porter starting talking about the city.

Betty and Holly exchanged a knowing look clearly sharing the same suspicion. "Does she know?" Betty whispered to Holly.

"You see it too, right?" Holly was grateful to have a confidant.

"The way he looks at her—" Betty pretended to fan her face with her hand.

"My sister is very stubborn. I think she doesn't *want* to see it, but then a part of me thinks she does, you know?"

"I'm sorry to tell you, but I think Miss Noelle might be crazy." Betty shook her head and sighed. "Love is wasted on the young." Holly laughed.

∞∞∞

Grant caught up to Noelle in the coat room. "Is everything OK?"

"Yes, fine. I decided to take a chance and submit my own recipe to the maple fudge competition this year. I need to finish my recipe and I'm really close. Besides I don't like being the center of attention with all these people and the mayor. Crowds aren't really my thing. I'll see you later at the Old Stein?"

"I think it's great that you're going to submit your own recipe! Meet there at eight o'clock? Let me know if you need a taster. I don't have much experience, but I was recently voted favorite elf by a very discerning expert," Grant joked.

Smiling, Noelle turned away for the door. About a half hour later, Holly found her at the bakery in the kitchen with holiday music blasting. Todd had taken Ava home so that the sisters could catch up. Noelle turned down the music

Christmas at Maplemont Manor

while Holly grabbed a piece of fudge.

"Is this the next award-winning fudge?"

"I hope so. What do you think? Ava thought it was too sweet so I toned it down with some cream, pretzels, and more butter."

Holly's face glowed with appreciation. "Oh Noelle! This is brilliant! It's better than Carol's and you know that I wouldn't say that if it wasn't true. This fudge is perfection and if you don't win the award this year, then I will be shocked."

"You think so? I don't know." Noelle's hands fidgeted nervously.

"You know this is amazing...And it's time. It's time to take a chance on your own recipe." She had been trying to get Noelle to submit a new recipe to the competition for years now, although she couldn't crack Noelle's reservations about making the change.

While both women knew that it was Carol's wish that Noelle would make the bakery her own, Holly knew that her sister still felt that changing the Sugarhouse submission to the competition would be a slight to Carol. She understood because she often felt that way when Ava called her 'mommy.'

Noelle smiled because she did think that this was gold medal-worthy maple fudge, and it was nice to hear Holly confirm that. Perhaps more important was Holly's permission that it was time to submit another recipe instead of the

'Christmas Carol' fudge that she'd been submitting. She smiled as Holly took another piece of fudge.

"Thanks. It means a lot to me that you said that. It needs a name. Any thoughts?"

"Well you could always go with the bakery name as Sugarhouse Christmas fudge, but this fudge is *epic*. It really needs a better name. It tastes like nothing else I've tried before. What about Christmas Kiss?"

Noelle looked unconvinced. "Maple Wonderland?"

It was Holly's turn to look unimpressed. She shook her head and they both continued to think. "Mistletoe Mystery?"

Sighing, Noelle rolled her eyes. "Please nothing about mistletoe—the theme for the gala is Miracles and Mistletoe."

Holly nodded that it would be too much to have them be so related. "I have the perfect fudge but no name seems right. I was hoping that tonight I'd walk in here and the right name would appear in my mind."

"If only we knew someone who was good with product development and marketing. You know, like Grant and that smooth-talking partner of his, Porter," Holly said, knowing that she was pushing Noelle. "They need to try this. Speaking of Grant, I'm confident the mistletoe was his—"

"It's only *business*, Holly, the most eligible

bachelor of Maplemont isn't interested in me."

Holly didn't look convinced. "I wouldn't be so sure of that."

"Even if he had the *slightest* interest, which I doubt he does, his mother would never approve. It would be exactly like Ewan all over again, only instead of a Scottish laird it would be the 'lord' of Maplemont Manor. I'm not going to make the same mistake twice. Grant is handsome and charming, but in the end, he'll choose someone like Imogen."

"Maybe it's time to take a chance on more than a new recipe, Noelle. You were always the brave one and you used to be fearless. That Noelle is probably dying to take a chance on Grant."

Disagreeing, Noelle shook her head. "It's easy to be fearless when you don't understand the risks. Ewan broke my heart and then Carol." She paused. "I just can't—" Noelle closed down.

"OK. We'll come up with a name on our own." Holly could tell by the tone in Noelle's voice that she needed to take the long way around the idea of Grant. "Exactly what is in that heavenly concoction?"

"It is maple fudge with maple syrup, an eggnog cream, dark chocolate, vanilla, cinnamon, pretzels, cranberries, and pistachios."

Holly sighed contentedly. "It is a Christmas dream, that's what it is."

"That's it! Christmas Dream! You are a genius!" Noelle hugged Holly.

"It's the pretzels that really put it over the top."

"Actually, it was Grant's idea...Well an accident caused by him."

Holly raised an eyebrow. "Grant inspired you, did he?"

Noelle shook her head. "I wouldn't quite put it that way and I didn't say that."

"You two sure have been spending *a lot* of time together and it seems like you get along very well. He's buying the old shoe store and his office will be steps away. I think he's getting serious about you."

"Don't be ridiculous. He's probably dating Imogen or someone like her. Money always seeks out money. Please drop it, Holly. I'm stressed enough as it is with this competition."

Holly knew when to drop it. She picked up another piece of fudge. "Carol would love this, you know, she really would be so proud of you. I love you, you know that, right? I only want the best for you."

"I know." They hugged again, thinking about their sister and how they held her close in their hearts.

On Comet and Cupid!

At Maplemont manor, Porter and Grant were getting their jackets on waiting for Dean to pull up to the door with the car. "I'm taking Skye to the opera in the city tomorrow," Porter said. Grant looked surprised. "Is it all right if Dean takes us there and back? You'll be in Maplemont all day."

"Of course! No problem. You're not wasting any time, are you?"

Smiling broadly, Porter nodded. "When you know, you know. I thought that was something to which you could relate. Not all of us take our time when we find our unicorn. Skye and I have been out on two dates already. Turns out we both love the opera." He pulled the gloves out from his jacket pockets.

Grant and Porter got in the car as Dean drove them over to the Old Stein. "Dean, Porter needs a ride to and from the city tomorrow, could you please take him?" Grant asked politely, yet knew what the answer would be.

Grant always preferred to treat staff as his grandfather had, as if they were very helpful family. He was grateful that his grandfather had been such a good model to follow, in contrast to his mother whose staff routinely quit because she was so difficult to work for.

"I'd be happy to take them, sir." Dean always appreciated that Grant asked him even though he always said yes. He'd worked for Grant longer than anyone else, because of how well he was treated.

"Thanks, Dean. It will be a long day for you, so please take the following day off."

"I will. Thank you, sir." Dean knew that Grant didn't really need a driver now that he'd move to Maplemont, but Grant told him very clearly that his job would remain in place as long as he wanted it. Knowing it was hard for Dean to keep other steady work with his condition, he never gave up on him. It was the least he could do, Grant thought, knowing that Dean was a hero who continued to struggle with PTSD. Fiona was planning to retire soon and Grant knew that Dean would be a good replacement as the estate manager and Dean agreed that he was eager for the opportunity. Dean loved the quiet and peace in Maplemont.

"I'm impressed that you *finally* invited Noelle out for a date tomorrow," Porter said.

"It's not a date."

"It involves food and you two sitting by

yourselves, so yes, it counts as a date. Wouldn't you agree, Dean?"

Dean shook his head. "It's not my place to comment, sir."

Grateful for Dean's loyalty, Grant smiled. "It's not a date, because she doesn't think that she *accepted* going on a date. It's simply two civically-minded people out to help the community." Porter shook his head.

∞∞∞

Holly stopped by Noelle's house to pick up Ava in time for Noelle to leave for the Old Stein. "Thanks for taking Ava."

"You know that she's always welcome here. She's playing her video game. Did Santa's elves finish all of their business?"

"Yes, thanks. Everything is under wraps. Is that what you are wearing for your double date?" Holly looked her sister up and down, clearly disapproving of her fashion choices.

Noelle wore a black turtleneck sweater and jeans. Her hair was pulled back in a ponytail. "It's not a *date*. And what's wrong with what I'm wearing?"

Holly frowned. "At least let your hair down." Holly pulled at Noelle's hair to remove the ponytail holder and her hair fell down in loose waves. "Are you sure that you don't want it

Julie Manthey

to be a date? I mean, he's rich, handsome, and the way Grant looks at you—"

"What are you talking about? If he does ever look at me, I'm sure it's only an attempt to frighten me with his contempt." Noelle didn't appreciate Holly trying to add drama to what was purely a business deal between them.

"Is he *still* the last man on the planet that you'd ever consider dating or maybe you might have been too quick to judge?" Holly wanted to know if things were starting to thaw.

"Holly, please. He doesn't have the slightest interest in me, at least not really."

"Miss Betty is right, you are crazy."

Noelle groaned. "You have not been talking to the town gossip about me and Grant, have you? Please tell me that is not what is happening."

"Oh Noelle! Grant likes you. Even the astronauts on the space station can see that. You decided on the first day you met that you didn't like him and now you refuse to see it, or you are too afraid to acknowledge it, or just too stubborn." Holly knew that she was lecturing, but she also knew that she was the only person to whom Noelle might actually listen.

"Maybe I shouldn't go."

Holly shook her head. "Chicken!" Holly whispered. Then calling for Ave, soon Ava bounded down the hallway and gave Holly a hug. "We'll get out of your way," Holly said.

Christmas at Maplemont Manor

Ava asked if they could stay longer so she could finish her game, but Holly explained that they had to go because Auntie Noelle had a date. Noelle made a face and shook her head. Holly laughed and quickly ushered Ava out the door. Noelle stopped to check her hair by the mirror near the door and decided to leave it down, when she put her jacket on.

"It's *not* a date," she whispered to herself.

∞∞∞

At the manor house, Dean and Fiona sat at the kitchen table for dinner. Grant encouraged the staff to eat there, considering it was so much more convenient and he hated to see any food go to waste.

"Evidently he's asked her out on a date tomorrow," Dean reported.

"You don't say! I heard that there was quite a scene at the bakery between Noelle and Imogen. A friend of mine was there the other day when Imogen came storming in and trying to take over the gala. Noelle stood her ground and wouldn't budge! I think she does like him," Fiona said with confidence. Fiona and Dean shared a knowing smile.

"For his sake, I hope so. I like working for Mr. Fitzgerald, but I'll quit if he marries that Imogen. Noelle is so nice. She brought out hot coffee and fresh fudge to me when she saw me waiting in the car the other day. He was out looking at that office building downtown and she recognized the car. She said it was our secret."

"Noelle is exactly like Carol—as sweet as fudge."

"Perhaps they need a cupid to help them along?" Dean suggested.

"*Two* cupids are better than one." They started to brainstorm on how they might be able to help the couple realize that they were perfect for each other. Fiona knew that, however they intervened; it must be subtle enough to avoid detection by either party.

Tinsel in a Tangle

Noelle was the last to arrive at the Old Stein, where she found Skye, Porter, and Grant sitting at a table. The band had started playing a fast tempo song that had enticed many out to the dance floor. The drummer threw his sticks in the air as part of a dramatic drum solo. Skye sat next to Porter, so the only empty chair was next to Grant.

"Sorry, I'm late," Noelle said. "I was watching Ava while Santa's elves completed some of their tasks."

Grant noticed how pretty her hair looked when it fell across her shoulders. He had only seen it pulled back and this was the first time he saw it down. He tried not to stare at her, but he had trouble looking away.

Skye smiled. "Perfect timing, Porter and I were on our way to the dance floor. You can keep Grant company." She stood up while Porter pulled her out onto the dance floor.

At the table, Noelle and Grant shared an

awkward silence for a few minutes, while they waited for the other to say something.

Noelle broke first. "What do you think about the band?" she asked, shifting uncomfortably in her seat.

"I like them."

"Great. Is this the type of band that you were hoping to find for the gala?" she asked, trying to gauge Grant's response. Seemed to her that a cover band probably wasn't what most of the people attending a gala thrown by Grant Fitzgerald would expect; the band certainly would never have been chosen by Imogen. She also thought Holly was crazy. He didn't look at her any differently than he did anyone else.

"I must say that I didn't know exactly what to expect." He smiled watching everyone dance to the music. "We want to make sure that the event isn't like typical benefits." He would rather eat broken glass than attend another stuffy event that centered on classical music and small food portions. In the invitations and on the web pages, they had emphasized it would be a fun gala that would be filled with surprises. "Thanks for the recommendation for the florist. We've already met with Suzanne and she has a terrific plan for the gala."

Noelle smiled. "That's great." She hoped it was convincing. Grant sensed that something was wrong because Noelle had been agreeing with whatever he said and not offering her own opinions, which was very unlike her.

"Did you finish your recipe?" His gaze connected with hers and his eyes softened.

"Yes." Noelle tapped nervously on the table in front of her. She thought about Holly calling her a chicken and how the look in Grant's eyes suddenly stirred something up in her. His eyes held an unasked question, something she hadn't noticed even a minute ago. It caught her off guard.

Grant noticed a slight shift in her eyes, where she seemed to return his gaze at the same frequency. He felt a sudden sense of hope and a spark of euphoria. "Of course the best way to test out a band is to dance to their music. Would you like to dance?" Grant stood up from the table and extended his hand.

Noelle felt cornered and unsure. Turning down Grant Fitzgerald for a dance in front of the rest of the bar would cause more gossip by far and away than agreeing. She took his hand and the connection made her feel a little lightheaded. Once they reached the dance floor, the song had ended and a new, slow song had begun.

Grant pulled her close, placing one of his hands on the small of her back. She could smell his cologne, which had a musky scent like leather, cedar, and sandalwood combined. The butterflies in her stomach didn't seem to care if she acknowledged them or not; they weren't going away. The song was about finding true love and how easy it was when one stumbled upon the right person.

"The band plays this song very well," Noelle finally said, without knowing what else to say. The awkward phrase reminded her of learning a foreign language. For the first time since she returned to Maplemont, Noelle felt disoriented as if the direction of her quiet life had been a steady compass needle and Grant was a magnet disrupting her focus.

"If we were to become a couple, *this* would be our song." Grant's voice was a low whisper in her ear as his cheek touched hers.

She closed her eyes and breathed in his cologne while they swayed together in sync. Her heart raced. Everything about Grant at the moment was warm, inviting, and natural. Everything about that moment felt like home until panic set in. Despite nature's best efforts, Noelle's insecurities overpowered every other instinct and she found herself pulling back, confident that he would only break her heart later.

Grant couldn't help but notice the new distance that felt to him like an icy blast of winter. He was desperate to know what was on her mind, but mostly he ached to get closer to her.

"I've been starting to wonder if perhaps Imogen was right about the gala; maybe we are erring on the side of too informal." She tried to spare his feelings by softening her well-practiced words from the drive over. Noelle sounded so formal and distant as if reading the news on the radio.

Grant felt hurt that after making somewhat of a bold move that Noelle would bring up Imogen, while they danced so closely together. The last thing in the world that was on Grant's mind was Imogen. All he wanted at that moment was more of that closeness with Noelle. "*That* is what you are thinking about?" Grant asked with disbelief, taking a step back. He wondered why she was willfully misunderstanding the situation and purposefully pushing him away.

"She has more experience at events like—"

Having spent hours of his life attending similar benefits, yet to have his judgment questioned still by Noelle made Grant angry. Being rejected hurt his pride. However, what had bothered him the most was that Noelle not only didn't trust him, but she seemed to have been spooked to trust Imogen over him. He knew from experience that nothing good in his life ever resulted from the phrase, 'perhaps Imogen was right.'

"So, you don't trust my judgment." He let go of her hand.

Noelle stopped dancing and stepped back further, matching his movements. Had Grant only known how much she hated siding with Imogen under any circumstances, he might have been more open to an actual conversation about her concerns.

"Why did you even ask for my help if you had no intention of hearing my point of view? You already know everything. What am I but the kitchen help?"

Porter looked over at them, sensing that something had gone terribly wrong when Noelle and Grant stopped dancing in the middle of the song. Unfortunately, he realized that all he could do was watch the slow-moving train wreck, as intervening at all would only escalate the scene and cause more gossip in town the next day. Skye likewise looked concerned especially since she knew Noelle would only dig in further to hold her ground; World War I trench builders had nothing on Noelle when she was convinced about her views.

Grant had also made a decision; he would hire that band if only to spite both Noelle and Imogen. "Well I think this band is excellent and I'm going to hire them, regardless of what you think!"

"Fine!"

"Fine!"

Noelle walked over to her coat and then out the door without another word. Grant sat down at the table in a huff.

Porter left Skye on the dance floor and sat next to Grant. "That could have gone better."

"She is being impossible," Grant said. "We disagreed about the band and then she inferred that I was stubborn."

"You *are* stubborn."

"Not as much as she is. Hire the band for the gala; I'm going home."

Skye walked over to the table and reached out for Porter's hand. "Those two are made for each other." Porter nodded in agreement, standing up to return to the dance floor.

∞∞∞

Dean looked surprised to see Noelle storming out of the bar, only to have Grant soon follow her lead. "Early night, sir?" he asked, observing that Grant was in a bad mood.

"You could say that."

Realizing that now was probably not the right time for any additional questions, Dean simply drove back to the manor in silence. He reminded himself to relay the scene to Fiona in the morning.

O Little Town of Matchmakers

Skye arrived late at the bakery the next morning, having slept in after a late night out dancing. Noelle looked up at the clock when Skye scuttled into the bakery.

"I know, I know! Sorry I'm late, but some of us actually stayed to dance."

"Dancing is overrated," she grumbled.

"What exactly is going on between you and Grant? It looked to me like you two have a connection."

Noelle gasped. "A connection? With that impossible man? Hardly." Skye waited. "He's so…so—" Noelle struggled to find the words.

"Handsome, rich, charming, and smart?" Skye said, finishing her sentence. Noelle glared.

"Stubborn, rude, closed-minded, and a pompous know-it-all."

"I think you like him and I think he likes you." Skye folded her arms as if to emphasize her point. "Everyone on that dance floor last night could see that."

Shrugging, Noelle turned for the kitchen where Skye heard several pans slam onto the stainless-steel counter. Skye looked pleased, knowing that she was right. Fiona's entry into the bakery was accented by the jingling bells from the wreath on the door. She waved to Skye with a wink.

Skye went into the kitchen and told Noelle that she needed to run home quickly because she had forgotten her cell phone. Noelle said that would be fine and then walked into the shop to take over. She took a deep breath to compose herself.

"Hello, Fiona," she said with a smile. "I wish that I knew you were coming in today. I would have made currant scones. Today we only have the plain scones, I'm afraid." Noelle knew that Fiona's favorite treat was a currant scone, but she usually called ahead with an order before dropping by.

"I was hoping that you had some of your famous black cherry clafouti, like what you served at the manor earlier this week." The request made Noelle suspicious, especially since she had gotten the recipe from Fiona a few years ago.

"That's a surprise, especially considering that you bake a mean one yourself. Usually it's only a scone for you...maybe a macaron."

She knew her customers very well in this town and once someone found their favorite thing in the bakery, they rarely changed their order after. When Noelle stopped baking rye bread, the local fire chief parked one of the fire trucks in front of the bakery until she agreed to put it back on the menu. As a result, Sugarhouse bakery makes and sells two loaves of rye bread, four cinnamon rolls, and one rum raisin Bundt cake each week for standing orders. Pastor Thomas did not know how the church could ever get through a coffee hour without a rum raisin Bundt cake, often joking that it couldn't be Sunday if they didn't have their cake.

Fiona had her explanation already well-rehearsed from the drive over. "Well, Mr. Fitzgerald prefers the one that you made. He told me that it was the best he'd ever had."

"I'm sure that he meant it only in politeness."

"Oh, I disagree! Quiet men like him rarely bother with insincere praise. He's exactly like his grandfather in that way. No, I am sure that he meant it. He's been moping around the manor all morning, feeling glum I think. I wanted to get something a little special for lunch to cheer him up." Fiona waited for Noelle's reaction.

"I do happen to have one. Would you like the whole clafouti or only a slice?" Noelle refused to comment or ask about Grant's glum mood. Although she found it nice to know that he was also in a bad mood after their argument.

"I'll take a whole one, since you have it. Thank you," Fiona said. Noelle found a box for the clafouti and transferred it carefully. "You know that I've known Mr. Fitzgerald since he was a child and he was absolutely one of the sweetest and most thoughtful boys in the world."

"Well, people do change as they get older." Noelle closed the cake box and brought it to the cash register. She passed along a scone separately, noting it was a gift. Fiona felt discouraged, but did not give up.

"I have not found that to be true. I believe that those who are sweet as children do remain so, like your dear sisters and yourself. Mr. Fitzgerald may not be as smooth talking as other young men, however, he is one of the good ones."

"Well I'm sure that is good news for the army of women like Imogen Prescott clamoring to date him." Noelle put the cake box and scone into a large paper bag after Fiona paid for everything.

"Pish posh! He pays no attention to any of those ladies. His mother puts them into his path and he is courteous, but keeps them all at arm's length. Not *one* of those ladies would cause him a millisecond of moping around the house."

Noelle understood her meaning, although she didn't much appreciate the meddling, but she knew only too well that meddling was an

Olympic sport in Maplemont. Dean tapped the car horn outside, waiting to take her back to the manor. "Thank you, Fiona. It is always a pleasure to see you."

"You too, love. I'll see you tomorrow at the community center for the cookie swap?"

"Yes. I'll be there. See you then."

Before the hubbub of Grant's arrival in town, Noelle agreed to help Fiona with the annual holiday cookie swap at the community center. Each person brought five dozen cookies and swapped them out with others to take a home a mix of different cookies. It allowed each baker to play to their strengths and bring their best cookies to the swap.

For the five dozen they bring, everyone brought home four dozen of a mix of cookies that they chose at the swap and the remainder of the cookies were donated to the local shelter. Noelle always enjoyed the event and she also made Holly's contributions as well.

Fiona picked up the bag and met Dean outside. When she got into the car, Dean asked how it went. She relayed the conversation on the drive home and they both agreed that it had gone very well indeed.

Skye returned shortly after Fiona left and found Noelle gazing out the window, deep in thought. Noelle thought about Grant's cheek on hers and his low whisper in her ear. She closed her eyes for a second remembering how her spine tingled with his hand on her lower back. Her heart still panicked at the memory and she had to admit that she was afraid of falling for him, despite herself. She sighed loudly and hoped that the feeling would pass.

∞∞∞

Dean read the paper at lunch while Fiona worked on a crossword puzzle. Grant met them in the kitchen after being tempted by the smell of caramelized onions for the French onion soup. Fiona popped out of her chair and readied a bowl with some bread for him while Dean continued reading the latest sports scores. Grant spotted the Sugarhouse Bakery cake box sitting on the kitchen island and it sparked his curiosity. He wondered if Noelle had sent it.

"Is that from Sugarhouse?"

"Indeed, sir. I was so busy this morning with polishing the silver punch bowl for the gala that I lost all track of time. Dean was kind enough to drive me into town to pick up a dessert for our lunch and dinner today."

Grant felt disappointed that Noelle hadn't sent it. "Thank you for that." He continued to stare at the box as if it would tell him a secret.

Dean peeked over the top of the paper and then quickly returned to reading. "It will be a shame when she sells the bakery and moves to Los Angeles," Dean said.

"Los Angeles?" Grant looked concerned. Dean set the paper down casually on the table while Fiona set the soup on the table. Grant sat across from Dean.

"Now Dean, that's simply wild speculation. She also had an offer in Madrid," Fiona said, stoking the fire. "But sir, you mustn't say anything to Noelle about this. We wouldn't want her to think that she couldn't trust us with her confidence. I have no doubt that the fire chief would find a way to detain her in town for the rye bread alone."

"Maybe he'll follow her to Los Angeles or Madrid so he doesn't lose his rye bread supplier," Dean joked and Fiona chortled.

"Yes, what a real shame to our community when she moves." Fiona sighed. "Whenever I'm feeling a little homesick, Noelle makes me currant scones and I feel suddenly transported to my Nan's kitchen in our tiny country village. It's funny how food can do that."

Nodding, Grant tried not to display his keen interest in the topic. "Your secret is safe with me. I'm surprised that she would consider moving with Ava and Holly here." Picturing a Maplemont without Noelle, Grant's stomach fell. He wondered why she didn't mention anything about the offers to him.

Fiona watched their words at work,

through Grant's facial expression. "Her reputation precedes her and she gets offers all the time from some of the best venues. Now that Ava is older and in school, she doesn't need her around as much and Holly's family has an established rhythm."

Dean nodded. "Without any other reason to stay, I would move if I was her and getting offers like that." He picked up the paper again.

"Would you?" Grant asked offhand trying not to look like the news impacted him but failing. "This soup is wonderful. I'm going to take it to the office. Thanks, Fiona...Dean."

As Grant stepped out of the kitchen, Fiona winked at Dean over his folded newspaper. He winked back conspiratorially.

In his office, Grant stared out the window. The green holiday sweater that Noelle gave him when they first met sat on his desk, neatly folded. He knew that he should return it, but he couldn't part with it. He had no doubt in his mind where Noelle belonged.

Oh Ho the Mistletoe

Fiona called Holly in a panic. The manor ovens were on the fritz and she had no way of baking her holiday cookies for the next day's swap. She and Betty had already planned to bake theirs together and, as luck would have it, Betty's oven was being replaced. Naturally, Holly was happy to help out since the farm's kitchen was big enough to host them.

That was the story that Holly conveyed to Noelle, anyway. As a favor, Holly asked Noelle if she couldn't come over to help with her cookies for the swap also which would be a fun ladies night in. Todd took Ava to the latest cartoon movie so they would have the place to themselves. To Holly's surprise, Noelle agreed to help without reservation or suspicion. She thought it would be nice to enjoy some good conversation and take her mind off of Grant.

Betty arrived first, rolling into the kitchen with two large bags of supplies. The bag included a sprig of mistletoe tied with a red bow.

Christmas at Maplemont Manor

"I'm giving everyone mistletoe this year to decorate the whole town like the manor house gala will be decorated! Isn't that fun? Oh! You should put yours here above the sink, Holly."

They exchanged a conspiratorial wink while Holly hung the mistletoe and Noelle was busy in the pantry checking on baking supplies. Betty planned to make her usual snickerdoodles and Fiona was going to make her highly sought-after shortbread cookies.

When asked what she would be baking this year, Holly looked at Noelle. "I'm baking maple brown sugar cookies for Holly, with Maplemont River syrup naturally. I've already made the candy cane meringue cookies."

"I look forward to those candy cane meringues every year, Noelle! I spoke with Fiona on the phone when I parked the car and she should be here any minute. She was running late after having to regroup from the oven fiasco. Thanks a million for letting us move our operation here. Talk about Murphy's Law of holiday baking! Whatever can go wrong—"

"No problem, Miss Betty. Tonight will be fun with just us girls," Holly said.

Miss Betty poured herself a glass of eggnog and asked Noelle where she could find the bowls and measuring cups. As Noelle squatted to pull the extra bowls from the lower cabinets, the doorbell rang and Fiona entered followed by Grant.

"Happy Christmas, everyone! Sorry we are late." Fiona announced their arrival while they both removed their snowy boots in the mudroom.

Upon hearing the word 'we' Noelle cringed. She decided to spend extra time researching the lower cabinets to buy some time while Grant and Fiona entered the kitchen.

"Grant, you already know everyone, right? Is this all of us then?" Fiona's voice trailed and she sounded a little disappointed since she thought Noelle was going to be there.

Noelle stood up from her hiding place knowing that she couldn't avoid detection for much longer. "I found the pans." She acknowledged Fiona and Grant with an edgy grin. Noelle set the pans onto the counter with a slight clang as if filing a polite protest. She didn't appreciate the ambush. She blinked for a long few seconds to compose herself after seeing the mistletoe hanging in the middle of the kitchen.

Miss Betty was delighted that Fiona had persuaded Grant to come. "I think it's terrific that you were able to join us, Mr. Fitzgerald. Very few men are brave enough to bake for the cookie swap. It's nice to see you leading the charge."

Noelle cleared her throat. "*You* are baking cookies for the swap tomorrow?" She made it clear by the tone of her voice that she thought it was ridiculous. He didn't know the difference between a spatula and a measuring cup.

Christmas at Maplemont Manor

Holly elbowed her for being so rude and stepped ahead of her. "We are so glad that you could join us, Grant. Please ignore my sister. She takes baking way too seriously and she can be terribly rude and annoying." Holly turned to give Noelle a look.

Grant winked and smiled. "Noelle is right to be apprehensive. She's had a front row seat to my cooking disasters, but I have been practicing. Yesterday I made toast without burning it. I think I'm ready to level up to Christmas cookies." He rolled up the sleeves of his flannel shirt carelessly like he did throughout boarding school, as if by reflex.

Miss Betty laughed as if it was the most hilarious joke that she'd ever heard in her life. "Not only are you handsome, but you are funny too!" Holly handed him an apron that said 'kiss the cook' and Noelle rolled her eyes.

"All right then, let's get started." Noelle helped everyone find mixing bowls, measuring cups, and whisks and they started on the dough.

Grant saw her break an egg with one hand and he was impressed. "Can you show me how to do that?"

She nodded and set a bowl on the table in front him. The other ladies hovered together at the other side of the kitchen, pretending to look at Miss Betty's vacation photos. Noelle took his hand, placed the egg in the middle of his palm and then held his hand below the egg to show him the proper finger placement. As his thumb graced hers, she pretended not to feel the electric connection that made her catch her breath. Still holding his hand, she then flipped his hand over to tap the egg on the side of the bowl to crack it.

"It has to be cracked in the middle, not the side. That's the secret." Guiding his fingers on how to separate the top half of the shell with the thumb and index fingers, the egg then dropped perfectly into the bowl and she set the shells aside. Letting go of his hand quickly, she exhaled. "And that's all there is to it. You try it now."

Handing him another egg, she watched him try out the process on his own and most of the egg shell broke into the bowl. They both laughed.

Grant shook his head. "I'll never be able to do this." His mind also focused primarily on how Noelle's fingers felt on his hand. He wondered if her hands were also warmer now from that touch, as his were. Spying the mistletoe over the sink, he also wondered if he'd have the courage to kiss her if they stood underneath it.

"Anyone can do it. It takes practice. Keep going. I bought plenty of extra eggs." She smiled and edged the egg crate toward him and then returned to making the dough she had started.

The other ladies soon returned to mixing their own batches and conversation in the kit-

Christmas at Maplemont Manor

chen turned to Miss Betty telling them about local gossip. Evidently Zoe Davis, the local beauty, had started dating a doctor at the hospital and he already asked her to spend Christmas with his family. All the ladies agreed with Zoe that such an invitation was too much, too soon. Opinions were evenly split across the group as to whether or not she should break up with the guy for being too clingy. As usual, Holly wanted to give him a second chance and only saw the best in the situation.

Grant looked bemused at being included in the local chit chat. "I like being included in the local gossip."

Miss Betty looked at him very seriously. "It's not gossip—it's *news*."

"I stand corrected." Noelle gave him a sympathetic look and he returned to his egg project, having nearly finished a dozen eggs without success and feeling more stupid with each attempt.

All of his hopes relied upon being successful with the twelfth egg. Slowly he went through each of the steps and spent extra effort not to think about Noelle's hand on his. When the egg fell perfectly into the bowl without any of the shell, he performed an end zone dance. "Yes!"

Everyone laughed and Miss Betty started to dance along, which caused the others to join in a little victory dance lap around the kitchen island.

Fiona spotted it first. "Look who is under the mistletoe!" Noelle and Grant looked up to find the mistletoe dangling above them.

"You know the rules," Miss Betty said as if nothing could be done outside of Grant kissing Noelle.

Noelle waved a hand. "Oh Miss Betty! We have too much to do tonight to play these reindeer games! You don't want poor Grant to think that I walked over here purposefully. What would he think of me?" She opened the drawer for a spoon and then returned to the island.

Holly soon stole Fiona and Betty to tour them around the den after the remodel, sensing that Noelle needed a break from the block watch and also wanting to give the pair some time alone. Noelle set out two cookie pans and started spooning out drops of the maple brown sugar cookie dough onto the pan. Grant assisted with adding them to the other pan.

"I heard that you have gotten offers to sell the bakery and that you might be moving. Is that true?" He had to know.

"Well, it's true. I haven't taken any of the offers seriously, if that's what you're asking. Holly would kill me if I moved."

"I'm glad to hear that. I can't imagine a Maplemont without...you." He moved closer to her. "Most women would be quite happy to be caught under the mistletoe with me. I'm just saying."

Christmas at Maplemont Manor

"I'm sure—looking like you do."

"What's that supposed to mean?" He stopped adding dough to the pan and pretended to look offended.

"You know." Noelle likewise stopped to look at him.

"I don't think I do." His eyes challenged her to say what she didn't want to say out loud. She tried to look disinterested.

"Fine. I'll say it. You are objectively handsome."

"So, you think I'm handsome." His eyes flirted in concert with his mischievous smile and he leaned over, closing the gap between them.

Noelle's pulse quickened. "*Objectively*...as in generally people would say you are handsome. Like how everyone agrees that puppies are cute. It's mostly about...science...you know and...math." She reminded herself to get a grip and that she was still mad at him about the other night with the band. She also knew better than to take Grant's flirting seriously, but as he stepped closer and her breath became shallow, that knowledge seemed immaterial.

"I always liked science, especially chemistry. How one thing can be undeniably attracted to another." Grant gently pushed some stray hairs behind Noelle's ear, stopping to keep his hand there.

Feeling unsteady, Noelle willingly leaned

into the vortex of energy that pulled them closer together. Miss Betty's laugh rang out, indicating that the ladies were around the corner. Grant stepped back and quickly resumed adding dough to the pan. He didn't want their first kiss to be in front of the neighborhood watch. His eyes twinkled with a knowing look.

Noelle started to stir the dough with the wrong end of the wooden spoon that she picked up absent-mindedly.

Holly looked at her strangely and whispered. "I don't know much about cooking, but isn't that spoon upside down?"

Realizing her mistake, Noelle touched her hand to her forehead and then wiped her hands on a towel. Grant gave her a knowing smile that she returned. He felt encouraged that this time, she didn't pull away. Noelle could no longer deny her attraction and she didn't want to. She suddenly longed for mistletoe. "Can you hand me a...um...another...you know...to stir the bowl."

Holly handed her a spoon. "Do you mean a *spoon*?" She chuckled. Holly wondered what exactly transpired between Noelle and Grant while they were in the other room, but based on how they both were blushing and looking at each other she had some idea.

Claus for Concern

The next day at the community center, it seemed like all of Maplemont converged to exchange holiday cookies, wrap toy donations for the needy, and learn who won the gingerbread house competition. Always a lively event, the room buzzed with holiday music and neighbors catching up on "news." Grant and Porter arrived together, but Porter soon split off after finding Skye. They went off to wrap presents, while Grant found Noelle by the gingerbread houses.

"Hey! Did they announce the winner yet?" He placed his hand on her lower back and her spine quivered. His hair looked askew after he removed his hat. She smiled at how it stuck up funny on one side. "What? Oh, my hair from the hat? Can you fix it?"

She nodded and reached over to run her fingers through his wavy hair to even it out. "There you go."

His eyes connected with hers. "Thanks."

Grant's phone buzzed and he fished it out of his pocket to find a text message. Noelle couldn't help but see that the name on the screen was Imogen's. He returned the phone to his pocket without responding to the message. "One of my mom's friends," was his only comment. Noelle's heart fell. "I have a surprise for you." He took off his jacket to reveal the green sweater with the Christmas tree that had blinking lights when he pushed the button on the cuff.

Noelle laughed. "I was wondering what happened to that sweater."

"I thought it was appropriate for today. I've been meaning to find an excuse to return it to you."

Victor hollered out for Grant and soon appeared, pressing a light punch to Grant's shoulder. "Hey! Now that's a great sweater! You literally light up wearing it." Victor laughed. "You are exactly the man I was looking for!"

"Really, why?"

"I need a favor. Our Santa Claus got stuck in the snow behind an accident on the freeway. There's no way that he'll make it on time. Can you fill in? Your grandfather always loved that job and I thought you might be willing to step into his boots."

Grant thought about it for about half a second before agreeing to help out. Each day in Maplemont he had started feeling more and more a part of the community. He and Victor were becoming good friends and the ladies had let him into their gossip circle. Cookies that he helped bake sat on the table for the swap and the donation to the shelter. He had something great planned for his talk at the school and he'd help build some of the gingerbread houses on display. He was honored to be asked to play Santa.

∞∞∞

Noelle, on the other hand, was surprised that he had agreed to be Santa. When she first met him, he wore only tuxes and suits, but now he wore flannel shirts, ugly sweaters, and now a Santa Claus costume. He seemed to have changed so much, and yet Noelle remained hung up on Imogen. She couldn't let go of her suspicion that Grant would end up with Imogen and she would be the lady of Maplemont Manor as it had been planned since they were children.

Grant beamed at Noelle, excited to be part of the show. She returned the smile, but her reservations about his interest in her added space between them. Victor took Grant to the back room where the Santa costume hung on a hook. Victor then returned quickly and started the presentation for announcing the winner of the gingerbread competition. Holly, Todd, and Ava soon joined Noelle.

"Where's Grant? I saw him drop the

cookies off earlier and I thought he came over here." Holly looked around, surprised to find that he wasn't with Noelle.

"He got a text message from Imogen."

Holly looked surprised. She had no idea why someone like Grant who was obviously in love with her sister would even have Imogen texting him. "That doesn't mean anything."

"Doesn't it?" Noelle looked insecure and Holly tried to look encouraging.

Victor stepped up to the podium and the crowd gathered for his announcement. "Merry Christmas, everybody! I'm happy to report that Maplemont will be donating over one hundred dozen cookies to the local area shelters this year and almost two hundred toys for the children! That's a new record and it couldn't be achieved without the support and generosity of every single one of you. I'm so proud to live here in Maplemont where the community takes care of each other and we can celebrate these moments together. Please give yourselves a round of applause."

The crowd cheered and clapped, pleased with their achievement. Victor continued. "Before our special guest arrives, I also want to announce that the winner of this year's gingerbread house competition is...Jurassic House submitted by Cole Bletchley!" Holly and Noelle giggled that the winning gingerbread house ended up being the one that Grant had wanted to

Christmas at Maplemont Manor

win, with the dinosaur.

Victor explained that the gingerbread house fund raiser also exceeded expectations, raising over five thousand dollars for the community center which was also a new record. Noelle suspected that Grant had influenced that total as well, especially since that was over four thousand dollars more than the amount raised last year. Victor thanked Sugarhouse Bakery and Noelle by name, for supporting the event. Everyone clapped and young Cole Bletchley did a little dance upon receiving his award of a gift certificate for the ice-skating rink.

The sound of jingle bells soon could be heard throughout the room, accompanied by a very jolly and deep 'ho, ho, ho!' Grant appeared disguised as Santa Claus and he looked very convincing with a plush white beard, velvet suit stuffed with two pillows for a big stomach. Ava squealed with delight to see Santa Claus sit down on the stage in a special chair by the mayor, who helped him with a large sack filled with small bags of candy.

The kids started to line up to tell Santa what they wanted for Christmas, including Holly and Todd who stood in line with Ava. Noelle couldn't stop staring at Santa, thinking how incredibly endearing he was in that suit and how sweet he was being with the kids. Noelle waved at Ava who had started a serious discussion with 'Santa Claus.' He winked at Noelle without Ava noticing, waking the butterflies in Noelle's stomach.

Santa asked Ava what she wanted for Christmas and she motioned for him to bend his head down so that she could whisper into his ear. "I want to see the reindeer for Christmas, Santa." Nodding his head with a jolly 'ho ho ho' thrown in on the side, Ava happily accepted a candy cane and shuttled back to Holly and Todd.

Imogen appeared wearing a very expensive cashmere sweater dress and fancy leather boots that were completely inappropriate for such snowy weather. She found Porter whose shrug could be seen from across the room and he pointed to Noelle. Imogen looked displeased.

"Have you seen Grant? I texted him that I was on my way and he didn't respond. Porter said that he was here near you earlier, which is odd because we were meeting up for our date." Imogen saw the line of children waiting for Santa and didn't notice he was being played by Grant.

Noelle looked at him and crossed her arms. Clearly Grant had invited Imogen to the event as his date, probably based on what she was wearing and the amount of smoky gray eye shadow she wore. That was all Noelle needed to interpret the situation that he had been waiting for Imogen to arrive and that the flirting from the other day wasn't anything serious.

"Yes, I have. He's up front wearing a very

red suit." Noelle grabbed her coat and went outside to walk home.

Betty intercepted her on the way out. "Miss Noelle, where are you going? Santa only got here a few minutes ago and isn't he doing a terrific job? I mean he's the whole package, that man."

"His girlfriend, Miss Prescott, arrived for their date." Noelle looked at her boots and then started again for the door.

Miss Betty looked completely shocked and seemed as heartbroken as if it had happened to her. She clutched her heart and gave Noelle a sympathetic look.

"Tell Holly that I'm going to walk home. I could use some fresh air."

Making Spirits Bright

Noelle arrived at the school promptly at two o'clock with several big trays of award-winning fudge. At the door to Ava's first grade classroom, she struggled with the fudge while trying to pull open the door. Her attention focused entirely on balancing the trays while also not spilling her coffee. By the time she freed up a hand, someone had opened the door. She looked up and was shocked to see Grant standing there in an army 'dress blues' uniform.

"Grant," she said, unable to cover her surprise, grabbing the coffee cup back from the precarious stack of trays. A blind woman would have noticed how handsome he looked in his uniform.

"Noelle." Grant took a tray without saying anything further and followed her inside. He was hurt that she had left the community center without saying anything, especially after he had volunteered as Santa. He wanted to talk to her about the Jurassic house winning the gingerbread competition and he was looking forward to picking Christmas cookies out with her in the swap. Instead he got trapped by Imogen and ended up having to listen to the dramatic events that unfolded at her hair salon that morning, involving her usual stylist deciding whether or not to buy a new car or a used one. He would have stayed in the Santa Claus suit all afternoon if he could have avoided that entire session of wrapping the donated toys with Imogen.

The teacher motioned where to set the trays and then introduced Grant as the first speaker of community day. Noelle sat down on a small chair in the back of the room, trying to look composed while feeling like a giant sitting on a miniature chair as Grant stood up in front of the class.

The teacher introduced Grant. "Class, today we get to learn from Mr. Fitzgerald about the exciting world of software application development, like those games you like to play on your phones. Mr. Fitzgerald is the great-grandson of Henry Fitzgerald, who founded Maplemont in 1825."

"Good morning," Grant greeted the class and Ava waved at him. He smiled and waved back. "Today I thought we'd do something special and I hope that Mr. Bailey won't mind." The teacher smiled and motioned that whatever Grant had planned would be perfectly fine. After all, no one in their right mind would deny a Fitzgerald anything in this town. Porter and Dean appeared, wearing Santa Clause hats and carrying boxes. "Oh good, my assistants have arrived. Does anyone know what kind of uniform I'm wearing?"

Ava's hand shot into the air. "It's a soldier's uniform."

"That's right. I was a soldier many years ago and the army sent me to Afghanistan." Grant walked over to the large wall map and pointed to Maplemont and then to Afghanistan to show the students how far away that was.

Noelle wondered where his presentation was going and was also surprised that Grant, with such a privileged background, had served in the army. Then she remembered the tour at the manor and his family's tradition of serving in the military that ran back to the American Revolution. She questioned her assumptions about Grant and had to concede, at least to herself, that she had been wrong more than right.

One of the children raised her hand and Grant called on her. "My mommy went to Afghanistan."

Grant smiled. "I met a lot of mommies and daddies over there. When I was there, it was Christmas time and I was feeling a little homesick." Grant went on to describe what homesick meant and how his job was to take care of other soldiers. He then went on to explain that the best gift he received that Christmas wasn't from Santa; it was from someone he'd never met.

Another student raised his hand and Grant called on him. "How did you get a gift from someone that you've never met?"

"One of the soldiers in my company...a company is a group like this class. Anyway, one of the soldiers had a young son who was also in the first grade, like you. He asked his classmates to send holiday cards to all one hundred and fifty-two soldiers in our company. I received this card from a girl named Annie from Birmingham, Alabama."

He held up a handmade card of red paper and a crayon drawing of a Christmas tree. Pointing on the map again, he showed the students where Birmingham was compared to Maplemont. "When I got this beautiful card in the mail with a note from Annie that Christmas, I suddenly felt so happy. That someone I didn't know took the time to make sure I had a good day and something nice to open in the mail was one of the best gifts I've ever received. I've kept this card a long time. All the soldiers in my company also received cards from students like you and we decorated our mess tent with them."

Grant explained what a 'mess tent' was and how it didn't matter if the soldiers celebrated Christmas or another holiday, they were all happy to receive a card that a student had worked so hard on. It was the thought of not being forgotten by someone at home that was the main point.

Noelle recognized the card from her tour of the manor, realizing that had she bothered to ask more questions of Grant instead of assuming that she knew everything, perhaps things would be different. Of course, she was attracted to him and the more she learned about him, the more she wanted to know. But she realized that this was all too late. Grant was dating Imogen, and if she once had a chance with him, then that window had closed.

Porter started unpacking construction paper in every color of the rainbow on the teacher's desk, along with new boxes of crayons. He showed the students how to fold the paper and Grant explained that, instead of a discussion about community history, the students would be creating cards for servicemen and women serving abroad. The students rushed up to the table, as Grant and Porter helped them pick out paper and crayons.

The teacher walked over to Noelle. "Noelle, do you mind helping with the cards instead of doing a presentation about the history of local maple syrup farming?" the teacher asked.

Noelle smiled. "I don't mind." She set out the fudge on another table as a snack for the students while they worked on the cards and then started helping students find crayons.

Christmas at Maplemont Manor

Porter also set up one of the empty boxes as a 'mailbox' where the students could drop their completed cards; Grant and Porter would mail them later that afternoon. Grant still felt spurned by Noelle, when she left the community center without a word. It frustrated him that when he thought they were moving closer together; she seemed to change her mind. He took a piece of fudge and sat down near Noelle in the front row of the class. He seemed like a giant in the small desk.

"Let me help with that." He reached out for construction paper to fold, helping a student..

"I didn't know that you were in the army," Noelle said to Grant while she helped cut out a Christmas tree.

"There's a lot that you don't know about me." He stood up and went to the back of the class to help another student.

The student Noelle was helping left to get some glitter and glue from the back of the room. He was followed quickly by the student Grant had helped who left to get some fudge. Dean overheard their discussion, sat at a desk near Noelle and helped a student cut Christmas trees for their card.

"Kevin, why don't you run over there and get us both some fudge?" Dean asked the boy he was helping, who quickly fled toward the fudge leaving Dean and Noelle alone in the front row of desks. "What he didn't tell the class today was that he received that card the day of his grandfather's funeral. It tore him apart that he couldn't be there and that card really made him feel better. Grant was my Captain out in the field. When I told him that I couldn't keep a job because of my PTSD, he hired me on the spot. He can be a difficult person to get to know, but he's worth the effort."

Noelle nodded as Ava rushed up to her asking for help with spelling the words in her card. As she helped Ava with the message, her mind turned over how wrong she'd been about Grant. He was right that there was a lot that she didn't know about him. She turned to see him laughing with Porter and she realized that the only way to ever know if he'd choose her or Imogen would be to take a risk with her heart. Noelle knew that there was only one way to find out.

∞∞∞

At the end of the hour, Noelle returned to the bakery. Grant, Porter, and Dean sorted the cards into large mailing envelopes in batches. Grant saw Ava's card on green paper of a tree decorated with gingerbread cookies that she showed him earlier. He then noticed the next card was written in marker and looked like it had been completed by an artistic adult. The front of the card was a hand drawn picture of a candle with holly leaves around it. He knew that it was completed by Noelle and opened it to read the note.

The card said:

'May this card remind you that there is always a light on to guide you home and even the harshest winter cannot break a holly tree. Thank you for your service.'

Grant quickly rubbed his eye, moved by her message, and shared the card with Porter.

Porter also looked touched by Noelle's card. "She did that quietly. I didn't see her put a card in the box."

"She probably had Ava do it. They were together in the stack."

Seeing an opportunity, Porter stopped to ask a question. "Grant, you had already decided to hire the cover band before you heard them, didn't you?" He knew that Grant's decisiveness meant that he routinely made decisions without Porter's input, which was often a point of contention between them.

Grant nodded. He had wanted a cover band for the gala and didn't really care which one. The recommendation from Skye alone was enough for him to decide. "Yes, I did."

"That means Noelle was right when she

said that you weren't interested in her opinion about the band." Grant continued adding cards into the envelopes silently without responding. "And Imogen showing up at the community center the other day...Skye said that Noelle saw the message. She thinks you two are an item."

"Me and Imogen? Why would she—"

"Oh, I don't know." Porter paused for effect. "Maybe because when she met you, Imogen was your dinner date at the manor with the dragon lady, then she was at the bakery trying to take over the gala, and then she showed up again dressed to kill like you had a date at the community center. Or it could be because you two had a big argument on the dance floor that featured Imogen. I'm not sure there are so many possibilities to choose from." Porter couldn't believe that Grant didn't comprehend how Noelle might come up with such a theory.

Grant shrugged his shoulders. "I simply mentioned the cookie swap in a text to Imogen because she asked me to go skiing and I said that I couldn't go because I had other plans."

"Rookie mistake. Give someone like Imogen Prescott a millimeter and she'll take a mile. You need to deal with her, Grant. Imagine if the situation was reversed and you had seen Noelle with some clingy, handsome guy at almost every turn."

Grant didn't want to deal with Imogen because that would mean dealing with his mother.

He preferred to avoid them both. Surely Noelle should have seen that he was serious about *her* and not interested in Imogen. Grant felt frustrated, thinking that Noelle hadn't ever really given him a chance. He looked at his best friend. "But Imogen doesn't mean anything to me."

Porter looked him squarely in the eye, putting his hand onto Grant's shoulder. "I don't think Noelle knows that."

A Cup of Cheer

Grant and Porter mailed the cards at the post office. Porter received a call from the caterer that they hired who was at the manor to understand the layout options for the food, but no one was there to let him in. Porter checked his watch.

"We can be there in fifteen minutes." He hung up the phone. "That was the caterer. Ready to go?"

Thinking about Noelle and the argument about the band, Grant shook his head. "Why don't you go? I have some errands to run in town. I'll ask Dean to come back to pick me up later."

"OK, see you back at the ranch."

Grant stopped first for coffee at the local coffee shop. There wasn't much of a line since it was pretty quiet so late in the afternoon. He stepped in behind Betty who was deep in conversation with the owner, Jocelyn Weston.

Upon seeing Grant, Betty stopped to address him. "Mr. Fitzgerald! How nice to see you!

We were talking about how excited the town is about the gala and how wonderful it will be to get the cancer clinic running again. Miss Jocelyn, this is Mr. Fitzgerald from the manor."

Jocelyn waved. "Pleasure to meet you. We are so glad to have someone living full-time at the manor again. I always thought it seemed such a shame to have it vacant. What can I get you, Mr. Fitzgerald?"

"Please, call me Grant. I'm buying a coffee for a friend and I'm not sure what I should get."

Miss Betty's eyes twinkled. "Perhaps we can help. Is it anyone we know?"

She shared a look with Jocelyn on the side. Grant shrugged. He wasn't accustomed to having people know his business and in the city he operated mostly anonymously. But life in Maplemont meant making adjustments and he did want to become a part of the community.

"Do either of you happen to know what type of coffee Noelle prefers?"

Miss Betty smiled. "Yes, that's easy. She always buys the cup-of-cheer latte this time of year, with soy milk and extra cinnamon."

"OK, thanks. I'll take two of those please." Reaching for his wallet, Jocelyn put a hand up for him to stop.

"These are on the house. My cousin has been driving to Ridgewater for his cancer treatments and it will be such a help to us all when the local hospital can help him again. We are all

Julie Manthey

taking turns to drive him there and back, and I can't tell you how grateful we are that you are taking this project on."

She reached out to hold his hand briefly. He nodded and put a twenty-dollar bill in the tip jar with a mischievous wink to Miss Betty who winked back as if he was being wicked.

"We were talking about Jocelyn's nephew, Mr. Bruce. He invited Miss Jocelyn over to their house in Montreal for Christmas, but she's staying here to help her cousin and to attend the gala. I think the whole town will be at the gala."

"I hope so, Miss Betty. We are planning a terrific party."

Jocelyn set the coffees on the counter. "Tell Noelle that I said hello and if she could bring over some more macarons later today that would be great. We're almost sold out."

"I will, thanks."

Miss Betty couldn't help but comment. "I saw her leave the cookie swap early the other day. She met your lady friend, Miss Prescott there. Miss Noelle told me later that Miss Prescott had gone to the cookie swap to meet you there for a date. I don't think that I need to tell you that Miss Noelle is one of the kindest women we have in Maplemont, Mr. Fitzgerald. A gentleman should make his intentions clear, especially to a woman who has already been through so much like our Miss Noelle."

"You are correct, Miss Betty. A gentleman

should make his intentions clear."

Grant put his leather gloves back on and picked up the two coffees. "Have a nice day, ladies."

Naturally Betty and Jocelyn dissected the conversation as if digging through an archeological site once the door closed behind Grant. As he walked down the street toward the bakery, his stomach turned in knots from nerves.

∞∞∞

Grant appeared at the bakery, carrying two lattes. When he arrived, Skye pointed him toward the kitchen where Noelle was pulling a big tray of sugar cookies out of the oven. She looked over upon hearing his footsteps.

"I brought a peace offering. It's the cup-of-cheer latte. Jocelyn said hello and asks if you could bring more macarons." Grant set the coffee on the counter, while he sipped his own.

"Already the Maplemont messenger, I see. I didn't realize that we were at war." Noelle ignored the herd of elephants in the room.

"I wanted to apologize about the band. You were right that I had already made my decision about them without consulting anyone else. Porter reminded me that I have a tendency to make decisions and forget to consult others first," he said, leaning against the counter.

Noelle set the oven mitts on the table and started transferring the cookies onto a cooling rack with a spatula. She stopped for a moment. "I'm sorry for second-guessing the vision of the event. Both you and Porter made it clear that you wanted a lively holiday party. When you mentioned the amount of money people were donating, I guess that I got spooked." Noelle returned to transferring the cookies to the cooling racks.

"I hope that you'll still join me this evening for that project with the mayor."

"I thought maybe you decided to invite Imogen instead."

"Imogen is my *mother's* friend, Noelle, and it's complicated. I asked you and not Imogen. I thought that my intentions were clear."

Noelle stopped again and pushed some stray hairs away from her eyes. His words, tone, and the way his eyes connected with hers made her think that perhaps she overreacted to Imogen appearing at the community center. He stood in front of her and had sought her out, not Imogen, and Noelle wanted that to mean something.

She took a sip of the coffee. "This one is my favorite."

Grant beamed. "That's what Miss Betty said. She was in line when I got there. I like it because it reminds me of you. It smells of cinnamon and vanilla."

She laughed. The butterflies in her stomach returned for the air show they performed every time Grant appeared now. "Yes, that's the perfume of all bakers. Hey, what did Ava ask Santa for her Christmas wish?"

"I believe that's covered by child-Santa confidentiality." He shrugged as if indicating that there wasn't anything that could be done about it. Noelle knew that he was teasing.

"I'm pretty sure that's not a real thing."

He shook his head to disagree. "It *is* a thing."

She pretended to look mad. "OK fine. Keep your confidentiality then. It was probably something like a trip to the North Pole or something like that. She keeps asking all these questions, wanting proof. We've been on the fence about telling her this year, but we all agree that we'd like her to believe in the magic if only for one more year."

"I agree. They should hold onto it as long as they can. You and I both know only too well how quickly that sense of magic can be lost. But I do think that we find the magic again when we grow up. If we let ourselves believe in it."

Noelle wondered if he was dancing around the idea of romance between them. There was no question that an attraction was there, but something more seemed out of reach. "Magic can be quite seductive, but as grown-ups, we learn that it isn't real."

"Isn't it? I liked the card you made the other day. It was beautiful and I was a jealous of the soldier who will get to keep it." He set his cup down and walked over closer to her purposefully, making her pulse beat faster. "Porter accused me of holding this entire gala for the sole purpose of vying to get added to your Christmas card list."

At two feet away, he stopped and waited. His eyes challenged her to meet him halfway and she hesitated. Noelle took a step forward to close the gap further. Their eyes locked and she couldn't deny how she felt. She was like a piece of iron helplessly pulled toward a magnet.

"You want a Christmas card?"

Grant took another step forward, his face now inches from hers. "I'm greedy. I want a lot more than that."

Noelle caught her breath. He leaned in. Her heart raced as she breathed in his cologne and she convinced herself that this was real. She leaned, drawn to him and unable to think about anything except his lips soon meeting hers.

"NOELLE! Help please!" Skye appeared in the doorway of the kitchen with cake boxes stacked in her hands, blocking her view.

They stepped apart quickly, knowing that the moment was lost. Noelle's heart beat quickly. She rushed to help Skye by taking some of the boxes.

"I'm always telling you not to take so

many boxes in one trip." Noelle sighed. Her eyes returned to Grant's and he smiled then shook his head, clearly frustrated.

"I'll pick you up at seven o'clock then? We have a thing with the mayor," Grant clarified for Skye who still didn't know that she interrupted anything.

"Is there some sort of a dress code? Where are we going?" Noelle asked.

"The important thing is to dress for warmth. The location and activity will remain a surprise." He brushed by her arm on the way out. Her heart beat a little faster and her face blushed. He spun around. "I'll pick you up at your house."

Noelle nodded. "OK."

He reached out for her hand. "It's a date, then."

Skye gave her a look, noticing her face and how she watched Grant walk out of the kitchen. "You're blushing!"

Noelle fanned her face with her hand. "It's the ovens back here, they get so—"

"Sure...Right. It probably had nothing to do with that handsome man who is picking you up for a date."

Noelle waved a hand. She covered her mouth to hide a beaming smile. Grant had asked her out on a date, without question.

∞∞∞

Back at the manor, Porter got ready for his opera date with Skye and asked Grant for advice on the options he'd settled on for their dinner before the show. "Of course, you would recommend the least formal option," Porter grumbled. "I want to impress her."

Grant nodded. "The food is better there than that fancy place; you should impress her by choosing a place with good food." Despite their close friendship, they often disagreed between matters of quality and style. "Why even ask me if you've decided already?"

Porter grinned mischievously. "It's annoying, isn't it?" He laughed.

"Touché."

"Skye said seven and a half, by the way," Porter said.

"Thanks." While Grant knew that he should have spoken with Noelle about it directly, he preferred it to be a surprise.

"You like, Skye, right?"

"I don't really know her, but you like her and so does Noelle, so I'll say yes, by association, I like Skye."

Porter made a face. "Of course, you couldn't simply say, 'yes Porter, she's lovely.' Leave it to the great Grant Fitzgerald to make it more complicated." Porter was frustrated that Grant hadn't supported his relationship with Skye more enthusiastically.

Grant, however, knew that Porter frequently fell in and out of love quickly and that he was unlikely to actually settle down with anyone in the near future. It was only last week that Porter was planning on moving to Los Angeles to win back his ex-girlfriend, Madison, who had left him two weeks ago to pursue an acting career. Grant found it difficult to believe Porter was really that serious about Skye. Besides, he thought, Porter and Skye were more about opposites attracting than anything else and he didn't think Skye was serious about Porter either. Grant deemed the whole relationship doomed and he was more worried that Noelle would get stuck in the crossfire and have another reason to not like him.

"OK then, if you must know, I think Skye is an inappropriate match for you and a rebound girl. She is a free spirit and you are a focused over-achiever. Right *now* you are attracted to her patchouli-scented lifestyle, but what do you actually have in common? I'm worried that in a few days you'll be desperately calling Madison and leaving poor Skye in the dust."

"Don't hold back. Tell me what you really think. I sometimes wish that when I asked you a question that you would tell me what I want to hear."

Julie Manthey

"Like I said, if you like Skye, then I like Skye," Grant said, exasperated.

"Touché. What if Noelle fails the skating test?"

"She won't." Grant always took his dates out skating at some point, to see if they loved the sport as much as he did and also because he found how someone approached skating to be similar to how they approached life.

"I still think it's a ridiculous test. How someone skates does not reflect who they are."

"Of course it does! If they fall and then quit, I'll know that they can't be counted on when things get rough. If they hold onto the rails the whole time, then they are afraid to take risks and try new things. And if they don't dress appropriately for warmth, then they are more concerned about their looks and fashion than anything else."

Porter shook his head. "You and your tests! I think you manufacture reasons not to date someone."

"Says the man who has his own opera test."

"You can tell a lot about a person by how they are at the opera," Porter defended himself. "It's not a test, as much as a survey." Grant looked unconvinced. "For example, if they fall asleep during the opera, then I know they aren't interested in the finer things. If they start talking about the opera like it's an academic assignment, then they are too serious. I'm looking for someone who enjoys the opera and other fine things, without being a pedantic bore about them."

"Hence, the opera test."

"Survey," Porter clarified. Grant laughed and lifted his hand for a high five. Porter responded in kind.

"This is why we are friends. I almost kissed Noelle today."

"What? Way to bury the lead. When did this happen?"

Grant relayed the story and how Skye interrupted them at the last minute. Grant fell down on to the sofa, pretending he had been shot in the heart.

"I take it back. I don't like Skye."

Porter laughed.

Rockin' Around the Skating Rink

Noelle had gone home to change into a thick white and blue wool sweater from Finland and navy turtleneck, assuming that they would be volunteering outside at a tree lot or something like that where El Toro would be serving nachos from a food truck. She also updated her makeup, daring to wear a bright lipstick and mascara. She curled her hair and let it fall down across her shoulders. All she could think about was standing close to Grant as he leaned in and her heart beat quickly at the thought. She stopped to see Holly.

"What do you think about the hair, makeup, the whole outfit? Is it too much?"

"You look very glamorous! And no, it's only lipstick and mascara. It is not too much. Exchange the sweater and turtleneck for a sequin shift and no man would be capable of denying you. Wait! Are you saying—"

Christmas at Maplemont Manor

"That I have a date with Grant and he almost kissed me in the bakery today? Yes!"

Holly squealed. "I knew it!" Noelle blushed.

"He's taking me somewhere with Victor tonight to volunteer. He said dress warm. Do I look OK? He's picking me up here."

"You look beautiful."

"I don't even know how it happened. He's so…and in his uniform, Holly! Then he apologized for being a jerk. He explained about Imogen, well, I think he did anyway. At least he made his intentions crystal clear. He brought me coffee, my favorite latte, and looked at me like—" Noelle exhaled and smiled so wide that every tooth could be seen. "I'm suddenly so nervous. He's all I can think about. This is crazy. I feel like I'm thirteen years old. What am I doing? People from his world don't date people like us."

Holly looked confused. "What do you mean people like *us*? He's a business owner, as are you. He lives in a house that he inherited and so do you. You are equal here in Maplemont."

"I live above the garage and he lives in a mansion. And the same woman who does my laundry, also cooks for me and manages my schedule." Noelle pointed a finger at herself to emphasize the point. "He has a staff that takes care of things like that for him. Who am I kidding? This can't be a *real* date."

"You have mascara on. It's a date." Holly

could practically watch Noelle second guess herself. "Noelle, life isn't risk free. You have to take a chance."

"I'm afraid that he'll break my heart," Noelle said quietly.

Holly smiled and reached out to hug Noelle tightly. "Mom always said that the heart is a muscle: It only gets stronger and it cannot break. Now get going, girl. You have a date with the—"

"Don't you dare say it," Noelle protested.

"The most eligible bachelor of Maplemont." They shared a laugh while Noelle put on her coat and jacket.

∞∞∞

Grant appeared promptly at seven o'clock, finding Noelle waiting for him outside the garage. She was bundled up in several layers of winter gear. Grant held open the car door for her, impressed that she already passed one of the tests based on her outfit alone.

"You didn't have to wait outside. I would have come to the door." He turned up the heat.

"I saw the car lights in the driveway."

"It's a beautiful house. I only saw the kitchen before but I can tell it's a nice house."

"Thanks. We grew up here. I live in the apartment above the garage and Holly, Todd,

Christmas at Maplemont Manor

and Ava live in the main house." Noelle watched his reaction, expecting him to flinch at her inferior circumstances. She knew that his driver lived in the garage apartment at the manor house, so this news was bound to remind him that she was part of how the other half lived.

"It must be nice to have your own space. I really enjoyed my small condo in the city. It was great to have the place to myself without any staff around." The news didn't faze Grant. He didn't care if she lived in a mansion or an apartment. All he cared about was that she was with him.

Still, Noelle found that statement impossible to read. "I suppose. Carol inherited it and Holly moved in after...We thought it would be easier for Ava although she was only a year old at the time." Noelle sighed. "And now I'm still living in the house I grew up in and the town I swore I'd never stay in, running the bakery."

"My dad passed away over the holidays when I was eleven and I was shipped off to boarding school, college, and the army after that. Mother's new husband, William, never really cared for children."

"I'm sorry. I didn't know that you were so young." Noelle reached out to touch his sleeve without thinking about it and then pulled back. She remembered the framed photo in the manor's hallway and realized that was probably the last photo of them all together.

"Thanks. I don't tell people that very often." Grant actually couldn't remember the last woman he had told. He found it easier to keep a little distance in relationships, but it was effortless for him to talk to Noelle. He felt like he could be himself around her and he didn't need to play the role expected of 'the young Fitzgerald millionaire.'

"I was fourteen and Holly was sixteen when our parents passed away. Carol was eighteen and she stepped in to take care of us so we wouldn't be sent to foster care. I don't know how she managed it. She didn't go to college, but made sure that we went, and she kept both the farm and the bakery going. We both owed it to Carol to take care of Ava, without question."

"Ava is a really great kid."

"She is and she's so much like Carol. Holly and I made a pact after it happened that we'd be there for Ava and that she'd always know how much her mother loved her, even though she's gone. Poor Ava, she always has two doting, and usually crying, aunts at every milestone of her life." Noelle laughed to avoid getting choked up. "She insisted on taking the bus for the first day of school this year because she said she'd be too embarrassed to see us crying at her school."

Noelle sniffed. Thinking about all the moments that Carol never got to see in Ava's life and how Ava would never have those moments with her mom always made her tear up. She missed her sister.

Grant could tell that this was difficult for Noelle to talk about. "She's a lucky kid. My mother sent the driver." They shared a laugh. "I was that kid, dropped off at school by the valet. I still send him a Christmas card every year and I call him Uncle James. My mother is…my mother and I love her but she's not warm, not like how you are with Ava. My dad was though and when he died, I felt alone. I've never told anybody that before."

Noelle thought about how something that happens to people as children can shape their entire lives. It was something she worried about all the time for Ava, but Grant also lost so much and he didn't have anyone to swoop in like Ava did. She realized that he was aloof as an adult because of something that several decades of time hadn't yet healed. Noelle found it easy to talk to Grant, especially knowing that they shared a bond through their childhood grief to which few others could relate.

"That must have been really hard for you. I'm sorry to hear that. My mom always used to say that strong people aren't strong because they want to be."

Grant nodded. He felt like he could Noelle anything and that she'd know the exact right thing he needed to hear. Feeling vulnerable, he wanted to change the subject. "Do you work on the maple syrup farm too or only at the bakery?"

"I work at the bakery, although I pitch in during sugaring season. Holly and Todd manage the farm. They really do make the best maple syrup in the area. Dad always used to say it was because of the trees. He said that the strongest maples make the sweetest syrup. I don't know if that is true, but I like the idea. You should come by when we tap the trees. It depends on the weather, but usually between February and April."

"If that's an invitation, then I accept. I want to spend a lot more time with you, Noelle."

The words made her heart beat a little faster. She blushed. "Now will you tell me where we are going?"

"You'll find out soon enough." They drove along silently until they reached downtown where the holiday lights on the buildings made the snowy roofs glitter. "Did you get that hat on your travels?" He noticed that the pattern woven into the wool hat looked Scandinavian.

"Yes, I got it when I lived in Finland, a town in the north called Kemi. That's where I learned how to make the cardamom rolls and rye bread."

Grant smiled at the memory of the smell of the cardamom rolls. "I love those rolls. Maybe you could teach me how to make them. I'm becoming a pretty good baker now. My resume includes a new special skills section that says 'can crack an egg open with one hand.' Ask Fiona! I've been practicing and I'm very good at it now."

She giggled. As they turned the corner, Noelle guessed their destination. "Are we going to the ice rink?" she asked. Grant winked and smiled. "The best nachos in town are at the ice rink?" Noelle looked unconvinced.

"Absolutely!" After parking the car, they walked toward the building's entrance to enter the rink. The building buzzed with holiday music as the staff seemed to hurry around, all wearing Santa hats as kids filtered in and out with their parents. Grant stopped at the concession area first for nachos.

"Dad said that you would be helping out today, Grant," said the teenage girl at the concession booth, referring to Victor, the mayor. "He's already out on the ice. Here are two nacho specials ready to go."

Grant laughed. "Thanks, Daphne."

He picked up one of the nacho trays and passed it to Noelle, then took the second for himself. Noelle followed him to the actual ice rink where a line of ten adults held onto the rails, trying not to fall down on their skates. Victor waved at them. Grant waved back, setting his backpack and nachos down on a bench. He took out two pairs of ice skates.

Noelle shook her head. "I don't know how to skate." She certainly didn't expect that they would be volunteering like this and hoped Grant would let her sit this one out, to watch by the sidelines. "I've only been out skating once with Holly when were little and all I did was fall."

"That's not a problem. Victor and I started teaching a beginner's class twice a week. This class is only the second one. Last week, we covered how to fall, so you are all caught up!" Grant grinned. "I hope you don't mind, but Skye told me your shoe size. These should fit," he passed her a pair of white skates that smelled of new leather.

He loved the rink and spent most of his winters here as a boy, skating with his dad and practicing for the hockey team. His dream occupation as a boy was to be a hockey player, naturally a profession of which his mother did not approve.

Worried that she'd end up looking more like an uncoordinated fawn on ice, Noelle still couldn't pass up a challenge. There was something about being around Grant that helped evoke her courage, which had been shelved for too long. She entered the recipe into the maple fudge competition, she was going to learn to skate, and she had opened her heart.

Grant put on his skates effortlessly and took a few bites of the nachos, while he watched Noelle put her skates on over what looked like elf socks. He smiled and she laughed, having noticed her holiday socks. Noelle tasted the nachos and nodded her head.

"These are great nachos. I can see why

you like them. You can't go wrong with extra cheese."

"They add extra cheese for me, which was how my dad always ordered them."

Noelle had assumed that Grant had an easy silver spoon sort of life, but she knew now that wasn't the case. It was clear to her that something broke inside Grant after his dad passed away and never fully healed. He skated and ate nachos here to remember that feeling of being whole. Noelle recognized it because she felt the same way when she made Carol's fudge recipe.

"Maybe we should wait and finish these first. It looks like Victor has the class well in hand." Noelle stalled.

Grant laughed. "I don't think Victor would agree." He pointed over to Victor, who was picking up one of the students who had fallen and nearly pushed down the rest in the line like dominoes. Victor's face begged for help.

"I don't think that I can stand up."

Smiling, Grant reached out his hand to help her up onto the carpet that led to the ice. "Don't worry," he said, with one hand on the small of her back and the other holding her hand. "Skating is as easy as walking."

Noelle held his hand tightly with her other hand clinging to his arm. "It's as easy as walking," Noelle repeated.

Grant perched her by the rail, so she could

hold onto that while he joined Victor at the front of the class. "Sorry, I'm late."

Victor elbowed him and made a face, only to quickly smile. They chatted briefly between them and then Victor explained the task.

"All right everyone. We are going to try gliding today. Grant and I will watch your form as you skate out to us, one-by-one."

Winking at her, Grant then skated over. "I'll start with Noelle, so watch us. What we want you to do is to bend your knees and step away from the rail gradually like we did earlier this week. Hold out your arms for extra balance, if you need it." He motioned to Noelle who was still standing at the rail approximately ten feet away.

Noelle made a face for dramatic effect and the class laughed as they watched her step away from the wall toward Grant.

"Very good, Noelle," Victor said. "Now, push off your blade and slowly moved forward. Lift up your arms a little to help balance."

Noelle thought that it was easier said than done, but she leaned into a tentative gliding step, while reaching out.

"Excellent! Look at her everyone and watch how Noelle is bending her knees and pushing off her blade. This is called stroking. Speed comes after we first master stroking."

When she seemed to be getting it, Noelle slipped and fell down onto the ice before Grant could reach her. She started laughing and Grant helped her up.

"Are you OK?"

"I'm fine, thanks. I think my pride took the brunt of it." He pulled her back up to her feet. They shared a brief moment where their eyes locked and their faces were only an inch apart, before she let go of his hand. "I think I almost have it. Let me keep trying while you help the others."

Noelle continued to glide toward the rail and then turned around to skate out, making it about twenty feet before falling again. She motioned to Grant that she was fine, as she stood up again and kept moving.

Victor hollered out to break the spell, where Grant's eyes were transfixed on Noelle. "That's right, Carrie, head over to Grant. He'll catch you if you slip."

Grant returned to his duties as one-by-one half of the class glided toward him and returned to the wall. Noelle had reached the other side of the rink and was starting back, when Victor waved and instructed the other students to follow her lead and take two laps around the rink.

"Try not to hold onto the rails the whole time," Victor said. "It's OK when you start, but we want you to follow Noelle's lead and learn to glide independently. If you need help, ask me or Grant." Victor then skated effortlessly between everyone, as Grant zigzagged around.

Julie Manthey

They helped to correct form and also occasionally to pick up someone who fell down.

Skating up to Noelle, Grant commented on her progress. "You are a natural. I'm impressed." He wanted to tell her that everything about her impressed him from her laugh to her debating skills. He also wanted to tell her how he got lost in her eyes and how he couldn't stop thinking about her.

Noelle scoffed. "You wouldn't say that if you had seen how many times I've fallen. But I have so far managed to get halfway across without falling." She slipped again but Grant caught and steadied her. This time he didn't let go of her hand. In her mind, she reasoned that it was only for balance but she knew that wasn't true. She liked being close to him and having her hand in his. "Thanks. How is that you teach skating here? Oh wait, let me guess. Not only did you graduate from an Ivy League university, but you were also in the army and an Olympic figure skater." Noelle laughed. "You probably speak three languages and your hobby is nuclear physics."

"Victor and I are on the same hockey team," Grant explained. "I *barely* speak Spanish and I like to say that my hobby is travelling, but mostly I plan vacations and then cancel them because of work."

"And the army?" Noelle was curious about how and why he enlisted.

Grant guided them expertly around the

curve. "After college I didn't know what I wanted to do and every Fitzgerald has served in the army since the American Revolution. I guess that I wanted to know that I could rise to the challenge. Those years were some of the best and worst times of my life. I worked with some of the most daring and amazing people. We achieved so much as a team; but not all of us came home."

Noelle placed her free hand on his arm and her eyes softened. She leaned her head onto his shoulder and they floated across the ice together, perfectly in sync. She didn't know how it had happened, but she was already in the middle of falling in love with him.

Victor saw them from across the rink and smiled.

Christmas Dream

At the end of the class, they sat on a bench changing back into their shoes. "Thanks for taking me here and for the skates. I'm definitely coming back to skate, now that I'm so great at it. I might even try out for the Olympics," Noelle said.

Grant laughed and Noelle noticed how his eyes lit up. She wondered if they always did that when he laughed. "You don't happen to know where we could get some maple fudge at this time of night, do you?"

Noelle was torn between wanting to run home to catch her breath and spending more time with Grant. He reached over to push stray hairs behind her ear. "Yes, I know a place."

∞∞∞

The bakery glowed softly with white twinkling lights until Noelle unlocked the door and flipped on a light. Grant followed her to the kitchen, where Noelle opened the refrigerator to retrieve a box of maple fudge. Grant's eyes widened when he saw the box.

"Is that what I think it is?"

"If you think it's possibly the next gold medal winning maple fudge of the Northeast Maple Tree awards, then yes. They called me today and it made the top five finalists. I'm taking this to Ridgewater tomorrow for the final judging."

"Congratulations! That's great news! Why didn't you say something earlier?"

"Thanks. I only told Holly. I guess I'm still uneasy about it. This is the first year I didn't submit Carol's recipe." Noelle popped open the box then set a piece of fudge on a plate for Grant. She passed the plate to him. "I used to be fearless, but after Carol died, I guess that I realized that anything can happen and it scared me to the core. I retreated into the safety of Maplemont's routine and maybe I got stuck."

He paused before tasting the fudge. "When I first inherited the manor, I refused to make even the smallest of changes. My grandfather instructed in the will that he didn't want it to be a museum; he wanted it to become my home. Still, it took me a few years before I could manage to replace the rug in the dining room that I never liked." Grant could relate to not wanting to rock a boat that didn't feel like it belonged to you, even when it actually did.

Noelle sat down and leaned an elbow on the counter. "Carol would have hated it if I left the bakery a museum. I know that, academically, but it's still been difficult for my heart to come to terms with making any changes." By replacing Carol's recipe this year with something new for the competition, Noelle still felt like the change made Carol feel less a part of her life and thinking about it made her cheeks flush. She stood up and fanned her eyes, taking a deep breath so she wouldn't tear up.

"I understand. I felt as if I was erasing a piece of my grandfather, by getting rid of that rug. I like to think that he'd approve of the change and he'd be happy that I was making it my home. Do you think she'd like the new recipe?"

Noelle's face was difficult for Grant to decipher. "I do. I know she'd love it and she'd be so mad at me for not taking the chance earlier. Actually, I have to thank you for your part in the recipe."

"My part?"

"That day you dropped in the pretzels and cranberries into the cooling fudge was serendipity. Without your utter incompetence in the kitchen, I'd never have made a breakthrough on the recipe." Noelle giggled.

Grant tasted the fudge and he savored it. The first time he and Porter visited the bakery they had some of Carol's maple pecan fudge and both of them had agreed it was the best that they ever had. However, Noelle's version somehow managed to exceed it in flavor. He was also partial to the pretzels and cranberries, knowing that he had played a part.

"Noelle, this is...it's like all the best flavors of Christmas in a maple fudge package. I'm glad that the pretzels turned out to be a stroke of genius! It's perfect." He was astounded at what she had achieved. "What are you calling it?"

"Christmas Dream. It was Holly's idea."

"I never met Carol, but I am *completely* certain that somewhere out there, she's looking over you and not only smiling, but cheering you on."

She nodded and took a piece of fudge. Grant took another as well. They sat for a minute in a comfortable silence.

Noelle regrouped. "Have you finalized the menu for the gala? I need to start planning for that." She assumed that she was catering the event.

"I thought Porter told you. We hired a caterer already and the menu has been set."

Noelle looked both surprised and hurt. She shifted in her seat, putting the top back on the fudge container and returning it to the refrigerator to buy time. "No, he didn't." Noelle felt upset that Grant didn't want her to cater the event. She didn't want to think that it was because he didn't think she was qualified or that her work wasn't good enough. Her mind tortured her, imagining that Imogen probably convinced him as much.

Grant stepped over to her and reached out for her hand, which she gave reluctantly, still reeling from the news. "I'm sorry. I asked him to find a caterer because I want *you* to be my date at the gala." Grant wondered if she was thinking of how to let him down because she didn't reply. He thought that things were going well with them, but suddenly felt insecure. Perhaps he was still the last man in the world that she would date. He took a step back.

"Me?" Noelle asked, stunned. She caught her breath while Grant waited for her to come up with an excuse.

"I'll understand if you don't want to...I mean don't feel obligated." He stopped himself and took a deep breath. "Noelle, I'm crazy about you. I think about you all the time and—"

"Yes." She surprised herself with the answer.

He looked up and it was his turn to be surprised. "Yes?" he asked, confirming that he did hear her say the word.

Noelle laughed and nodded. Grant beamed.

Reindeer Games

The next morning at Holly's house, the family had breakfast together before Ava got on the bus for school. Having taken the day off, Noelle made gingerbread pancakes with a side of bacon. Holly took the day off also to attend the maple fudge competition with Noelle in Ridgewater. All Holly could talk about was which boutiques they had to visit in Ridgewater to shop for the gala.

"The dress is *everything*, Noelle."

Noelle's stomach turned when she thought about shopping. She had spent months saving up for her trip to Cambodia and it looked like all of that money would now be spent on a dress that she'd wear for one night. She wasn't as willing as Holly to make that trade, however, Noelle agreed that she didn't have anything appropriate to wear to a black-tie event.

Holly helped Ava put on her hat and jacket, despite Ava's protests that she didn't need to wear a hat. "But it's very cold out today and it's snowing. You are wearing a hat, Ava." They often battled wills. It was the same with Holly and Carol. Noelle smirked, wondering it was like for Holly to argue with a smaller version of Carol.

Todd had been outside, shoveling the walk to clear a path to the door. He rushed inside the house with his boots on, shouting for everyone to come outside. "You won't believe it! Come on!"

They all followed him to the front porch in a rush and Ava squealed with surprise and pure delight. Snow floated gently in the morning twilight as the sky wafted between navy and periwinkle.

"Santa's reindeer are on our lawn!" Ava's face lit up and she couldn't believe what she was seeing.

The school bus pulled up quietly as faces plastered against the windows and the kids piled over each other to see the reindeer. Eight reindeer walked around their lawn, with red collars that had bells attached which jingled as they took each step. The adults looked at each other with questioning eyes, trying to see which one of them planned this. They all looked as surprised as Ava.

Louder jingle bells were soon heard with a 'ho-ho-ho' echoing across the meadow, behind a large patch of maple trees. All they could see from that far away was a flash of a red suit behind

Christmas at Maplemont Manor

some trees in the direction of the manor. The reindeer started to walk toward the noise.

"That's it Dasher, Dancer, Prancer, Vixen! Let's go Comet, Cupid, Donner, and Blitzen! Come on now! Ho-ho-ho! We must dash away back to the North Pole!"

Ava wanted to run after the reindeer, but Holly held her close. It was a magical moment as they watched the reindeer disappear into the thick grove of trees. "That's what I asked Santa Claus for! He *is* real! I asked to see the reindeer!" Ava was beside herself, completely lost to Christmas magic.

Noelle's heart melted, realizing the great lengths that Grant went to for this moment. Once the reindeer had disappeared into the snowy grove, Ava boarded the now rowdy bus teaming with other Maplemont Elementary School students who believed in Santa more than ever

∞∞∞

Back at the manor, Grant stood in a Santa costume in the driveway without the white beard or hat. Eight reindeer investigated the manor drive, trying to find anything edible. He exchanged high fives with Porter and with Eddie Fletcher, the owner of the Fletcher Reindeer Farm a few hundred miles away. They congratulated themselves on a job well done and Grant couldn't believe how seamlessly the reindeer behaved.

"Thanks again, Eddie. You gave a lot of kids a memory that they'll have for the rest of their lives."

"My pleasure, Grant! Things like this are exactly why my wife and I decided to buy the reindeer farm in the first place."

"I appreciate you coming out here with such short notice." Eddie didn't mind at all, especially given the very lucrative incentive that Grant paid him. He would have agreed to get the reindeer on the moon for that amount of money. He whistled and worked with his staff to load the animals into several large trailers.

Both Grant and Porter got to pet at least one of the reindeer, before they walked onto a trailer for the return to the farm.

Eddie returned for a final goodbye. "Thanks again, Grant. You sure have a nice place here." Eddie gazed up at the manor.

"Thanks, Eddie. It must be incredible to work with these animals all the time."

"We love these guys. They are fascinating creatures. Did you know that reindeer are the only mammals that can see ultraviolet light? They can find anything in the snow. We play games with them all the time. They are such a hoot!"

"I didn't know that," Grant said with a surprised look. "Don't forget to take the north road out of town. The south road goes right by the school and we wouldn't want any of the kids to see the trucks."

Eddie winked and gave a half-salute. "Roger that. We'll keep the secret safe! Don't worry."

As the trucks pulled out of the long driveway at the manor, Grant and Porter watched them go. Grant's phone buzzed and he fished it out of the Santa trousers. He read a text message from Noelle that made him smile.

Thank you for the Christmas magic!
He texted back.
What magic? ;) Good luck today.

A Thrill of Hope

The hour drive to Ridgewater was scenic with snow glistening on the trees in the distance. Holly volunteered to drive, which was greatly appreciated by Noelle because she was so nervous. They discussed Grant's text message, where he pretended not to know about the reindeer that morning. Both agreed that his denial and the wink emoji were charming.

"I knew he would ask you to the gala," Holly said.

"No, you didn't. You couldn't have known. I didn't know."

"I knew at the gingerbread house event at the community center. The way he looks at you! Even Todd said so." Holly giggled and Noelle blushed. "When did you finally realize?"

Noelle sighed. "I don't know. It all happened so slowly yet suddenly that I still can't make sense of it. He isn't anything like what I first thought."

Holly grinned. "You really like him, don't you?"

Smiling broadly, Noelle nodded. "I do."

The sisters laughed and Noelle looked out the window, thinking about Grant.

∞∞∞

They arrived at the hotel where the Northeast Maple Tree awards were being held with a half an hour to spare. Noelle had plenty of time to turn in the maple fudge to the administrative staff who numbered it and set in on the table along with four other submissions. Because it was a blind tasting by the judges, all the plates were the same and the fudge entries were numbered instead of associated with their names or bakeries.

Every effort was taken to ensure that the final decision would not be influenced by favoritism, including judges changing each year. The competitors also weren't allowed inside during the judge's taste test to ensure that an expectant look wouldn't give away an association to the baker involved. That the Sugarhouse 'Christmas Carol' fudge had won for so many years in a row with that type of competition said a lot about the quality of Carol's recipe.

"Now we wait." Noelle nervously tapped her foot while sitting on a leather sofa in the

Julie Manthey

lobby.

    Local press scurried around interviewing each of the competitors, knowing that only the winner's story would be featured. Noelle's phone beeped and she saw that Grant had texted a picture of the manor's living room, where he and Porter played air guitar on the stage setup for the band, which made her giggle and she shared it with Holly. He wished that he could have gone to Ridgewater to be there as support, however, he had to be at the manor to ensure the final decorations and deliveries were resolved.

    Although she had entered Carol's fudge each year for the last four years in this same competition, she never sat nervously waiting because it wasn't her recipe and also because Carol's fudge always won the gold medal. This time, however, she worried that she would let Carol down if she lost. Holly tried to distract her by talking about what kind of gown they should look for at the boutiques later and Noelle was surprised at Holly's in-depth knowledge of hem lines, skirt shapes, and fabric types.

    A reporter from the local press soon sat down near her to take some photos and interview Noelle for the paper in case her maple fudge entry won this year. He had large glasses that made him look very hip, along with a perfectly pressed blue oxford shirt. Holly had been joking that he looked like the 'before' of a super hero and then they had been speculating what his super powers were. He was serious about his job and recorded the session to make sure that he conveyed everything accurately.

Although he was only covering the regional maple fudge competition, the reporter made it seem as if he was working on a major news story that could end in a Pulitzer. He shifted papers around to find a clean sheet on which to take notes.

"Miss Kringle, is that right?"

"Yes, please call me Noelle."

He smirked. "Noelle...Kringle?"

She nodded sympathetically, since it was a common reaction to her name throughout her life and decided not to introduce Holly into the mix. "Yes."

"OK, Noelle, you own the Sugarhouse Bakery in Maplemont, New York and Sugarhouse has won the gold medal of the Northeast Maple Tree award for best maple fudge in the region every year for the last five years. But this year you have decided to submit an entirely new recipe. My questions are what inspired this new recipe and why change things up when you are clearly the established leader of maple fudge in the northeast?" The reporter pursed his lips and furrowed his brow, looking very serious about his hard-hitting questions.

"Well, this year I wanted to try something new. My sister's recipe for 'Christmas Carol' fudge is...her recipe and I was inspired this year to take a chance. I wanted to be able to condense all of my most favorite elements of Christmas sweets into maple fudge that would transport people to feel a sense of that holiday joy all year long."

"Can you tell us about this recipe? What makes it special?"

"It is maple fudge with maple syrup, an eggnog cream, dark chocolate, vanilla, cinnamon, pretzels, cranberries, and pistachios. I think what makes it special is that the maple flavor comes from the pure maple syrup that our family has made for generations locally in Maplemont. We also use that syrup in the 'Christmas Carol' fudge and I think it makes the difference when you have expertly crafted ingredients. The pretzels, cranberries, and pistachios also add a unique flavor pop."

"That sounds wonderful, Noelle. We wish you the best of luck in the competition this year with the new recipe." He stood up to shake her hand and take another photo, before quickly disappearing to interview another contestant.

Holly grinned. "Nice plug for our syrup. Noelle, even if you don't win this year, I'm so proud of you for taking the chance."

Noelle chuckled. "Thanks. I'm grateful that you are always in my corner, even when that sometimes means a kick to get me moving."

"What else are sisters for?"

The door to the conference room opened

and the fudge submissions sat on the table, with their related names and bakeries now associated with place cards. Everyone sat down in the rows, awaiting the final awards presentation from the president of the Maple Tree committee.

Holly leaned over to whisper to Noelle. "Remember, whatever the results, I'm proud of you and so is Carol. She's watching us now from wherever she is." Noelle thanked her and reached out for her hand. Nervous hope ran through Noelle as she awaited the announcement.

The president, a tall woman in a pink suit and silver hair stepped up to the podium. "I'd like to thank everyone for participating this year. As you all know, we take our maple fudge very seriously in this region and this year alone we received over one hundred entries. I can assure you that we all spend a lot of time at the gym to make up for it," she joked.

Everyone in the room laughed and she waited a beat before continuing. "These top finalists deserve a round of applause, simply for making it this far in the competition." As everyone applauded again, she got to the part that everyone had been waiting for, by introducing the independent auditor who would announce the winners. They started with third place, the bronze medal, which was awarded to a bakery in Connecticut for their maple bacon fudge.

The silver medal went to a bakery in Vermont that submitted maple fudge with marshmallow cream and white chocolate chips. The same bakery won the bronze medal the previous year. Noelle took a deep breath as she waited for the announcement of the gold medal, squeezing Holly's hand tightly.

"And last, but definitely not least, the winner of the gold medal Maple Tree award for best maple fudge throughout the Northeast region is Christmas Dream by the Sugarhouse Bakery in Maplemont, New York! This is the sixth gold medal win for Sugarhouse, but the first win for this newest maple fudge recipe."

Noelle walked up to the stage to receive the certificate for the award, and Holly took a picture and texted it back to Todd and Miss Betty, and left it up to Miss Betty to tell everyone else in town.

Did You Hear What I Heard?

After the big news about the award, Noelle and Holly left the hotel excitedly to find the perfect dresses to wear at the gala on Christmas Eve at the manor. Holly found her dress at the first store, a long deep green silk dress with a V-neck and kimono sleeves that looked very elegant and was on sale for a great discount. Noelle had a tougher time find the right dress and they went to some other stores and tried on several other options.

At the third fancy boutique they visited, Noelle selected two dresses to try on, mostly to appease Holly. The prices were exorbitant, but the dresses were gorgeous and very high quality. Holly sat outside the changing room door waiting for the big reveal and Noelle stepped out in a navy blue sleeveless velvet dress with a halter neck top and mermaid cut skirt.

The dress hugged each curve and Holly

couldn't stop talking about how elegant it was. Frowning at the price tag, Noelle wasn't convinced that elegance was within her price range. She tried on another dress that had an A-line cut with delicate embroidered mesh sleeves and the skirt was made in silk and tulle in two different shades of red and magenta. Holly said that was her favorite.

"They are so expensive and it's only one night. More importantly, I don't feel like myself in either of these," Noelle said, turning in the mirror in the magenta dress. She sighed in frustration. She wanted the perfect dress for the gala and felt that nothing they had found yet even came close.

They overheard a familiar voice and looked at each other in panic, jumping into the small changing room together to hide as Imogen Prescott entered the section. Hidden behind the curtain, they heard Imogen ordering around the staff and asking her friend for advice on her dress choices.

Imogen carried two dresses. "There simply *must* be a tartan dress somewhere in this town that matches this cummerbund. Grant and I must match, so everyone will know we are together."

Noelle and Holly exchanged a confused look.

"When did he ask you?" Imogen's friend, Rachel, asked.

"Well he hasn't yet, but he will. I went over to his house a few days ago after that terrible dinner with his mother and we were talking about the gala. His best friend made it clear that they didn't want me to lift a finger for the event and instead I could focus on which beautiful dress to wear. Of course, Grant means for me to be his date. We are *practically* engaged. I think he'll propose at the gala."

Noelle made a face and Holly raised her finger up to stay quiet.

The store assistant had a recommendation after looking at the cummerbund more closely. "We do have a silk mermaid dress in a deep emerald green that would match this perfectly. Let me get your size."

Noelle gave a Holly a telling look and Holly understood instantly that Noelle wouldn't buy either of these dresses. Soon enough, Imogen agreed to buy the green dress and once she and her friend could no longer be heard, Holly ventured out of the room to confirm that they had left.

"They're gone," Holly said. "That was close." Holly worried about how Noelle would interpret what Imogen had been rattling on about.

Noelle changed back into her clothes and left the dresses on the hangers.

∞∞∞

At a nearby coffee shop, they stopped for a break. Noelle looked sullen. "What am I going to do? I can't go there wearing something that Imogen Prescott would wear and I don't have anything that is nearly appropriate. Maybe I shouldn't go at all."

"Don't say that," Holly said. "We'll figure this out."

"Imogen said that she and Grant are practically engaged. She's expecting him to *propose* at the gala. How could she have that impression if they weren't dating? Why does it always come back to her?" Noelle mindlessly stirred her coffee, the spoon making a tapping noise in the mug.

Holly took the spoon from her hand. "She's crazy, that's how. He's in love with *you*, not her. Anyone with eyes can see that."

Noelle looked unconvinced. All she could think about was losing her last boyfriend to Lady Seraphina Breckenridge. "What if he didn't mean to ask me out and it was an accident? What if he asked me to attend the gala and I confused it as him asking me to be his date?" Noelle thought out loud. "Although he did say it was a *date*. I remember that very clearly." Noelle sighed.

"Of course you do. He asked you to plan

the gala, wore an elf costume to help you with the gingerbread house event, and he's almost kissed you at least twice already. Not to mention that he's throwing the gala entirely because you mentioned that the hospital needed money for the cancer center. Noelle, Grant Fitzgerald is in love with *you*, not Imogen. I'm sure of it. Every woman feels insecure at the beginning of a new relationship, but you have to trust in him and take a leap of faith."

"There's been all these '*almosts,*' but nothing concrete. He's never actually kissed me. What if I only imagined that he asked me out? He said that he and Imogen had a complicated relationship but he never actually denied dating her. Imogen had a cummerbund of his that she wanted her dress to match. How would she have gotten that if it wasn't true?" Noelle asked.

"She probably bought that cummerbund herself. She's delusional if she thinks Grant is going to propose to her at the gala."

Noelle wanted to believe her, but the situation played on her deepest insecurities and they were multiplying faster than snowflakes in a storm.

Holly's eyes went wide and she had an idea. "I know of the perfect dress in Maplemont. Leave it with me. Let's go home."

Ho-ho-home Again

When they returned to Maplemont, Holly took Noelle to the guest room in the main house to look at, what she billed as, the perfect dress for the gala. "If it's my hot pink prom dress that you are thinking of, then forget it."

Holly rolled her eyes. "Thanks for the trust, sis." She opened the closet and rifled through old jackets, Halloween costumes, and suits until she found what she was looking for. She pulled out a long silk scoop neck, A-line gown with long sleeves in a deep scarlet red with white faux fur along the edges that had belonged to their mother.

"I can't believe you still have this! I thought it was lost." Noelle remembered the dress fondly and became emotional from seeing it again.

"Mom wore this to the manor ball every Christmas. The faux fur needs to be updated and we'll need to take it in a little at the waist, but

I could get all the sewing done by then. Maybe even add a little organza to really make it pop. Come on, try it on!"

Smiling broadly, Noelle knew that it was the perfect dress. It meant more to her than any of the designer dresses that they found in the boutiques. She tried it on and Noelle pinned off sections to guide her alterations. "Thank you, it's perfect."

"Well it's not perfect yet, but it will be in time for the gala. I might have missed out on the cooking gene, but I got a double dose of the sewing gene." Holly felt proud that she could help her sister for this special occasion.

Looking in the mirror, Noelle did wonder if the dress wasn't too much of a Mrs. Claus vibe. "Is it too…I don't know…North Pole?"

"If Noelle Kringle can't go overboard at Christmas with a North Pole princess ball gown, then who can?"

They shared a laugh, knowing that was almost exactly what their mother had said about the gown when she had it made.

∞∞∞

The next morning, Noelle unlocked the bakery at her usual five o'clock start time early in the dark winter morning before the sun had even started to lighten up the sky. She was surprised to find red roses decorating each of the tables and counter, mistletoe hanging inside over the door, and the glass on the door etched with the phrase, 'home of the Northeast's gold medal award-winning maple fudge.' She ran her hand over the etched glass and smiled, wondering who had done it.

Hearing a noise in the kitchen, she walked in to turn on light.

"Surprise!"

Skye, Grant, Porter, Holly, Miss Betty, Jocelyn, Victor, and about forty of her regular customers and other Main Street business owners stood in the kitchen where a new espresso machine sat on the counter, already hooked up with a cup-of-cheer latte waiting for her in a white mug. A breakfast buffet was set out for them on the large island, with scrambled eggs, bacon, croissants, and some berries. Noelle couldn't believe it and she was overwhelmed by the gesture. That so many people woke up so very early that day to surprise her made a few happy tears drip from her eyes.

"How did you—"

Holly chuckled, pleased with the surprise. She bounced over to hug Noelle.

"Everyone pitched in. Jocelyn found the right espresso machine, which is your birthday and Christmas gift from us. I want you to spend the award money on finally taking that trip to Cambodia. Grant found someone to get the window etched late last night and Miss Betty coordinated everyone else. They all wanted to be here to celebrate."

Noelle hugged her again, grateful for such a supportive sister. Everyone else then walked up to congratulate Noelle, telling her how proud they were of her achievement. Skye turned on holiday music and it became a lively breakfast party with everyone chatting and laughing. Noelle brought out the 'Christmas Dream' fudge for everyone to try and they raved about it.

Grant stood back to be the last one to get Noelle's attention. "Congratulations!" He hugged her like everyone else, but he held her a little bit longer than anyone. Instead of his usual cologne he smelled like fresh linen and soap, probably more of a sign of the early hour.

"Thank you. This is incredible. I had no idea." She looked around the room and her heart melted to see so many people there to celebrate her success and to show her how much they cared.

"I...*We* wanted to do something special for you. I know how much it meant for you to submit a new recipe and take the risk. Hopefully this encourages you to take at least one more leap of faith."

Grant wished that he had been smart enough to place the mistletoe above the doorway between the kitchen and the shop where they were standing, instead of above the main door. His eyes connected with hers and said more than his words.

Noelle's pulse quickened and she started to feel a little woozy. Her cheeks flushed. The thoughts from yesterday about what they heard Imogen say in the store vanished completely once Grant stood near her again as everyone else the room seemed to fade into the background. "One more leap of faith?"

Grant winked, feeling buoyed by her response to him. "Falling in love is the biggest leap of faith we can take." He looked expectantly for a response, while Noelle caught her breath.

Victor bumped into Grant and his coffee spilled on the floor along with Victor's plate of eggs. "Oh! I'm such a klutz! I'm so sorry. I hope that your shirt isn't stained."

Skye and Holly were nearby and they instantly jumped in to help clean up. Grant looked down at his shirt and dried it off with a towel. "Don't worry about it, Victor." He then reached over to a bag on the counter and pulled out the green Christmas tree ugly sweater that he had planned to return to Noelle that morning. He put the sweater on and clicked the button on the cuff to make the lights on the tree blink. "I always have a backup in case of kitchen emergencies."

Noelle laughed so hard that she couldn't breathe. Miss Betty then stole Grant to get his opinion on which Maplemont T-shirts she should carry in her store in the summer. He couldn't help but look up to catch Noelle's eye a few times while he and Jocelyn reviewed the catalog with Betty. Each time he looked up, he found that her eyes were already seeking him out as well.

After almost an hour, everyone left the bakery to open their shops or start their work days. Grant and Porter were the last to leave. They were going skiing and tried to convince Noelle and Skye to close up early to meet them on the ski hill.

"Oh, can we close early today Noelle? I'd love to get some runs in on the hill. Today the weather should be perfect." Skye knew that Noelle had wanted to go skiing as well, and she could tell by the way Noelle looked at Grant that she would say yes.

"Why not? If we leave here at noon, we'll have plenty of time to get our stuff and meet you up there by one o'clock?"

Grant beamed. Any day that Noelle chose to spend more time with him was the best of days.

"Great! See you in a little while then."

Porter pulled Skye to the door to kiss her under the mistletoe and Grant wished he had done the same, but the move had already been taken. The men left the bakery and Skye watched them walk around the corner.

"I'm in love with Porter, but I'm worried

that he isn't in love with me." She sat down and sighed. "I know it's fast and seems rash, but I don't care. I'm all in."

Noelle sat across from her and looked concerned. "I've got to say that I've been jealous of how you two fell into a relationship so quickly."

"But will it last? He keeps talking about moving to Los Angeles and Grant let it slip that it's where Porter's ex-girlfriend Madison lives. Porter didn't mention her at all to me, but evidently, they only broke up a few weeks ago. I really like being with him and absolutely I'd be up for moving to California but not like this. Not to get there so he could win back his ex-girlfriend." Skye gazed out the window, lost in her thoughts.

Noelle reached out to take her hand. "What did Porter say when you talked to him about this?"

"He got quiet and didn't really commit to anything. I can't help but want to be with him, but I also want to move to Europe. I contacted Luke at that bakery you worked at in Paris and he agreed to take me on simply because I had mentioned your name. I want to move to Paris with Porter, but I think that he wants to move to L.A. with Madison."

Feeling nothing but empathy for Skye, Noelle understood that Skye wouldn't stay in Maplemont forever. "You're going to Paris, aren't you?" Noelle knew the answer to the question before she asked. Luke had emailed her a few months ago, asking if she would be OK about losing Skye to his shop and she already provided her blessing.

"Yes, I start right after New Year's. I'm sorry. I know that I should have told you earlier, but I didn't know how to tell you. I have really loved it here."

"I'll miss you, but I'm happy for you, not to mention, a little jealous. I miss the days when I could move like that. It's a great opportunity and a wonderful place to work."

"I asked Porter to come with me and he hasn't said that he will." Skye knew that meant something. She also knew that the kiss under the mistletoe meant something too. "I suppose that right now I'm enjoying it while it lasts."

Noelle didn't want to get Skye's hopes up too much. Porter's smooth-talking ways were always a red flag for her. She knew that Porter was loyal to Grant, but beyond that didn't know that he was ready for something more serious with Skye. Noelle wanted to say something to give Skye hope, but she wasn't sure and wanted to talk to Grant about it before providing any advice.

"Let me talk to Grant about it today. Maybe he has more insight or he can provide some encouragement for Porter to move to France." Skye gave her a look of appreciation.

As It Snow Happens

Noelle and Skye met Grant and Porter inside the ski lodge for a light lunch break before hitting the slopes. The men's cheeks were flushed from the cold weather and their morning out skiing. They all shared French fries and each had their own burger, chatting about the weather and their many different ski stories.

Noelle explained that she basically grew up on this ski hill since it was only twenty minutes away and that she started skiing when she was two years old. Grant looked impressed. He and Porter learned to ski together during boarding school. Porter told them a few funny stories about their early ski escapades and near misses.

After lunch they left the lodge and were putting their skis on outside. Grant noticed that Noelle wore jeans instead of snow pants. "You're wearing jeans to go skiing?"

"I have layers on. I'm not cold. I always

ski in jeans." She noticed that Grant was fully decked out in the most expensive skiing gear.

"But if you fall, your jeans will get covered in snow and then you'll freeze."

She smiled and skied up next to him. "That's why I don't fall."

"Then you probably ski too cautiously, if you never fall." His words had a double meaning that wasn't lost on Noelle.

She looked up at him, after snapping her boots into the skis. "Meanwhile you are decked head to mistletoe in the most expensive ski gear looking more like you are going to shoot a commercial than actually ski. I hope you can keep up." She winked at him and pushed ahead toward the ski lift while he laughed and hurried to catch up.

Grant loved how she challenged him and it excited him. "Oh, it's so on!"

Noelle beat Grant to ski lift by about one minute. "I was wondering when you were going to get here," she teased, holding their place in line for the lift.

He pretended to look upset. "You had a head start!"

"Yes, but wearing all that state-of-the-art ski gear, I thought you'd fly by me." She couldn't help but smile as she teased him and she liked how his eyes sparkled when he rose to the challenge.

They stopped for the chairlift, which

scooped them up for the ride up the hill.

"Are you willing to make a wager on this? We race down and the loser buys dinner." Grant thought he had added a dinner date into their day quite smoothly.

"You could simply ask me out for dinner now and save your pride."

Grant laughed. "My, you are very confident. I better warn you though that I find confident women to be incredibly attractive."

Noelle took a deep breath, trying not to get lost in his eyes. "OK. Loser pays for dinner." They watched the skiers below them as the chairlift continued up the hill. Noelle wanted to talk about Skye and Porter. "Skye told me this morning that she's moving to Paris after New Year's. She's going to be working with an old friend of mine at a macaron shop."

Grant looked surprised. "Oh really?

She wondered if this was the first time that he heard the news. "You hadn't heard? She asked Porter to go with her and evidently he's thinking about moving to Los Angeles."

"Well it would be *really* fast for them to be moving somewhere together, especially Paris. I mean they only met recently and they are so different."

"I once moved to Morocco after meeting a great guy on a plane. She's fearless and I admire it. But you don't approve?"

"It's not for *me* to approve. The decision is

Porter's. How are you so OK with this? Doesn't that create problems for you to find a replacement in such a short time?"

"Skye is a free spirit. I always knew that one day she would decide to move on without much notice. Holly can help me out at the bakery at least until sugaring season. Hopefully by then I'll find someone else."

"So, you think he *should* go then?"

"I know that she wants him to go and he seems to be quite taken with her. Yes, I think he's waiting for your approval or at least encouragement. Do you object because of Skye?" Noelle watched his reaction and noticed a twitch. "You don't think she's good enough for him."

"I never said that, Noelle." Grant looked frustrated.

"You didn't need to." She looked away from him.

The chair reached the top and they skied off to the side. They decided on which ski run to take and then moved to the top to start their race. Grant disliked having a negative energy between him and Noelle.

Noelle thought about their conversation and she knew that a direct line could be drawn to her own insecurities about feeling like she wasn't good enough for Grant and that Imogen was. She knew that she wasn't being fair to Grant and that he hadn't said anything negative about Skye.

"I'm sorry, that was all my own insecurity. I really like you and I can't stop thinking about you or about being with you. Frankly it scares me because I'm afraid that you'll break my heart. It doesn't make sense that you want to be with me and not someone like Imogen." She waited for him to respond, already wishing she hadn't said any of that out loud. She felt completely vulnerable.

He skidded down the hill so that he could stand closer to her and face her directly. Their skis pointed opposite directions. "As it so happens, I feel exactly the same way about you." He planted one of his ski poles and leaned over, close enough for his cheek to touch hers and she leaned over as well.

She could barely breathe, thinking about his lips touching hers and she closed her eyes in anticipation. Instead of hearing his low breath, she heard his skis sliding down the hill and a yelp, having lost his balance and control of his skis. He sped down the hill, backwards with only one pole and he started to freak out.

Reacting quickly, Noelle picked up his lost ski pole and flew down the hill after him. He was going too fast so she had to keep her arms tight to her chest and lean forward to increase her speed. Barreling down the mountain at speed she caught up to him, but only after he had crashed and rolled a few times. She stopped several feet above him so that she could pick up his other ski pole, both skis, and his hat that had gotten lost in the fall. She joined him and had only concern in her eyes.

"Are you OK?"

Grant lay on the hill with his arms splayed out on the side of him and his face covered in snow. Noelle stuck his skis in the snow like an "x" and then popped hers off as well, setting up clear signs for other skiers to go around them. Grant groaned. She walked over to him and asked him if he could sit up. She then helped him sit up and repeated her question.

"Yes, I'm OK." He started to laugh and so did she. "I lost my balance leaning over to kiss you and my skis—"

Noelle took off her gloves and dusted his hat off, placing it back on his head for warmth. Keeping her hands by his hat, she moved them to his cheeks and leaned in closer to him. They stopped laughing as Grant reached out to pull Noelle closer.

With his cheek on hers, he whispered in her ear, "I've, quite *literally*, fallen for you."

They both smiled and she pulled him closer. When his lips touched hers, neither of them could feel the cold of the snow. Their shared vulnerability and intense chemistry made Noelle's spine tingle and the butterflies in her stomach performed an air show. She felt every sensation and it seemed as if her skin even heated up to melt the snow. They stayed there for several moments completely locked together, as if they were the only people in the world. Noelle's hands trembled and Grant pulled away to warm her hands with his.

"That was...uh..." She didn't have the words to describe the intensity that they had shared together in that kiss. Her breath was shallow as her pulse still raced wildly.

"Extraordinary," Grant said with a quiet, low voice as he caught his breath.

They heard a swish and a man on the ski patrol appeared. "Are you two OK?" the ski patrol man asked.

"Yes, we're...extraordinary." Grant waved.

"You should ski down the hill and get out of the way."

"OK, yes, we were—"

The ski patrol sped away as Noelle and Grant stood up.

Noelle snapped her boots into her skis. "I don't think we should race down."

Grant laughed and agreed that slow and steady would be a better choice. He also insisted that he would be taking her out for dinner anyway.

When they reached the lodge, Noelle was freezing and Grant hurt from his crash landing. They decided to call it a day after only one run and go home. Grant texted Porter who soon met them at the lodge to get the car keys. Noelle drove her car back and dropped Grant off at the manor and they arranged to meet later that evening for dinner.

Jingle Bales

Holly was providing fashion advice while Noelle tried on a few different outfits for her dinner date with Grant. Holly had already vetoed two outfits.

"You should wear a dress."

"But it's freezing outside."

Holly shrugged. "Then wear tights with it." Noelle's phone buzzed with a text message from Grant. "Is that from *him*?"

Noelle picked up the phone and nodded with a grin that quickly turned into a shadow. "He asked for a raincheck. He says that he's still feeling sore from the fall on the hill and he'd rather meet up tomorrow when he's feeling better. I shouldn't over think this, right? Or was he repulsed by kissing me and he's now trying to disappear?"

Holly shook her head. "Don't be silly. He wasn't repulsed by you."

"You don't know that."

"You're right. He's probably packing up

the manor right now to put as much distance between you two as possible." Rolling her eyes, Holly continued. "You're being ridiculous."

"Maybe he forgot that he already had a date with Imogen?" Noelle raised an eyebrow.

Holly sighed, exasperated. "Was I this crazy when Todd and I started dating?"

"No, you were worse. Remember when he didn't call you for five days after your first kiss and you had me go to the hospital to see if he was there in a coma?"

Giggling, Holly remembered the insecurity of her early dating days. "That's right. Oh, I don't envy you, Noelle. The early days of dating are just the *worst*, but also the best. Join us for movie night then? Todd's making popcorn and hot cocoa." Holly smiled, hoping that would cheer her up.

"Sounds great. I'm going to change into sweats if that's the case. I'll be over in a few."

Later when they were all settled in the den on various sofas, the movie started on the screen. Ava got to pick the movie so it was a holiday cartoon that they had already seen a few times in the last two weeks, but it was still nice to hang out together and relax.

They heard a horn honk twice in the driveway and then carolers singing as they got closer to the door. Holly told Ava to run into the kitchen and get a bag of cookies. The carolers sat on hay bales in the back of an open truck and they all stood up after the truck came to a complete stop.

Miss Betty, Jocelyn, Victor, and few others wore thick coats and Santa hats, while they sang a holiday song with big smiles. At the end, Miss Betty accepted the cookies with a kiss on the cheek from Ava and the truck honked again as it pulled away to drive to the manor. The carolers were getting cold as they finished their round through town, with Maplemont Manor as their final stop before returning home. Noelle and the others returned inside to watch the rest of their movie, with Ava cozying up to her on the sofa as they shared a bowl of popcorn.

∞∞∞

At the manor, Grant welcomed his cousin Violet into the TV room where he and Porter were watching a hockey game that they had recorded earlier. A fire crackled in the large stone fireplace. Grant was surprised to see Violet standing on his porch, since he hadn't been expecting anyone.

"Hey cuz! Please let me in, I'm seeking asylum from Mount Briar." Violet, almost the same age as Grant, had long blonde hair and looked rather glamorous in her blue cashmere sweater and designer jeans.

Both Grant and Porter hugged her, having

spent a lot of time together fleeing their crazy relatives at various events. Grant moved slowly to the sofa and groaned a bit when he sat down abruptly.

"What's happening with you over there, grandpa?" Violet joked.

"I wiped out on the ski hill today."

"He's burying the lead again, Vi," Porter said. "He kissed Noelle Kringle for the first time today. He leaned in to kiss her, lost control of his skis and wiped out. She caught up with him and picked up his skis, poles, and hat. Finally, he kissed her."

Violet put her hand on heart, touched by the story. "What a sweet story and it's so *romantic*! Imogen Prescott is going to freak out when she hears that you two are an item. Puh-lease let me be the one to break the news. Pretty please?" Violet disliked Imogen almost as much as Grant did, if not more, ever since Imogen had stolen a boyfriend from her in high school.

Grant laughed. "Steady now. The last thing I want in the world is Imogen gunning for Noelle. She'll find out soon enough at the gala. Let us enjoy our bubble for now."

Violet crossed her arms. "If you say so. I certainly won't miss the gala now. I want a front row seat when Imogen sees you with Noelle. It'll be like Christmas and my birthday gift all in one!"

Grant waved a hand, thinking she was

being dramatic. He was confident that Imogen would move on and that she wasn't particularly invested in him as it was. "You're going to love Noelle, Vi. She's amazing and I can't wait for you to meet her."

"What about you, Porter? Last I saw you there was an actress that you couldn't stop talking about. What was her name?"

"It was Madison and we broke up. She moved to Los Angeles. But I have met someone new and she's asked me to move to Paris with her."

Violet looked surprised. "Ooh la la! Are you going to go? Now that you've sold the business, seems like you could do whatever you wanted."

Porter looked like he was on the fence. "I still haven't decided. We only met recently and I really like her, but Grant seems to think that we're not a good match."

Grant looked surprised and he wondered if Noelle hadn't been right. He wondered if Porter really was waiting for his approval. "I didn't say that."

"I distinctly remember that you said Skye was an inappropriate match for me and that I was only attracted to her patchouli-scented lifestyle."

"That does sound like you, Grant." Violet looked judgmental, in favor of Porter.

Grant sighed and looked exasperated.

"That was a long time ago and before the opera test. I was more concerned about you rebounding back to Madison then. A lot has happened since then. I think you *should* go to Paris. Skye seems to be great for you and I've never seen you happier. You should carpe diem and all that, after all, you are a man of means and leisure now."

"Really?" Porter looked both surprised and grateful to hear Grant say those things.

"Absolutely."

"Excuse me, what's an opera test?" Violet asked, trying to keep up.

"It's not a test...it's more of a survey," Porter replied, which cracked Grant up and he started laughing. "You can tell a lot about a date by how they respond to opera."

"That's ridiculous." Violet shook her head and chuckled.

"It's not as ridiculous as a skating test." Porter looked accusingly at Grant.

Violet couldn't stop laughing. "I'm so glad that I came to see you guys tonight. This is so much better than having my mom criticize everything from my clothing to grad school choices."

They heard two honks and saw lights in the driveway. Walking toward the door, the carolers voices belted out a holiday standard.

Grant opened the door and grimaced at the pain caused by the movement. "Ouch."

"I'll hold you up, Grandpa." Violet offered him a shoulder to lean on as they stood in the doorway listening to the carolers.

Grant waved at them. Towards the end of the song, Violet kissed Grant on the cheek and whispered how glad she was that he moved back to the area.

As the carolers pulled out of the driveway, Betty gave Jocelyn a concerned look. They both agreed that seeing the same Prescott woman from the community center also now at the manor and kissing Grant on the cheek would be terrible news for Noelle. Betty knew that they simply had to tell her.

Hearsleigh

Skye practically floated into the bakery. She wore her favorite blue sweater and had her hair pulled back into two pigtail braids. Wiping the snow off her large, cat eye shaped glasses, she hummed an upbeat holiday carol.

"You're in a good mood this morning," Noelle observed.

Skye jumped up and clapped. "I'm so excited! Porter called me last night and he's moving to Paris with me! I can't believe it and I'm so happy!" Skye shrieked in excitement. "He apologized for taking so long to decide. I guess he was waiting to make sure it was OK with Grant since he had wanted him to stay in Maplemont and start a new business, but they worked it all out."

Noelle grinned, happy for Skye and Porter and very pleased that Grant took her advice. "I'm thrilled for you, honestly." Noelle hugged her.

"So thrilled that you're OK with me leaving at ten o'clock today? We have so much to pack and organize."

"Absolutely."

The usual morning rush in the bakery made the time fly by and Noelle was pleased to see a few orders for the new maple fudge. Before they knew it, it was ten o'clock and Skye hung up her apron to meet with Porter and plan their big move. Noelle started some cardamom rolls and put some gingerbread cookies in the oven. The bakery smelled wonderful with the spicy sweet scents of ginger, cardamom, and cinnamon wafting through the air. Noelle's secret recipe for the Sugarhouse gingerbread used maple syrup instead of brown sugar and there simply wasn't anything else like it.

Betty entered the bakery on a mission to deliver some terrible news. She'd practiced her speech all night, working on the exactly the right words to use. Her facial expression looked as if she was planning to inform Noelle about a death.

Noelle looked up from wiping down a table to see Betty arrive and grew concerned. "Oh no! Who died?"

Betty pulled up a chair and motioned Noelle to sit down. "I'm afraid that the news is worse than that."

Noelle looked confused and sat down. The bakery was otherwise quiet and they were the only people in the shop. Betty knew to time her visit during the pre-lunch down time. "You're freaking me out, Miss Betty. Is it something about Holly or Ava?"

"They're fine, hon. Last night, after stopping at your house, we took the Jingle Bales over to the manor. That blonde Prescott woman from the community center was there with him and she kissed Mr. Fitzgerald's cheek. They seemed to be very cozy as he leaned on her at the door. I know that you two have become close and I thought that you should know."

The news hit Noelle hard. Grant had cancelled their dinner plans to spend the evening with Imogen Prescott at the manor. "Are you sure it was her?"

"Well it was dark but she had long blonde hair and a very expensive sweater." The description matched Imogen perfectly.

"Thanks, Miss Betty." Noelle's gaze moved blankly out the window.

"I'm so sorry, Noelle. I didn't want to tell you, but then I thought that you deserved to know."

Noelle managed a fake smile and Betty left, returning to her store. Noelle thought that she would have actually preferred not to know at all. For the rest of the afternoon, she walked around the bakery listlessly while half of her brain thought about what to do with Miss Betty's news and the other half thought about kissing Grant.

Several hours after hearing the news, Noelle still didn't know what to do about the situation. When her phone rang and she saw that it was Grant, Noelle debated whether or not to take the call. She answered.

"Are we still on for dinner tonight? I'm feeling better today and I've been looking forward to seeing you." Grant sounded sincere.

Noelle wondered which of those last statements was actually true. "Did you see the Jingle Bales last night? They stopped by the farm and I thought that I saw them turn down the road toward the manor."

"Jingle Bales?"

"I mean the carolers. That's what they call themselves."

"Oh yeah, in the truck with the hay bales! That makes sense now. I was surprised to see them. My cousin Violet had stopped by and she watched the carolers with me and Porter. Violet's mother can be even more annoying than mine, so she stopped over to get a break and watched the hockey game with us. She teased me by calling me 'grandpa' the whole time because I was moving so slowly. You'll meet her at the gala. She's the only family member I never have to apologize for."

Noelle's heart felt like it had been on a roller coaster, from a deep drop earlier to a new high. It was Grant's cousin that Betty saw and *not* Imogen. She was glad that she didn't overreact at the news earlier.

"Meet at seven o'clock? What about going to Ridgewell Cottage?"

The Ridgewell Cottage on South Street was a small, cozy restaurant that had two big fireplaces and wooden beams that served incredible food. The lights were always turned down low and candles on the table added to the ambiance.

"You read my mind."

The Fire is So Delightful

Grant's car pulled into the farm's driveway at exactly seven o'clock. He bounded to the garage entrance and knocked on the door. Noelle opened the door and he stepped inside.

"It's really coming down out there," Grant remarked about the snow. "I forgot how these upstate winters can be and for a while there thought I'd have to walk over in snowshoes."

"Yeah, tonight they say we might get another ten inches."

She already had her hat and coat on. She reached for a scarf from the rack by the door, but Grant grabbed it first. He wrapped the thick wool scarf around her neck and pulled her hat down tightly around her ears, before leaning in for a quick kiss.

"I've been thinking about doing that all day."

His low quiet voice in her ear along with the smell of his musky cologne made her heart race. He opened the door for her and they walked carefully to the car to avoid falling on icy patches, while snow fell in big clumps around them. They arrived at Ridgewell Cottage and were taken to a quiet table by the window in a cozy corner next to the fireplace.

As they walked in, every eye in the room looked and followed them to their table. "Well, I suppose Miss Betty will have a full report about this tomorrow morning." Grant smiled, slowly getting used to the gossip mill of Maplemont. He noticed how people were looking at them while they chatted at their tables.

"This is the first time anyone in town has seen us sort of together, together."

Grant's eyes took on a mischievous twinkle and he winked. "We might as well give them something to talk about."

He reached out and took her hand, then raised it up and kissed her hand. Noelle giggled and she didn't pull her hand away until the menus arrived.

"Do you think we'll make page six of the Maplemont Mirror tomorrow?"

"I think there's a good chance of that. What do you think the headline will be?"

Grant looked thoughtful as he thought about it and then his eyes lit up. "Hopefully it will be clever like, 'Amor at the Manor,' or something like that."

Laughing, Noelle brushed her hair behind

her ears and he noticed how the amber in her eyes reflected the candlelight. "That's a good one. I'm impressed. I was also happy to hear that Porter decided to move to Paris with Skye. She was on top of the world this morning."

"So was he. But enough about them—how was your day today?" He leaned forward in his chair, content to be having a private dinner with Noelle and being able to share simple, everyday things with her. He enjoyed their comfortable ease.

"It was good. Skye left early after the morning rush and then Miss Betty came in with her news. I supposed that you could say it was a typical Maplemont sort of day." She decided not to tell him about the confusion over his cousin and Imogen.

"And what news did Miss Betty have? Let me guess: Zoe Davis has kicked that guy to the curb for being too clingy or Victor finally caved to her request to add mistletoe decorations in between the library stacks. That last one I was *completely* in favor of, by the way."

Noelle giggled, remembering how irate Miss Betty had been with Victor about the library decorations and his stance that his daughter Daphne shouldn't be encouraged to kiss anyone in the library. "Something like that."

When he smiled, his blue eyes almost sparkled. "The longer I'm here in Maplemont, I definitely appreciate small town life more and

Christmas at Maplemont Manor

more each day. When I brought you coffee that day in the bakery, Miss Betty practically lectured me about making my intentions toward you clear. It was the first time that I think I finally understood what living in Maplemont meant. Everyone here reserves the right to comment on your life at any time."

"Yes, that's Maplemont for you. They mean well."

"I have a confession to make." Grant sat up a little straighter and Noelle looked apprehensive. A part of her waited for him to tell her that he had secretly married Imogen in Vegas. She was risking her heart and feeling brave, but no matter what she tried, Noelle couldn't stop feeling like Imogen haunted her as the ghost of Christmas Present.

"OK." Noelle was wringing her hands nervously under the table.

"When we first met, I overheard you talking to Holly. I won't ever forget hearing you say that you wouldn't date me if I was the last man on earth. Those words have tortured me."

Noelle winced as if feeling the sting of the phrase. "Please don't repeat what I said then. I didn't know anything about you and I never should have—"

He reached for her hand. "Don't mistake my intention. My behavior that night was unpardonable. I didn't tell you who I was, nearly wrecked your dinner, insulted you, and then I stood by shamefully when Imogen patronized you. You were justified for thinking me the last man on the planet that you'd ever date. I've tried over the last few weeks to change your opinion."

Noelle squeezed his hand. "We have certainly had a rocky start. I second-guessed you, insulted you, and made you wear an elf costume. Perhaps it is our imperfections that make this work? I can honestly say that today, you are at least in the top ten of men on earth that I want to date." She smiled wickedly.

"Top *ten*, huh?" He laughed and shook his head.

"Now that you said that, I've decided to keep that ugly sweater with the Christmas tree that lights up."

Noelle giggled. "Good. I think it brings out your eyes."

Grant laughed so hard that he had to catch his breath.

Everwreathing is Merry and Bright

At the manor, it was all hands on deck to complete the final decorations for the gala. The florist arrived with, very possibly, all of the mistletoe in the western hemisphere. Grant and Porter directed volunteers and staff to keep everything coordinated. Holly helped Noelle put mistletoe garland on the fireplace mantels and then they decorated the drinks table with floral arrangements in the TV room. They also set up the Jurassic gingerbread house in the middle of the room on a table with pride of place.

Grant went to check in on them in the TV room and he stopped at the doorway when he heard them chatting. He knew that he shouldn't eavesdrop, but he couldn't help himself. He promised himself that this would be the last time.

"This TV room is bigger than my living room and kitchen combined." Holly looked overwhelmed at the scale.

"I know and it's the *cozy* room in comparison to the main living room," Noelle said.

"If things work out with Grant, you could become the lady of the manor."

"Don't remind me. I'm in love with him, *despite* this crazy house. Besides, another perk would be that you and I would still be close neighbors."

Grant practically radiated with delight to hear Noelle say that. It was the best Christmas gift ever, to know that the woman he was in love with, didn't care about his money. He silently took a step back to announce his presence from the hallway.

"Noelle? Are you over here somewhere?"

"Marco!" she responded loudly.

"Polo!" Grant appeared at the doorway with a winning smile. "There you are. This looks great, ladies." He surveyed the room to see that it was almost completely decorated. "Porter and I were thinking it would be fun to have some snowmen as valets near the front door. Would you like to help us build them?"

Noelle and Holly shared a playful look and answered almost in sync to confirm that they would. While they bundled up into their outdoor gear, Grant made a loop through the house to find some things that the snow valets could wear. In the back closet of the old butler's room, he hit the jackpot. He pulled out two top hats, a jar of large buttons, black ties, gray flannel vests, and black jackets that hadn't been worn by anyone since probably the thirties.

Making a mental note that he should donate everything in that closet after getting it cleaned, he bundled it up and brought it downstairs. Fiona found two carrots for him in the kitchen, perfect for the noses and she smiled with delight handing them over. She hadn't seen Grant so free and happy since before his father passed. By the time Grant got outside, he found everyone had started to roll out the large snow balls that would make the snow valet's bodies.

He started one himself and soon they had two large bases of equitable size and two medium pieces. They stacked up each after spending time figuring out the proper placement. Holly and Porter volunteered to make the last pieces and they dispersed to find the best snow. While they waited, Grant and Noelle debated whether or not they were in the right places or if they were too close to the stairs. Grant didn't want to move them, but Noelle thought that the snow valet on the right side should be pushed over a few inches to the right.

Shaking his head, he volunteered that a snowball fight should sort out the winner. First one to get hit by two snowballs would lose.

"Oh, it's *on*, city slicker!" Noelle giggled and then quickly made a snowball but it missed

Grant by several inches.

"Don't worry, snow valet! There's no way you are moving!"

He threw a snowball that touched Noelle's leg and she squealed with laughter, running over to the side to pick up more snow trying to get a better shot. She lobbed another over at him, this time gracing his arm. She raised her arms in victory.

"That's one-one," she said announcing the score, only to get pinged by a second snowball on her arm.

"And the city slicker wins, ladies and gentlemen! That's two-one and the crowd goes wild!" He raised his hands to cup his mouth, making the sound of a crowd roaring for his triumph.

Noelle laughed so much that it made her cough as she dusted herself off. Porter and Holly returned with the snow valet's heads, as well as four small tree branches for arms, and the bodies were complete.

"OK you two laughing hyenas take that one and Porter and I will decorate this one." Holly pointed out the snow valet decorating assignments like a mom dealing with unruly kids.

Grant picked up the valet's clothing from the porch and they divvied out half of the buttons from the jar for each team. He insisted on adding the top hat first, so that they could then center his eyes beneath it. Noelle agreed and she sorted through the buttons to find the largest ones for the eyes and set them in place. He then added the carrot nose and they worked together on the button smile. Grant tied the tie and they worked together to get the vest and jacket over the unusual arms.

When both teams finished, they stepped back to appreciate their work. The end result was charming with two snow valets, both well over five feet tall, looking very dapper to welcome guests. The manor's exterior lights would feature them perfectly.

"This turned out better than I imagined!" Porter's eyes lit up with delight.

"They are perfect, especially the one on the right side—the location, especially." Grant winked at Noelle.

She smiled and shook her head, disagreeing playfully for the sake of it.

Two Calling Birds

The next afternoon, Noelle laughed at Grant on the phone. "I don't care if you want the Christmas Dream fudge. I told you that I'm making gingerbread macarons with an eggnog buttercream for the gala."

Grant pretended to gasp. "I don't even get an opinion?"

"Not about food." Skye motioned for her attention. "Sorry, I have to go."

"Noelle, I have to tell you something," Grant said.

Skye's hand motions became wilder and more exaggerated, as if she was miming that there was a baby lost in a well or something. "Can you tell me later? I really have to go." She hung up the phone. Skye looked concerned. "What is going on?"

"It's—" Skye started, motioning for Noelle to follow her to the shop room.

Noelle followed at Skye's heels, curious until she saw perfectly coiffed hair and designer red wool coats. Imogen stood with Mrs. Fitzgerald-Smythe, leaning over the specialty cakes menu.

"Noelle," Mrs. Fitzgerald-Smythe snapped. "I hope that you don't keep all of your customers waiting like this, it's disrespectful and this one," she pointed at Skye who turned and fled for the safety of the kitchen, "should be fired."

Noelle wondered what she had walked into. "What a coincidence! I was talking to Grant on the phone only a second ago. I'm sorry, Mrs. Fitzgerald-Smythe and Imogen. How can I help?" Skye had probably fled to Kansas by now at the rate she darted away, Noelle figured. Noelle knew how prickly the two calling birds were and she assumed that was the cause of Skye's quick departure. She'd have time to talk her down from the ceiling later.

Mrs. Fitzgerald-Smythe looked surprised to learn that Noelle had been talking to Grant. She stopped a beat and then figured out how to turn that to her advantage. "You were? Well, I imagine that he called to tell you the news himself since you two are such...*friends*."

"What news?"

"That Imogen and Grant got engaged this afternoon, of course. I can't *believe* he didn't tell you. We'd like to order a special cake for the gala where we'll make the big announcement."

Mrs. Fitzgerald-Smythe smiled while Imogen reached out her left hand to display an engagement ring large enough to collect solar power. If the bakery been swallowed by a whale at the very moment, Noelle could not have been more surprised.

"Engaged?"

Imogen squealed. "I know! He *finally* came to his senses and asked me this morning. It was *so* romantic."

Noelle staggered and leaned on the counter, trying to remember to breathe. The ladies kept grins on their faces, as if turning into fun house mirrors. Noelle's heart constricted and she struggled to breathe as if her heart was made of crystal and being crushed by a vice.

"Can you come back next week? We are closing early today for the holiday."

"I think we'll probably drive to Mount Briar. I prefer the bakery there," Mrs. Fitzgerald-Smythe said as Noelle nodded, following them to the door and locking it behind them.

She took off her apron and went to the kitchen where she threw the macarons into the garbage can before turning off the kitchen lights and locking the door behind her. When Skye returned after getting lattes from Jocelyn's for both of them, she found the bakery closed and Noelle had already left for the day. It was almost closing time anyway, so Skye figured that the stress of Imogen meant that Noelle had closed the bakery early and would see her tomorrow at the gala.

Noelle didn't cry. She drove home, baked a vanilla cake, and packed her suitcase. Setting the cake on the counter, she took two pieces for the road and left a note for Holly. With her suitcase in the trunk and passport in her purse, Noelle turned off her phone. Speeding down the highway, all she could hear in her mind was Grant's voice saying that he had to tell her something.

∞∞∞

Back at the manor, everyone at the house was shocked by the arrival of Mrs. Fitzgerald-Smythe and Imogen.

"What are you doing here?" Grant asked.

"Can't a mother visit her son at Christmas? Imogen was a doll to pick me up at the airport. I wanted it to be a surprise."

Grant knew that his mother preferred to make a scene so he didn't question the dramatic arrival or secret pickup by Imogen. He figured she couldn't help but attend the Christmas Eve gala.

Fiona cooked a lasagna dinner and Mrs. Fitzgerald-Smythe held court at dinner telling everyone about how lovely her time was in the Maldives in between critiquing how the manor had been decorated for the gala. She found all the red and mistletoe to be a distraction and agreed with Imogen that a green tartan would have been more elegant.

Grant didn't worry when Noelle hadn't returned his text, assuming that she was busy making the perfect macarons for the party. He pictured her dancing around the kitchen to holiday music, too much in the zone to be bothered by returning his message. Grant asked about his step-father.

"Why didn't William come back?" Typically, the two were inseparable.

His mother looked as if she had been caught in a lie, but quickly recovered. "Oh, you know that he despises snow. He insisted that I return by New Year's Eve, though. He'll spend Christmas with our lovely neighbors, the Havertons."

What she failed to say was that William didn't approve of this trip or her scheme with Imogen at all and he stayed in the Maldives in protest. William did not believe in such meddling and he had almost emailed a warning to Grant, but thought against it considering that meant getting involved. He preferred staying outside of the fray between Rosalind and her son.

Dashing Through the Snow

In less than two hours, Noelle arrived at the border and pulled up to the check point where a Canadian Mountie waved her over. His red coat, black trousers, and the signature hat made him look very official. She gave him her passport and he asked her how long she planned to stay in Canada.

"I'm not really sure," she said.

He gave her a quizzical look. "You don't know?"

"How long can I stay?"

"Six months without a visa, ma'am."

Noelle started to cry. "I'm sorry." She wiped her eyes. "Six months then, I suppose." The calming effect of baking vanilla cake having worn off, all of the emotions caught up with her at the border and Noelle couldn't seem to stop crying.

"Are you OK ma'am?" He handed her a tissue.

Tears streamed down Noelle's face "No,

I'm not OK. I fell in love with this guy and I thought he was in love with me, but then his mother said that he got engaged. And his fiancée…and this huge ring! It's exactly like Lady Seraphina Breckenridge. I was supposed to be his date for this gala tomorrow and wear my mother's dress. But now I'm here in Canada and tomorrow is Christmas Eve. I'm going to miss Ava on Christmas morning. I baked my sister a vanilla cake and she's going to be *so* mad, but I couldn't breathe in that town. You know what I mean?"

His look conveyed that he had no idea what she meant. His eyes softened in sympathy and concern. "Do you have a place to go?"

"I have friends in Montreal. I don't even know if they'll be home for Christmas."

Noelle blew her nose on a tissue. She hadn't called her friends in Montreal, but she knew that they'd let her stay at their house even if they weren't home. The Mountie stamped her passport and gave her the box of tissues with her passport.

"I put six months down, love. For the record, I think that guy must be a real jerk. I hope that you have a nice Christmas in Montreal."

"Thank you. Canadians really are very nice."

He waved her along.

∞∞∞

An hour later, she arrived at her friend's house in Montreal. The house glowed with Christmas lights and smoke puffed out the chimney. She parked the car and walked to the door. Noelle knew the address well because she had lived there for a month last summer. She met Martina and Bruce in Maplemont several years ago, since they spent time each year visiting with his aunt Jocelyn, who owned the local coffee shop. Since foodies always seem to magnetically attract each other, they became fast friends.

Martina and Bruce managed one of the best bagel shops in Montreal where the bagels are still made by hand. After agreeing to teach them how to make cardamom buns, they repaid the favor of teaching Noelle how to make Montreal-style bagels which are sweeter and denser than a typical New York bagel and baked in a wood-fired oven. Never one to cut corners, Noelle stayed with them in Montreal for a month to learn how to cook using a wood-fired oven. They chatted frequently and often exchanged recipes.

Martina answered the door and could not have been more surprised to see her. "Noelle!" She hugged her closely and noticed how red

Noelle's eyes were from crying. "Come in! Come in!" Martina pulled her inside and helped her take off her coat.

Bruce jumped up. "Joyeux Noël, Noelle! Did we know that you were coming?" His eyes questioned Martina, who shrugged behind him with a concerned look when he hugged Noelle.

"Please sit down. Can we get you a drink? We made eggnog." Martina nodded and Bruce fled to the kitchen.

"I'm sorry to drop in like this." Noelle accepted the glass of eggnog and took a sip. "I got in the car and drove. I didn't even know that I was coming here until I'd been driving for an hour." She explained her recent heartbreak and managed to get through the story without crying until the end. "I should have known better. Real life isn't a fairy tale."

Martina clutched her chest and shook her head empathetically as if it was her heart that had been broken instead. "Of course you will stay here. Bruce, get the guest room ready and her bag from the car. Have you eaten?" Noelle shook her head and Martina jumped up to reheat some beef bourguignon from the refrigerator.

A Rudolph Awakening

Holly wondered why Noelle hadn't already come over for their traditional Christmas Eve breakfast. When she didn't get an answer to her phone call or texts, she walked over to Noelle's and knocked on the door. As a baker, Noelle never slept in, so Holly let herself into the apartment with her key. She stopped cold when she saw the vanilla cake on the kitchen island and the note. She read the note immediately.

It said:

Holly – Grant's engaged to Imogen. Not sure when I'll be back. Give me space. Bah Humbug. –N.

"No! Oh, Noelle." She took the cake and spun around, dashing out of the house.

In minutes she stood at Maplemont Manor, beating on the door like a prize fighter. Grant opened the door wearing sweatpants from his morning jog and she pushed inside.

"Holly! Merry Chr—"

"How could you? Do you know what this is?" Holly held up the cake. Grant looked confused and had no idea why Holly was in a flaming rage and holding a cake in his face.

"Cake?"

"It's VANILLA CAKE, you big fat jerk!" Holly started to tear up and her face turned a shade of red. "How could you?"

Grant's eyes widened. "I don't know what's happening. Where's Noelle?" He spoke calmly, hoping that would help calm Holly down so he could get to the bottom of this.

"She's gone! She only makes vanilla cake when she moves away. The last time she made it was after mom's funeral. She didn't come home for *ten* years. Ten years, Grant! This is all *your* fault." Holly was inconsolable. She abandoned the cake on a table.

"What do you mean Noelle left? Why?" Grant looked panicked and reached for his phone to call Noelle. He left a message when the call went straight to voicemail.

"She won't answer. I've already left at least twenty messages. How could you get engaged to Imogen? I can't believe that I *defended* you." Holly crossed her arms.

"What? I'm *not* engaged to Imogen? Why would—"

Grant couldn't believe what was happening. That morning he woke up excited to spend Christmas Eve dancing with Noelle under the mistletoe and now suddenly she had disappeared. Holly gave him the note. He shook his head unable to comprehend where Noelle would get such an idea. That is until he stopped and remembered his mother's surprise arrival with Imogen at her side yesterday and Noelle not having called him back since.

"Mother," he said under his breath and then loudly, running to the dining room where she sat nervously drinking her coffee. Holly followed him. "Mother! What did you do?"

Mrs. Fitzgerald-Smythe admitted to going to the bakery after arriving from the airport. "I don't know how Noelle got the idea that you were engaged. Perhaps she assumed it from Imogen being there with me. These local women draw all sorts of conclusions based on town gossip. The last thing you need in your life is someone who is overdramatic."

Her plan was working out even better than she had planned with Noelle leaving town. Imogen could swoop in this afternoon and they would be an item at the gala.

Grant seethed, knowing that Noelle would never have left Holly without a word based on only the appearance of his mother and Imogen at the bakery. He smelled a rat and needed backup.

"Porter!"

Porter soon appeared from around the corner with his hair disheveled and cup of coffee in hand.

"Holly! What are you doing here?"

"Noelle left town. She thinks Grant is engaged to Imogen." Holly shook her head and started pacing out of nervous energy.

Grant motioned toward his mother. "Porter can you get Holly some coffee and keep her company for a few minutes while I have a chat with my mother?"

"Of course, Holly, come into the kitchen." Holly glared at Mrs. Fitzgerald-Smythe as she walked to the other room.

"And Porter please get Dean and Fiona. I'm going to need their help today."

The Naughty List

Grant sat down across from Mrs. Fitzgerald-Smythe at the dining room table and looked at her very seriously. He crossed his arms before he spoke.

"Mother, you are fired."

She found his statement incredulous. "You can't fire me, Grant. I'm your *mother*."

"OK. Have it your way. Then I quit, as your son. I have tolerated your setups and schemes for years. I finally found this amazing woman who makes me laugh and she challenges me. I'm in love with Noelle and I don't care if you support that or understand it. I choose her."

"But Gr—"

"Rosalind, I am going after Noelle. I'm in love with her and you had no right to do whatever it was that you did. You speak of family obligations, but then you don't honor them yourself. When you married William, I thought it was too soon after father's death and I never really liked William, but still I supported you. I even defended you to grandfather." Grant stood up. "Go home or to the Maldives. I don't care where you go, but you can't stay here."

Mrs. Fitzgerald-Smythe looked crushed. She understood him to be serious and he'd never spoken to her that directly before. Instantly she realized the cruelty of her scheme and felt very ashamed. The coldness in her son's eyes was more than she could bear. She knew that she had overstepped and William was right; she should have never intervened.

"I'm sorry, Grant. I didn't realize how you felt about her. Can you ever forgive me?"

"Rosalind, if Noelle returns and she manages to forgive you, only then will I even consider it."

She hated hearing her first name spoken by her son. He had only ever called her 'mother' and something had been severed between them, possibly forever if she couldn't fix things with Noelle. Grant joined Porter, Holly, and Dean in the kitchen. They sat at the marble island, moping over coffee. Fiona was on her way to provide help with the last-minute details on the gala that Grant wouldn't be able to work on.

Stopping for a second to look out the window, Grant was hit by the thought that Noelle didn't come looking for him. She left him. Here he was fighting for her and she left him without a second thought. The idea made him feel like he'd been punched in the gut. Everyone else noticed his injured look as he leaned on the counter. Porter walked over and patted him on the back.

"She didn't fight for me. She *left*, Porter."

Holly stood up and walked over to them. "My sister is in love with you. The only reason that she left without getting into a boxing match with Imogen must be that Noelle thought she had lost you. Your mother and Imogen must have been very convincing."

Porter agreed. "You've seen her manage Imogen before. Noelle isn't one to give up easily, and you of all people, know how manipulative the dragon lady can be."

Grant's breaking heart knew they were right. Most importantly, he knew that Holly would not give him false hope. The knowledge that Noelle felt as strongly about him as he did about her encouraged him. "Holly, where would she have gone?" Grant asked.

"I don't know. I wish that I did."

Porter scratched his head and got into problem solving mode. "Before we panic, let's start with what we know. Did she take her truck?"

"Yes, it wasn't in the driveway this morning."

Porter called Skye to find out when she last saw Noelle. "Thanks, hon." He hung up the phone. "Skye said that she saw her at the bakery around four o'clock yesterday and that Noelle closed early. So, we know that, wherever she went, she drove there and left quickly probably last night around six o'clock."

"She probably would have taken a taxi if she went to airport," Dean said. "It wouldn't make sense to take the truck if she didn't know what flight or how long she'd be gone. It's expensive to park there."

Porter nodded. "Excellent! That's great, Dean. Where would Noelle have driven to last night? Somewhere within say a few hours' drive? Who would she decide to spend Christmas with if she didn't want to be here?"

Grant was grateful that he could rely on the others to brainstorm the options. His mind was completely occupied with thoughts of Noelle, especially the panicked ones that told him he wouldn't see her again.

Holly looked thoughtful. "Her best friend from college lives in Greenville, Vermont and that's only two hours away. She probably went there."

Grant started to see a plan develop in the haze and he stepped up to the plate. "OK. Porter, you and Holly go back to Noelle's house to find the address of this friend's house and call them. I'm going to get the helicopter on stand by and once you have an address, we'll leave. Dean, please drive my mother to Highgate House in Mount Briar."

Mrs. Fitzgerald-Smythe stood in the doorway. "I'd like to help. What can I do?"

Grant stared at her for a full minute before speaking. "I don't want your help, Rosalind." His words had clearly stung her.

"Grant, please, I know that I made a terrible mistake. Please give me a chance to fix this."

It was Holly who moved over to Rosalind, taking her hand. "My oldest sister, Carol, said that family must always be forgiven...no matter what." They both looked expectantly at Grant, whose eyes softened.

Grant knew how hard it was for Holly to take Rosalind's hand and he knew what Noelle would want him to do. She wouldn't want him to cut his mother out of his life, even over something like this. "You can come with me in the helicopter to apologize profusely to Noelle and then drive her truck back, once we find her. She'll come back with me in the helicopter so we can attend the gala."

"But wouldn't Dean be better at driving the truck back than me?"

Sighing loudly, Grant's voice oozed of frustration and a lack of patience. "No. As far as I'm aware, your helicopter didn't crash in Iraq and you didn't walk two miles after also being shot in the arm, carrying the pilot to safety. That Purple Heart means that Dean doesn't ever need to fly in a helicopter for the rest of his life."

His mother took the offer and didn't ask any more questions. If Grant needed her to drive

Noelle's truck on Christmas Eve, then that's what she would do. She had no idea about Dean's heroism and she felt embarrassed for trying to get out of driving, given the circumstances.

Grant's phone rang and he picked it up. "Noelle? Oh, it's *you*, Imogen. Before you say anything, there is something that I must make clear. I'm in love with Noelle and you need to leave me alone and find someone else. If you don't leave us alone, then I'll get a restraining order."

He hung up the phone and Holly snickered. She could see that he was nothing like Ewan. Grant would fight for Noelle every step of the way. Most importantly, he would forgive his mother for this, which was harder than turning down Imogen. Holly was impressed by how much Grant had changed since they first met.

Blue Christmas Eve

Bruce disagreed with Martina over coffee while Noelle slept in.

"We should call my aunt Jocelyn and make sure someone in Maplemont knows where Noelle is. She'll know what to do."

"Bruce! No. When Noelle is ready, she'll call. We shouldn't interfere."

Sighing, he nodded in agreement. "You're right, as usual. I've got to go. See you later." He kissed her on the cheek.

Once in the car, however, he called his aunt and woke her up. He knew that Maplemont was a small town where everyone took care of each other and, more importantly, that his aunt would probably disown him if he didn't call her with headline news like this. She had already told him all the gossip about the gala and he knew that the town believed the pair was in love.

Julie Manthey

∞∞∞

Noelle was woken up by Sadie, Martina and Bruce's golden retriever, that stood next to her face, blasting her with dog breath and then jumping on the bed. "Merry Christmas, Sadie." Noelle patted the dog on the head. "I was supposed to be going to big gala tonight to dance under the mistletoe with Grant. But instead, I'm here with you. I'm sorry to say, but this is already the worst Christmas Eve and that includes the one I spent in the airport in Tunisia."

Noelle felt depressed. Her heart ached and her mind was tormented with memories of Grant. She heard dishes clattering in the kitchen and decided to get up to investigate. Martina finished unloading the dishwasher and had set out plates of cookies for them to decorate.

"Oh! You're awake. I hope Sadie didn't wake you. She can be such a pest, but we do love her. Let me get you some coffee." Martina patted Sadie on the head and set out her food bowl along with new water.

"I thought you and Bruce were going to his parent's house today." Looking at the microwave clock, Noelle noticed that it was already afternoon. She had slept a long time, yet still felt exhausted and beaten down.

Martina handed her a mug of coffee. "You

gave me the perfect excuse to stay home. I didn't want you to wake up with only Sadie for company on Christmas Eve. Besides his mother would have only spent the whole morning criticizing my fashion choices and asking when we are planning to have children."

"I should probably go home tomorrow. I don't want Ava to miss anyone at Christmas. She deserves to have all of us there." Noelle sighed. "Martina, I don't know how I can go back to that town and live next door to the Manor…and to him. Maplemont is too small. I can't stay there and I can't leave Ava or Holly. What am I going to do?"

Martina reached out a hand to comfort her. "I know that things seem impossible right now, but you'll get through this."

Nodding, Noelle took a sip of coffee and surveyed the cookies on the counter. She didn't want to talk about anything else at that moment.

"I can help you decorate those cookies."

"I was hoping that you would say that." With an encouraging smile, Martina handed over a tube of frosting.

∞∞∞

Jocelyn was in Ridgewater, taking care of her cousin and helping to get his house ready for everyone else to visit that day for Christmas Eve. While not surprised to hear from her nephew on Christmas Eve, the early hour of the call was somewhat unusual. She knew that they always spent Christmas Eve morning at her sister's house and they were probably on the road to get there.

"Noelle Kringle is at *your* house in Montreal?" Jocelyn couldn't believe the news. "Leave it with me. You were right to call because I know exactly what to do." Jocelyn called Betty after she couldn't reach Holly.

Betty, still wearing her pajamas, ran to her car and drove to the manor. She knew only too well that news like this couldn't wait. After racing to the manor, Betty parked in front behind Holly's car and honked the horn to announce her arrival. Then she rushed up the steps and knocked loudly on the door.

Grant hurried to the door, hoping against hope that it was Noelle and everyone else followed him. "Miss Betty? Please, come in. It's freezing outside."

"Mr. Fitzgerald! Miss Holly! I'm so glad that I found you. I know where Miss Noelle is. Please forgive my outfit, but I rushed over as soon as I heard."

Looking relieved, Grant hugged Betty and lifted her up from the floor. "Thank you, Miss Betty. Thank you. Where is she?"

Betty handed him a note with Bruce's address. "Montreal. She's staying with Miss Jocelyn's nephew and his wife."

"You have single-handedly saved my Christmas, Miss Betty." He kissed her on the cheek and she blushed.

"Save that for your girl, Mr. Fitzgerald."

Everyone laughed. The new plan was for Rosalind and Grant to take the helicopter to Montreal. Holly would get home to make sure that Noelle had her dress and everything else ready for the gala, while Porter would manage the final details for the gala that night coordinating all the other moving parts with help from Fiona and Skye.

Then Arose Such a Clatter

Martina and Noelle took Sadie out for a walk, after finishing up decorating the cookies. Martina thought that the fresh air would help Noelle, although she wasn't sure that anything would cheer her up. They laughed playing 'catch' with snowballs with Sadie. Sadie never learned to actually retrieve anything so they had fun throwing the snowballs for Sadie to chase around the field down the street from Martina's house. Sadie started barking and ran over to them.

"That's strange. Sadie never barks," Martina said. "Do you hear that?"

Noelle listened and heard it before she saw it. "Sounds like a helicopter."

"Look over there! It's landing in the field!" Sadie kept barking while the two women stood in disbelief. "What should we do? Maybe we should stay in case they need help. I've never seen a helicopter land here before."

They decided to wait and see. "Maybe

one of your neighbors has a celebrity relative?" Noelle suggested.

Martina shrugged, but agreed that would be exciting. They then went back and forth on which celebrity that they hoped it would be. They watched expectantly as the helicopter landed in the field and the passengers disembarked.

Noelle recognized the green-blue plaid shirt and the red wool coat. "It *can't* be." Her shock was evident.

"Is that your—"

As the pair walked towards them and the helicopter blades stopped turning, Noelle had no doubt who it was, yet she still didn't believe her eyes.

"Yes. It's Grant...and his mother. Did you know about this?"

Martina looked shocked and then angry. "Bruce must have called Jocelyn. How else would they know how to find you?"

Grant and Rosalind reached them.

"What are you doing here?" Noelle couldn't believe that Grant stood two feet away from her.

"I'm not marrying Imogen."

"You're not?" Noelle looked accusingly at Rosalind. "Why did—"

"I'm very sorry, Noelle. I lied to you because....well it's a long story. But I know now that I was wrong, very wrong."

Noelle didn't know what to think. "It's freezing out here. Let's go back to the house. I need a minute to think."

Martina tried to make conversation on the way back, but Grant looked at Noelle, worried. Noelle walked several steps ahead of all of them. At the house, Martina set out coffee and Christmas cookies for everyone. Noelle left for the guest room where she packed her suitcase. Grant started to get up to follow her, but Rosalind signaled that she wanted a moment alone with her first.

She pushed the door to the guest room open and saw Noelle putting things back into her suitcase. "Noelle. I know that you don't want to talk to me right now."

"You are right. I *don't* want to talk to you, Mrs. Fitzgerald-Smythe."

Rosalind sat down on a small bench at the end of the bed. "What I did was inexcusable and my son wants nothing to do with me. He only let me come with him so that someone would be able to drive your truck home. He's been punishing me all morning by calling me 'Rosalind' instead of 'mother.'"

Zipping up the suitcase, Noelle set it upright. "Are you actually trying to make *me* feel sorry for *you*?"

"No. Please sit down."

Noelle sat down next to her at the farthest end of the bench and crossed her arms.

"I grew up at a time when all a woman could do to secure a future for herself was to marry well. After Grant's father died, I re-married a wealthy man who could take care of me. William didn't really want children so I sent Grant away to boarding school and eventually he grew up and I missed most of it. I suppose that, over the last few months, I overcompensated trying to match him to the 'right' sort of girl to marry."

Noelle nodded. "Imogen Prescott."

"Grant humored me, letting me think that I was still in the game as his mother. He listened to me when I talked at him on the phone but I had stopped listening to him. Grant hasn't needed me since he was eleven years old. I suppose that I wanted to feel like he needed me to find the right woman and Imogen made me feel like I was a part of things. She made me feel like I still had a chance to be part of his life. I love my son. I've made so many mistakes with our relationship though. Please don't let my mistakes ruin your relationship with him. Can you ever forgive me? I promise that if you take him back that you'll never see me again. Please, take him back. Please don't break his heart. None of this was his fault. I'm the one to blame for everything."

Noelle took a deep breath. Rosalind looked sincere. They sat in silence for a minute while Noelle thought things through. Finally,

Noelle spoke. "I forgive you."

Rosalind looked shocked. "Really? But I was so terrible to you."

Noelle reached for her hand. "If things work out with Grant…then I'll want our kids to have grandparents. My parents are—"

Tears streamed from Rosalind's eyes as she reached over to hug Noelle. "Thank you. Leave it to Grant to find a woman who is one million times better than anyone I had in mind for him."

Noelle stood up and went to her purse. She took a key off the key ring and offered the key to Rosalind. "You're going to need to buy gas."

Rosalind laughed. "Oh Noelle, I'd buy you a new car if you wanted one." Noelle shook her head.

"Don't you dare! I love that truck. Besides, I think that I already have everything that I want for Christmas."

Rosalind stood up, taking the key. "Well, I'm going to get some coffee. It's a long drive to Maplemont. Besides, there is a certain someone who is desperate to talk to you."

She left and very shortly Grant appeared. Noelle stood up to meet him.

"I hope that she apologized," Grant said.

"You could say that we reached an understanding."

"I'm sorry that I let this get so out-of-hand. I had no idea and I thought Imogen and Rosalind were harmless. Had I known—"

Noelle reached for his hand. "I know."

He clasped her hand and looked deeply into her eyes. "You left me." Seeing the pain in his eyes, she felt that same twist in her heart.

"My heart didn't leave you. It stayed back in Maplemont."

He pulled her into a tight embrace and didn't let go for what felt like a long time. Their hearts beat in sync and on a frosty winter day they found their home in each other.

"Let's go home. We've got a party to get to."

Noelle nodded and they went to say goodbye to the others. Mrs. Fitzgerald-Smythe hugged him goodbye and thanked Martina for her hospitality before going out to Noelle's truck. They watched her pull the truck out of the driveway.

"Thank you, Martina. And don't be mad at Bruce. Without his intervention...well, things wouldn't have worked out as they have. Merry Christmas!" Noelle hugged Martina tightly while Grant grabbed Noelle's suitcase.

"Joyeux Noël, Noelle!" She then whispered in French how sometimes life is like a fairy tale and that they will both have crazy mothers-in-law in common.

Noelle giggled and when Grant asked what she said, Noelle purposefully didn't translate it accurately. She told him that Martina asked her to send the new fudge recipe. At the helicopter,

Grant gave her suitcase to the pilot who loaded it up correctly.

Noelle looked amazed at the helicopter. "I can't believe that you came to get me in *this*," she said as she sat down and pulled the seat belt tight.

"Well, you are the first woman who's left the country to avoid a second date with me, so I figured that I had to pull out all the stops." He laughed.

"What were you going to tell me on the phone the other day? Before I saw your mother and Imogen at the bakery we were talking about the macarons and you said that you had to tell me something. After I saw them, I thought that you were trying to tell me about the engagement."

"I wanted to tell you that…I'm shamelessly in love with you."

Noelle kissed him on the cheek. "The helicopter kind of tipped me off to that."

She winked and they shared a laugh. The pilot started the helicopter and said that they'd be arriving at Maplemont manor in approximately forty-five minutes.

Don We Now Our Gala Apparel

Holly arrived at the manor with Noelle's dress and shoes for the ball and Porter showed her to one of the spare bedrooms. She and Todd were already decked out for the gala. Todd donned a tuxedo like all the other men and Holly wore the deep green silk dress with her hair up in a braided bun. Most of the gala attendees were already gathered near the band playing holiday tunes, with only a handful of the most observant noticing the helicopter land in the back.

Once inside, Noelle rushed over and hugged Holly, before returning her attention to Grant. "Thanks for the ride. I've got to run and get ready. I have a hot date tonight and I don't want to keep him waiting."

His face flushed to bright red when he grinned before leaving to change into a tuxedo.

After Noelle and Holly settled into a room

upstairs, Holly went to the closet to grab the dress. "I've decided that I'll wait to be mad at you about the vanilla cake until after Christmas."

"Jeez, thanks." Noelle opened her suitcase to find her makeup bag.

"Drum roll please!" Turning around, Noelle saw Holly hold their mother's dress and she gasped.

"It's even more beautiful! How did you do it?"

Noelle reached for the red dress that had been updated with white plush faux fur along the edges and a luxurious layer of deep red organza over the silk that made the dress practically shimmer on the hanger. She couldn't believe how beautiful Holly made the dress within such a short time.

"I stayed up all last night to finish it. Although I burn toast, I guess that I got all the magical sewing powers." Holly giggled. She was clearly proud of her achievement. "I can't wait for you to try it on."

"But first, help me with my hair. I have helicopter hair!"

"Don't panic. Come here and I'll braid it into a French lace braided up-do, like what I had at my wedding."

"Thank you and I'm sorry about the vanilla cake."

"You promised me that you weren't going

to leave AND that you would *never* make vanilla cake again," Holly said quietly.

"I know. He came to pick me up in a *helicopter*." She blushed with a big smile. Noelle still couldn't believe it.

"That's *nothing*. He threatened to get a restraining order against Imogen if she didn't leave the two of you alone."

"You're kidding!"

They shared a wicked laugh and gossiped about everything that had happened over the last two days. When her hair and makeup were finished, Holly helped her with the dress. Holly was pleased to hear that Noelle had forgiven Mrs. Fitzgerald-Smythe. They both knew that is what Carol would have wanted. The one thing that Carol always impressed upon them during their teenage drama years was that family must always be forgiven, no matter what. That simple rule was something that they lived by, even decades later.

"You look like a princess from the North Pole. Mom would be so happy to see you wearing her dress, especially here at the manor."

Noelle spun around in the dress and said that she felt like a princess. The dark crimson dress contrasted with the bright white faux fur accents and she really did look like royalty from the North Pole. It was the perfect dress for a certain Noelle Kringle to wear to a Christmas Eve ball.

Once Holly approved that she was ready, they left the room for the party where Todd and Grant waited for them downstairs in their tuxedos. As they made their way downstairs Grant caught the movement in the corner of his eye and his attention focused completely on her as if she was the only person in the room.

Miss Betty and several others followed his gaze and thought that Noelle looked every bit like her lovely mother. The band played a lively holiday song that had several out on the dance floor. Grant held out his hand at the bottom of the stairs and Noelle took it.

"You look so beautiful."

Noelle blushed.

Season of Giving

Porter took to the stage and called out for Grant and Stan, from the hospital, to join him. The band had taken a well-earned break and they now mingled with guests near the buffet tables. With over three hundred people at the manor, the house hummed with activity even after the band took a break. Tapping the microphone, Porter asked everyone to join them for an announcement.

"I know that everyone is enjoying the gala, but please could we ask you to join us in the main room. We have a special announcement that you won't want to miss. Yes, please everyone make room so we can all squeeze in. Thank you!"

Holly, Todd, and Noelle had been talking to Miss Betty and they all moved closer to the stage to be there for the big announcement. Grant winked at Noelle from the stage and she smiled, her heart ready to burst from happiness. Before he handed the microphone to Grant, Porter introduced him as the 'guy who knows how to throw a house party' and he placed a Santa hat on his head. The crowd laughed and applauded. A few people whistled.

Grant was delighted that they had managed to throw a gala that was truly a fun holiday party and not a stuffy, society event. "Thank you, Porter, and thank you to everyone here who has supported this event. We sold all three hundred tickets for this gala in record time, with outstanding support from the local community and those who learned about the gala through our outreach efforts online and elsewhere. I won't waste time making a big speech, but I will tell you that we surpassed even my own wildly optimistic expectations for tonight. Stan, please join me. I'd like to present this check to Maplemont General Hospital for twenty-five million dollars!"

The crowd was elated and everyone clapped and cheered. Stan looked gobsmacked. He accepted the ceremonial check and hugged Grant in place of a handshake. Picking up the microphone, Stan's face still displayed the complete shock of the moment.

"I want to thank Grant and Porter, and everyone involved in this on behalf of Maplemont General Hospital. It's heartwarming to know that so many people who have never even visited our town or knew it existed contributed so much to help us rebuild the cancer clinic. Less than two weeks ago, I told Grant that we would need at least twenty million dollars to re-open the clinic and I had hoped that maybe in a few years we could do so. Thanks to this outpour of support we will now be able to re-open the cancer clinic next year. This means so much to the community, thank you. Thank you!"

Stan raised the check up into the air and everyone cheered and clapped loudly. He waved at the crowd to have them settle down for a second so he could say one more thing. "As many of you know, Grant has recently moved back to Maplemont and, while many of you might not know him, I'd like to be the first to properly welcome him home. Please join me in applause. Welcome home, Grant."

The crowd roared again and Fiona had tears in her eyes. She knew that, more than anything, Grant wanted to fit in and be part a community that considered him one of their own. She had seen him always reserved on the sidelines, but now officially embraced by a community who loved him. Fiona also saw how Noelle looked at Grant and she knew that it would be only a matter of time for the manor to gain itself a new lady. Her tears were happy ones, knowing also how Grant's grandfather was somewhere looking down with pride, love, and joy.

Grant noticed her tears and walked over to her as the band returned to the stage and the crowd dispersed into the many other rooms open for the party. "What's wrong, Fiona?"

"My dear boy, these are the happiest of tears. How proud you've made your grandfather and father. Wherever they are, I know that they are smiling."

Grant's eyes started to tear up as well and he wiped them with a corner of his sleeve. "Come on, now, Fiona. It's a party. Dance with me." He extended his hand as the band started up a lively holiday tune.

"It would be my honor, Mr. Fitzgerald."

Where the Love-Light Gleams

Grant found Noelle talking to Skye and Porter about their big move to Paris. He took Noelle's hand.

"Excuse me, but I've been waiting all night to dance with Noelle."

Porter and Skye grinned, waving them off.

"I thought you'd never ask," she said.

They walked out onto the dance floor. Grant signaled the band with a wave and the music changed to the same slow song that had played at the bar for them that night. Grant pulled her in close.

"It's our song. That's why I really wanted this band. No other band would play this song exactly the same." Noelle looked at him like it was the sweetest gesture in the world. "Aren't you now glad that I was right about the band?"

Noelle straightened up and challenged him with a look. "I still think that—"

Grant kissed her under the mistletoe-covered ceiling before she could finish her counterpoint.

"Don't think that you are going to get out of future debates so easily."

He pretended to look surprised and then smiled roguishly. She kissed him back while the room turned around them and snow gently fell outside, glittering in the twinkling lights of the manor.

Elfterward

Over one year later, the engagement ring burned a hole in Grant's pocket. He wanted the proposal to be perfect and memorable, but so far it was one unmitigated disaster after another. First, he baked cupcakes for Valentine's Day and hid the ring in one of the cupcakes, but lost track of which one so he had to dig through all of them to find it, which only resulted in a mess. He also burned the cupcakes in the oven which set off the manor alarm that automatically summoned the fire department. On the plus side, he got invited to join the department's bowling league.

Needless to say, Valentine's Day came and went without a proposal although they did enjoy a nice dinner out at Ridgewell Cottage. During sugaring season, when they helped out tapping the maple trees for syrup, Grant thought it would be clever to put the ring on a spile for Noelle to discover when adding the tube, only he dropped the ring on the ground and it was lost for almost two weeks during an especially snowy March.

Porter laughed with a loud, hearty belly laugh when Grant relayed these misadventures to him on the phone. He and Skye were happily settled in Paris and they planned to visit Maplemont in June.

"Grant, buddy, you are overthinking this. All you need to do is ask her already and stop stalling with these ridiculous grand gestures." Porter knew that sometimes Grant spun his wheels when trying to create the perfect event, which he assumed was simply the result of years of trying to get Mrs. Fitzgerald-Smythe's notice as a child.

"I know that you're right, but—"

"I am right. Noelle doesn't care about a big gesture. She's crazy about you, although if she finds out what a mess you are, she might change her mind. You better lock down this deal before she hears about your shenanigans." Porter laughed again.

"Thanks for the support." Grant chuckled.

"What are friends for?"

"I should have asked her in Cambodia, but I didn't have the ring with me. How did you ask Skye?"

"We were walking home after dinner in Saint Germain and I asked her if she would marry me and she said yes." Porter smiled at the memory.

"You make it sound so easy."

"It *is* easy. The *hard* part is finding the right woman to ask, which you've already managed and, by some miracle, she is crazy about you. I've got to run. Promise me that you'll ask her *today*." Porter knew that without a deadline Grant could often put things off.

Grant hated it when Porter was right. "I'll think about it." After hanging up the phone, he pulled the ring box out of his pocket and opened it to look at his grandmother's art deco engagement ring. His two Siberian husky dogs lay near him on the office rug.

He closed the box again and called Noelle. "Hey, I was thinking we could have dinner at the manor tonight. I'll make macaroni and cheese from a box."

∞∞∞

Noelle arrived closer to half past six and she flew into the kitchen door. "I'm sorry that I'm late! I had to stop home first to change."

Grant greeted her with a kiss and then pulled back with accusing eyes. "You smell like pizza...pepperoni with extra cheese. Did you bring backup pizza, assuming my dinner would fail?"

Noelle knew that she was caught red-handed. "How do you do it? You are like a blood-

Julie Manthey

hound! I left it in the car."

"We won't need it. I promise that this will be the *best* macaroni and cheese you've ever tasted in your life."

She noticed that the kitchen looked like a rock band had left minutes ago after a party in the kitchen and wondered how such a mess was possible. "I'm sorry, Grant. You're right. I shouldn't have stopped for pizza. Let me taste what you made. I'm sure it's perfect."

"So?" Grant waited anxiously.

Her face said it all and she spit it out into the sink. "Something went wrong."

"What are you talking about? I followed the directions exactly, minus a small substitution."

"Let me guess—You ran out of milk and opted to use the vanilla coffee creamer instead?"

Grant looked shocked that she had guessed exactly what had happened. "Now who's the bloodhound? How could?" He tried it himself and then quickly spit it out into his hand. They both got the giggles and couldn't stop laughing. "Please get the backup pizza."

Noelle kissed him on the cheek and started for the door.

"Noelle?" She turned around to find him kneeling on one knee, holding the ring box in his hand. "You are the love of my life. Will you marry me?"

She put a hand over her heart, touched by the

heartfelt proposal from her perfect guy where they first met. "Yes!"

Book Club Guide

While this novel takes place during the Christmas season, do you think that it could be said that Christmas itself is almost a character in this novel? Why or why not?

Much of the novel emphasizes the close relationship between Holly and Noelle. What could you relate to about the relationship between these sisters?

This is the first novel in the Maplemont series. Did you find it a fun introduction to this quaint town? Which of the secondary characters would you have liked to learn more about?

Each chapter in **Christmas at Maplemont Manor** has a light-hearted, unique title with a holiday pun that relates directly to the events in that chapter. Which were your favorite chapter names and why?

Let's talk about the food! Food takes center stage in this novel, from award-winning maple fudge to cardamom rolls and a tagine dinner. What did you want to try out the most? Do you have a favorite recipe for maple fudge? What are your favorite holiday treats? *Julie's favorites are the cardamom rolls, which she makes from scratch herself rather routinely!*

The fellow residents of Maplemont (even those *relatives* of Maplemont residents) help to drive the story, as well as, to bring the couple together via their matchmaking. Which character was *your* favorite matchmaker in town? Why?

About the Author

Julie Manthey believes that holiday snow is magical and hopes you've enjoyed spending Christmas at Maplemont Manor. Julie is an independent author and has self-published this novel. If you enjoyed reading it, please tell *all* your friends and librarians. Please also consider writing a review. Thanks for your support!
JulieManthey.com
Author photo @Heather Crowder